THE THING....

Blade ducked aside and crouched, instinctively drawing his right Bowie, turning to confront his enemy, prepared for anything.

Or so he thought.

Blade hesitated, gaping in astonishment at his attacker. It was the size of an average man, on the lean side, and essentially humanoid, being bipedal and possessing two arms and a face, but after that any human resemblance ended. Its skin was light gray and leathery, its nose narrow and pointed, and its ears tiny circles of flesh on either side of a bald, hawk-like skull. The mouth was a thin slit, and the eyes were endowed with a bizarre hypnotic effect because of their bright red pupils. The creature was naked except for a brown loin cloth covering its genitals and a metal collar around its squat neck.

In the second Blade delayed, overcome by amazement, the thing pounced....

THE ENDWORLD SERIES
by David Robbins:

#1: THE FOX RUN
#2: THIEF RIVER FALLS RUN
#3: THE TWIN CITIES RUN

DAVID ROBBINS

ENDWORLD

THE KALISPELL RUN

LEISURE BOOKS   NEW YORK CITY

Dedicated to . . .

*Al & Bea & Al & Barb, for the respective
gleams in your eyes;
John Carpenter, for some of the best writing
music this side of the Milky Way;
and to my Guardian Seraphim, just because.*

A LEISURE BOOK

Published by

Dorchester Publishing Co., Inc.
6 East 39th Street
New York, NY 10016

Printed in the United States of America

1

The three men were huddled together several feet from the roaring fire, conversing in hushed tones, idly watching the blonde woman prepare their evening meal: rabbit stew. All three wore a tunic and cloak made from bearskin, stitched together using deer sinew. All of the men were filthy, their long hair and beards matted with sweat and grime, their bodies reeking from neglect and a devoted aversion to water and bathing. The tallest of the grubby trio was armed with a Glenfield Model 15 bolt-action rifle, snugly cradled in his brawny arms. The oldest carried an axe, and the youngest a crude spear consisting of a lengthy straight branch with the tip sharpened and hardened in the smoldering ashes of a fire.

"Can't figure it out," the youngest commented to his companions. "Where could they all be?"

The tallest shook his head. "We've looked and looked. If they don't show up in a week, we'll go south."

"Why south, Grant?" the oldest inquired.

Grant gazed at the stars filling the sky. "Winter comes in a couple of months. I'm tired of cold. I heard it's warmer in the south."

"What about her?" the youngest asked, jerking his

left thumb in the direction of the woman.

"What do you think?" Grant replied. "We have some fun, and then we kill her, just like all the rest."

"I'm looking forward to the fun," the youngest admitted, licking his thick lips.

"Me too!" the eldest cackled.

The blonde woman provided a stark contrast to her bestial captors. She was lean and lithe, attired in skimpy, tattered rags. Her entire demeanor was marked by dignity and composure, despite her perilous predicament. Although she was covered with cuts and scratches, and there was a large welt above her right eye, she bore the pain patiently and resolutely. As she stood to take the metal pot of stew to the men, her own stomach growling from her prolonged lack of nourishment, she steeled her mind, refusing to give the bastards the satisfaction of seeing her buckle.

"Move your ass, woman!" Grant contemptuously bellowed.

"Yeah, Sherry!" the oldest added. "We're hungry! Give it to us."

Sherry's green eyes flashed. I'd love to give it to them, all right, she mentally told herself. Right in the groin! She crossed to them and held out the metal pot, taken from the ruined remains of a nearby building.

Grant lunged and grabbed the pot. He screeched as his fingers made contact with the scorching metal and he inadvertently dropped the pot. The steaming contents spewed over the ground.

"Damn your hide, female!" Grant surged upward and gripped her by the flimsy fabric of her torn yellow blouse. "You made me drop the food! It was hot!"

"What did you expect, you congenital idiot?" Sherry retorted, forgetting herself. "It just came off the fire."

Grant savagely backhanded Sherry across the face, knocking her to the grass at his feet. "Forget the food.

The fun comes first." He began to hitch his tunic up his legs.

"I hate to spoil your fun," a voice intruded, "but I don't think you want to meet your Maker with your dingus flapping in the wind."

"Look!" the youngest of the trio blurted, pointing.

The newcomer stood on the other side of the fire, directly across from them. He was a blond man with a sweeping blond moustache, and he wore buckskins and moccasins. Strapped around his slim waist were a pair of pearl-handled revolvers.

Grant froze, momentarily stunned.

"Where are they?" the newcomer asked.

"Who?" Grant responded, perplexed, uncertain of his next move. He didn't like the way the blond man's hands hovered near those revolvers. A glint of light from the fire revealed the newcomer had a rifle hanging across his back, suspended from a rawhide cord slanted crosswise over his chest.

"I'm not in the mood for games, pard," the newcomer warned icily. "Where are they?"

"Who?" Grant replied, genuinely confused. He let his tunic drop. The Glenfield was in his left hand, and he toyed with the notion of shooting this stranger, but something in the newcomer's manner deterred him.

"You're Trolls," the stranger stated. "The slime of the earth. Scum. Vermin . . ."

"Liar!" the youngest Troll screamed, throwing his right arm back, the one with the spear. "Liar!"

He never completed the throw.

Grant saw the newcomer's hands flicker and the revolvers were in his hands, appearing faster than the eyes could follow. The two shots sounded as one, and the youngest Troll was flung backward, the rear of his head exploding blood and brains and hair in every direction.

Grant held his breath, afraid to move.

As miraculously as they were drawn, the revolvers were returned to their holsters.

"As I was saying," the stranger continued, "you're Trolls. If you've survived, then others have too. Where are they?"

"Survived?" the eldest Troll interrupted. "What do you mean?"

"Obviously, you weren't here when some of my friends and I took on your buddies," the newcomer explained. "Your buddies lost."

"I don't understand," the graying Troll said, looking at Grant.

Grant did. "You mean you killed them all?" He couldn't believe it.

"Not all," the stranger reiterated. "You've survived. . . ."

"But we weren't here!" Grant declared.

"Case in point. Some of those who were here managed to escape, and I'm looking for them. Where are they?" The newcomer moved a step closer to the fire.

"I don't know," Grant admitted. "We've been looking for them too."

"You expect me to believe you?"

"He's telling the truth." Sherry, still on the ground, spoke up.

The stranger glanced at Sherry. "You're backing his play?"

Sherry shook her head. "No. I hate them as much as you. . . ."

"Bet me!" the newcomer snapped, cutting Sherry off.

". . . but I know they're telling the truth," she resumed in a subdued voice. "They've drug me all over creation looking for their missing clan ever since we came back here to Fox and discovered no one here."

"How long have they had you?" the stranger inquired.

"Over two weeks," Sherry replied, glaring up at Grant.

"Have they abused you?" the newcomer demanded, his tone harsh and grating.

Sherry attempted to answer, but the disgusting memories overwhelmed her, her eyes moistening at the corners, and she simply nodded.

"Figured as much." The stranger stared at Grant and the other Troll. "If you don't know where the rest went, you're of no further use to me."

"What do you plan to do?" Grant asked a shade nervously.

The buckskin-clad gunman glanced at Sherry. "Get out of the way. Don't stand up! You'll be in my line of fire. Roll to one side, away from them, and then stand," he directed.

Sherry obeyed.

"Now," the stranger said to the Trolls, "the next step is all yours. I'll let you make the first move."

"What if we just turn and walk away?" Grant offered hopefully.

"I'll shoot you in the back," the gunman promised.

Grant looked at his companion and nodded. The eldest Troll began to circle the fire to his left, hefting his axe. Grant walked to his right, gripping his rifle.

The newcomer remained immobile.

"You have a name?" Grant asked, his right hand inching toward the trigger on the Glenfield. There was already a round in the chamber.

"Hickok," the buckskin-clad man replied.

"Well, Hickok," Grant stated, trying to distract the gunman with conversation as he came around the fire, "I find it hard to believe most of my brother Trolls have been killed. What about our leader, Saxon? What happened to him?"

"A friend of mine turned him from a bull into a

heifer," the stranger recounted, still making no move toward his guns.

Grant and the other Troll were clear of the fire, only feet from the newcomer. "Maybe we can return the favor," Grant mentioned sarcastically.

"Just hurry it up!" Hickok rejoined. "I'm gettin' bored."

Grant glanced at the elderly Troll and nodded again, and both men went into action simultaneously.

Hickok finally moved, the Colt Pythons in his hands, and he swiveled to his right and fired, aiming for the head as he almost always did, the two heavy slugs catching the senior Troll right between his brown eyes and exiting out the top of his head. The Troll silently slumped to the ground, even as Hickok turned, the Pythons held low, at waist level, and the Colts boomed again as Grant was bringing the Glenfield barrel to bear on the gunman.

Grant felt a tremendous impact in his groin area and he involuntarily doubled over, still holding his rifle, as the shock and the excruciating agony hit him.

"That's for Joan," Hickok said grimly, walking over to Grant.

Grant's vision was spinning and he dropped the Glenfield. He managed to croak a few words as blood trickled down the right corner of his mouth. "Don't! Please! No!"

"That was for Joan," Hickok repeated, reaching the Troll. "This is for me."

"Don't!" Grant pleaded.

Hickok ignored the entreaty. Instead, he jammed the barrels of his Pythons into Grant's eyes and slowly cocked the hammers of the .357's.

Grant frantically attempted to pull away from the revolvers.

Hickok pulled the triggers.

It was as if the Troll was smashed in the head with a sledgehammer. He jerked backward and toppled on the grass, twitching.

The gunman grinned. He twirled the Colts back into their respective holsters. "Piece of cake," he commented.

A heavy silence filled the night.

Hickok sighed, stared at the fire for a moment, then walked around it, bearing east.

"Wait a minute!"

Hickok kept walking.

"Hey! Hickok!" Sherry yelled. "Hold it!"

He apparently entertained no notion of stopping.

"Damn it!" Sherry angrily exclaimed. She ran up to him and grabbed his left arm, spinning him around. "Hold it!"

The gunman glared at her in annoyance. "You want something?" he demanded.

"What the hell is the matter with you?" she barked, peeved.

"What's it to you?" he retorted, pulling his arm free. He began to leave.

"You're going? Just like that?"

"I have a score to settle," he informed her.

"You'd abandon a helpless woman in the middle of nowhere?" Sherry questioned him.

Hickok stopped in midstride. He faced her and thoughtfully studied her from head to toe. "I doubt you're the helpless type."

"Like what you see?" she asked, a hint of possible pleasures to come implied in her tone and her expression.

"You offering yourself to me?" Hickok asked, his tone laced with unconcealed digust.

Sherry stepped up to him. "I'm sorry," she hastily apologized. "But you've got to understand my position.

I don't want to go it alone. I thought if I offered my body to you, you . . ."

"You thought wrong," Hickok interjected distastefully.

"I'm sorry," she stressed. "I misjudged you."

"Did you offer your body to the Trolls?" Hickok asked.

Her temper flaring, Sherry aimed a slap at his right cheek. He easily gripped her wrist and prevented the blow from connecting. "They took what they wanted!" she answered. "They . . ." she began, then hesitated, swaying, her ordeal catching up with her. Two days without food, and the harsh treatment accorded by the Trolls, combined with the emotional excitement of the past few minutes, all conspired to take their toll at this particular moment. "I think I'm going to pass out," she announced weakly.

She did.

Hickok caught her as she fainted and carried her over to the fire. He gently laid her on the grass and stared at her lovely face. "You remind me of someone," he told the sleeping form, then grinned. "But, lately, every woman I run into reminds me of her. Guess it's only natural." His mind drifted, recalling another beautiful woman, a soldier with the Nomads in the Twin Cities of Minneapolis and St. Paul, a feisty female named Bertha. "She has the spunk, but not the looks," he absently mentioned. "You've got the looks, but I wonder about the rest. . . ."

Sherry groaned.

The gunman smiled. "Reckon I put my quest on hold for a spell." He gazed into the darkness. "But not too long. I've got a debt to collect, honor to satisfy, and a dummy to find."

Hickok set about ministering to her wounds. Just great! Just what he needed! He seemed to have developed a knack for attracting women in distress. Shaking his head, he looked straight up.

Why me?

2

Hundreds of miles to the west, another man was reflecting along similar lines. Why couldn't I stay at the Home this trip? Why must I constantly be separated from my beloved Jenny? Why couldn't Rikki or one of the other Warriors go for once? He sighed, knowing the answer. None of the others had his experience with the SEAL.

He was a large man, this malcontent, with bulging muscles, black hair, and piercing gray eyes. He wore a green T-shirt and green fatigue pants. Hanging in leather sheaths from his belt, one on each hip, were two Bowie knives, his favorite weapons. Absently avoiding ruts, holes, and cracks in the road, he steered the SEAL west on U.S. Highway 2.

The vehicle was a green van, constructed with a bulletproof and heat-resistant plastic body. Its tires were huge, over two feet wide and four feet high. A pair of unique solar panels were attached to the roof, and suspended under the transport was a lead-lined case containing the revolutionary batteries used to store the converted solar energy and power the vehicle. The transport was called the SEAL, an acronym for Solar Energized Amphibious or Land Recreational Vehicle.

Although no one outside the vehicle could view the interior because of the tinted plastic, the four current occupants were able to enjoy the scenery. The big man behind the wheel praised again, for the umpteenth time, Kurt Carpenter's foresight.

Kurt Carpenter. The man responsible for constructing the compound in northwestern Minnesota intended to serve as the survival site for his followers. The thirty-acre plot became known as the Home, and Carpenter's followers adopted the title of the Family. Carpenter spent millions building the walled, fortified Home, and providing the provisions and supplies the Family would require after World War III. He wanted to ensure the Family would persist in a world run amok. The SEAL was built according to his precise specifications by auto-makers eager to take his money. They viewed him as another harmless, but immensely wealthy, eccentric. Carpenter wanted the engineers and scientists to fabricate a vehicle capable of enduring a century if necessary. He had the transport hidden in an underground chamber, leaving instructions that it was to be left alone until needed. Ironically enough, one hundred years after The Big Blast, as the Family referred to the nuclear conflict, the current Leader of the Home, Plato, had the SEAL uncovered and put to use.

Plato wanted to send three of the Family's Warriors, the trio known as Alpha Triad, to the Twin Cities in the hope of locating certain medical and scientific equipment he required. The Family was suffering from a form of premature senility, and Plato was optimistic he could discover the cause and develop a cure if he only had the right implements and resources. Alpha Triad success-fully reached the Twin Cities, but it returned to the Home without the items Plato requested. To compound the matter, the Warriors hadn't really looked. For one thing, they had been too busy staying alive.

The muscular giant frowned at the memory of Plato's scathing rebuke after they came back. True, he was badly beaten and not in any condition to go traipsing all over Minneapolis and St. Paul, scouring the dilapidated structures for the articles on Plato's list. But, as his kindly mentor loudly noted, in a rare display of anger, the others weren't seriously hurt and they could have searched if they had really wanted to do so.

That was the crux of the issue.

"If you had sincerely desired to do as instructed, Blade," Plato had emphasized.

Blade sighed, knowing Plato had correctly assessed the real reason for their failure. Unknown to anyone else, Hickok had wanted to return so he could go after the remaining Trolls, the ones responsible for his darling Joan's death. Blade couldn't tolerate being separated from his fiancee, Jenny. And even the normally dependable Geronimo, it turned out, had entertained an ulterior motive for wanting to head back to the Home; he intended to assist a woman and her daughter named Rainbow and Star.

Geronimo. Hickok. Himself. Alpha Triad. They had all changed in recent months, Blade reflected. Hickok was off somewhere, filled with a burning need for revenge, searching for the barbaric Trolls. Geronimo was quieter than usual on this run to Kalispell, and Blade wondered why. He knew Geronimo was the only remaining Family member with any vestige of Indian blood, and he also knew Geronimo had speculated on whether he was the last Indian left alive after the Big Blast. It must have come as something of a shock to learn there were thousands of Indians still residing in Montana, and probably elsewhere as well.

Blade could scarcely believe the sequence of events since they had returned from the Twin Cities. First, Plato verbally lambasted them for not complying with their orders. The Family Leader gave them two weeks to mend and prepare for their next run to the Twin Cities. Before the two weeks elapsed, however, circumstances conspired to prevent their departure for Minneapolis and St. Paul. While Alpha Triad was engaged in its initial trip, with Family member and Empath Joshua and Bertha, the colorful black woman raised in the Twin Cities, one of the Family had vanished from the Home. He was an aspiring Warrior, a youth named Shane, and he had left a sealed note for Hickok. The Family's pre-eminent gunfighter read the note, then angrily tore it to shreds. The very next night, Hickok disappeared from the Home, leaving a letter of his own, explaining he was going after Shane. Apparently, to impress Hickok, his hero, the inexperienced Shane had decided to hunt down the Trolls himself. In his note, Shane told Hickok he would return to the Home with the location of the Trolls' new headquarters by the time Hickok came back from the Twin Cities. Hickok, in his own letter, apologized for leaving without permission, but stressed he could not, in all conscience, leave Shane away from the Home alone.

Plato hit the proverbial roof!

Blade smiled at the memory. In all the years he'd known his gray-haired mentor, he could count the number of times he'd seen Plato mad on one hand. Hickok's abrupt departure disrupted their planned trip to the Twin Cities. Plato wanted three Warriors, one of the four Warrior Triads, to make the run, and Alpha Triad was the only one familiar with the SEAL and experienced in its use. Alpha Triad would be unable to leave until Hickok returned.

About this time, Geronimo requested a conference with Plato and the other Elders. Rainbow actually did the talking. She formally expressed her gratitude to the Family for taking her in after Hickok had saved her from three men in green uniforms. Rainbow explained her situation and requested aid. Those men Hickok had killed were part of a much larger military force attempting to exterminate her people, the Flathead Indians. These soldiers were based at a place called the Cheyenne Citadel. An army had attacked the Flathead Indian Reservation—as it was designated before the Big Blast—and slaughtered hundreds of the Indians before they could rally and retreat. The Indians withdrew to Kalispell and were surrounded. Four Indian warriors, along with Rainbow and Star, managed to escape the encircling troops, but they were followed, expertly tracked, and the four braves were shot. Rainbow and Star fled, and were about to be killed by the patrol sent after them when Hickok intervened and engaged the patrol in a gunfight, with fatal consequences for the unfortunate men. During the hundreds of miles of flight, Rainbow had neglected to eat and rest regularly, wearing herself down, and she had developed pneumonia. While the Family Healers supervised her recovery, Geronimo visited her regularly, becoming attached to both Rainbow and Star.

Blade glanced in the rear-view mirror at the two Flathead Indians, mother and daughter. They were sitting in the seat behind him. The SEAL was arranged with a pair of bucket seats in front, divided by a console. A comfortable seat the width of the transport was immediately behind the bucket seats. In the spacious rear was an ample section devoted to carrying supplies and storage.

Rainbow was the mother, a laconic woman with rich black hair and dark eyes. She wore homemade buckskins, decorated on the back with a realistic embroidered representation of a rainbow. Her twelve-year-old daughter, Star, was the perfect image of her mom.

Blade's mind drifted to that fateful conference

between the Family Elders and Rainbow. At the conclusion of her speech, Rainbow made a proposition. "I asked to meet with all of you for a reason," the Flathead woman had said. "I need to return to Kalispell. It was a mistake for me to leave. It's too far to try alone, with only my daughter along. I know your vehicle, the SEAL, could make the . . ."

"The SEAL is our only means of transportation," Plato promptly replied, "aside from our horses. We can not risk damaging the SEAL, so we only utilize it when absolutely necessary and we have no other recourse. I'm sorry, but I can't allow what you're about to suggest."

"Hear me out," Rainbow patiently urged him. "I realize how important the SEAL is to you. I also know how much you want to find some scientific and medical things. Am I right?"

Plato nodded, his brow furrowed.

"If you will let someone take me back to Kalispell in your SEAL," Rainbow offered, "I will let them know where they can locate the items you need."

Blade and Geronimo attended that meeting, held in one of the concrete blocks in the Family compound, in E Block, the library. Blade recalled how Plato leaned across the table he was seated at and drilled his blue eyes into Rainbow.

"You know where the equipment and supplies we need can be found?" Plato asked skeptically.

"I do," Rainbow affirmed.

"You'll excuse me," Plato bluntly stated, "if I don't believe you."

Rainbow straightened. "I do not lie," she retorted.

"I meant no insult," Plato informed her. "But you must appreciate my stance. The SEAL is too valuable to the Family."

Rainbow slowly stared at each of the fifteen Elders, seated at the long table with Plato. To qualify as a

Family Elder, a member of the Family simply had to attain a forty-fifth birthday. The high mortality rate made the forty-fifth birthday a legitimate milestone. "And what about your problem?" Rainbow asked them.

No one answered.

"Geronimo has told me about your aging problem," Rainbow went on. "He also told me you'd hoped to find the things you need in the Twin Cities. You heard him. The Twin Cities are in a shambles. Those groups—what were their names?—and the crazies, the ones fighting over the Twin Cities for the last one hundred years, have left the place a shambles, the buildings in ruin, and everything of any real value destroyed." Rainbow suddenly faced Blade. "You were there. What chance do you have of finding the things Plato needs?"

Blade, caught off guard, squirmed uncomfortably. "I don't know. . . ."

"Be honest," Rainbow said, goading him.

Blade stared at Plato. "Realistically, I'd have to admit our chances are pretty slim."

"See?" Rainbow declared triumphantly. "Even if Alpha Triad goes back to the Twin Cities, you're not guaranteed they'll find what you've sent them after."

"It is still our wisest recourse," Plato said, dissenting.

"No, it isn't," Rainbow disagreed. "There is a hospital in Kalispell, and it may well have the items you've been looking for."

"Why should the hospital in Kalispell be in any better condition then the ones in the Twin Cities?" Plato asked.

Rainbow grinned, sensing she was winning her argument. "Because, unlike the Twin Cities, after the Government evacuated all the towns and cities at the beginning of World War Three, there weren't any gangs left in Kalispell to tear the place apart. I visited it several times in my youth, and it was essentially deserted, except for occasional drifters and scavengers. I can vouch for the fact that, when I left Kalispell, the hospital was still standing and its contents were still intact. I've seen the inside of the hospital. There's a lot of abandoned equipment all over the place—covered with dust and dirt, but still there. It just may be what you're looking for."

"What about the battle?" Plato inquired.

"The army from the Cheyenne Citadel has Kalispell surrounded," Rainbow elaborated. "They prevent my people from leaving, but they haven't attacked yet. At least, they hadn't before I was forced to leave. They're just sitting there, apparently trying to starve us out, watching and waiting."

Blade abruptly sat up, all attention. "Watching?"

"Yes." Rainbow seemed puzzled by his reaction.

Blade glanced at Plato and knew the Leader was thinking similar thoughts. "Have you ever heard of the Watchers?" Blade asked Rainbow.

She shook her head. "Why?"

"We had a run-in with a military organization in Thief River Falls," Blade expounded. "The people in the Twin Cities call this organization the Watchers. I wonder if they're related. . . ."

". . . to the ones trying to wipe out my people?" Rainbow said, finishing for him. "Could be."

"And you maintain the hospital in Kalispell and the equipment inside it are undamaged?" Plato asked her.

"They were when I left," Rainbow replied.

"Hmmmmmmm." Plato leaned back in his chair and pulled at the hairs in his gray beard with his left hand. "Would you be so kind as to step outside? We must discuss your proposition in private."

And here I am, Blade ruminated, on my way to Kalispell, Montana. His dearest Jenny was hundreds of miles behind him. All because Plato and the Elders decided a mission to Kalispell might be worth it, after all. *Something* must be done about the creeping senility, and the sooner, the better. Family records revealed that each generation of Family members was evincing evidence of a particularly debilitating form of senility at an earlier and earlier age. If the cause and a cure weren't discovered, the prospects for the Family's future were exceedingly grim.

Blade gazed at Geronimo, sitting in the bucket seat on the passenger side, intently scanning a map. "How many miles do we have left to travel?" he inquired.

Geronimo, attired in a green shirt and pants sewn together from the pieces of an old tent, glanced up, frowning. "That's what I'm trying to figure out," he explained. His stocky body was hunched over the road map, his left hand absently scratching the short black hair above his left ear, his brown eyes reflecting his deep concentration. "It's not as easy as it was when we went from the Home to the Twin Cities."

"How so?" Blade questioned him.

"It was simple to compute the total distance from our Home, in northwestern Minnesota, to the Twin Cities, in southeastern Minnesota," Geronimo elaborated, "because they're both in the same state. It was a snap to add the mileage listed on this map and determine there were three hundred and seventy-one miles between the Home and the Twins. But this time . . ." He left the thought unfinished as he studied the map again.

"It's a good thing Hickok isn't here," Blade noted. "He might offer to take off his moccasins so you would have more to count with."

Geronimo grinned and looked at Blade. "I miss him," he admitted.

"So do I," Blade acknowledged.

"I'm surprised Plato let us come on this trip without

Hickock," Geronimo commented.

"Plato wasn't kidding when he said it was urgent," Blade remarked.

"Anyway," Geronimo said, "I think I have the mileage calculated."

"Let me hear it," Blade responded.

"Well," Geronimo said, glancing at the map, "bear in mind we're traveling across several states this time, so I may be a little off. We've already left Minnesota behind, we're in North Dakota now, and the next state we'll hit is Montana. We took Highway 11 to Highway 59, cut across to U.S. Highway 2, and, according to this map, we can follow Highway 2 all the way to Kalispell. Amazing."

"And the mileage?" Blade reminded him.

"The total is somewhere in the range of eleven hundred miles," Geronimo replied.

"We knew that before we left the Home," Blade noted. "What I need to know now, Einstein, is how far have we come, and how far do we have to go?"

Geronimo smiled. "We passed through what was left of Minot this morning," he replied. "According to my calculations, we've traveled about four hundred and seventy miles, and we have something like six hundred and sixty to go, give or take a few."

"Give or take a few," Blade repeated, sighing.

"At our average speed, about fifty miles an hour," Geronimo stated, "it's taken us a day and a half to come this far. If we continue driving seven or eight hours a day," Geronimo detailed, "we'll reach the vicinity of Kalispell in three days. Maybe even sooner, if I've over-estimated the distance remaining."

"So soon?" Rainbow spoke up from the back seat. "Four or five days? Do you know how long it took me to reach your Home from Kalispell with those men after me?"

"How long?" Blade inquired.

"Over two months!" she answered. "Of course, I had to watch out for wild animals and the blistered ones. . . ."

"The blistered ones?" Blade reiterated.

"The creatures you call mutates," Rainbow elucidated.

Blade involuntarily shuddered. The damn mutates! He hated them with a passion! One of them was responsible for slaying his father, the Family Leader prior to Plato. The origin of the mutates was unknown, most Family members speculating they were the result of the radiation and the chemical weapons unleashed on the environment during the Big Blast. Mutates were once normal animals, altered through a mysterious process to become monstrous caricatures of their former selves. Their hair dropped off, their skin turned brownish and dry, cracked and covered with blistering sores, oozing pus all over their bodies. Each mutate was endowed with a voracious appetite and undiluted ferocity. Mutates attacked and devoured any living thing they encountered, including one another. Even just a single mutate bite could prove fatal, if any of the yellow pus entered the bloodstream.

"I've got a few questions I'd like to ask," Blade said to Rainbow, eager to change the subject.

"Go ahead," she said.

Blade glanced in the mirror, observing Star asleep in her mother's lap. "She's a little angel," he remarked.

Rainbow proudly stroked her daughter's forehead. "That she is."

"You really haven't told us much about your people," Blade commented. "For instance, you've never mentioned your husband."

"What would you . . ." Rainbow began to say.

"Look out!" Geronimo suddenly shouted in warning.

Blade's eyes darted forward.

The SEAL was at the top of a small hill, and lined up across the road at the bottom were over a dozen armed men.

Blade slammed on the brakes and the transport lurched to a stop.

Tall trees bordered the highway on both sides. More armed men came rushing from the woods, closing in on the vehicle.

"It's a trap!" Rainbow exclaimed in alarm.

Blade caught sight of men closing in behind the SEAL. He glared right, then left, and pounded his right fist on the steering wheel.

Damn!

3

Sherry woke up with the sun high in the sky, a light breeze on her face, and birds singing in nearby trees. The September air was warm. She remembered the events of the night before and sat upright, fearing the gunman had abandoned her.

He was still there.

Hickok was by the fire, sitting up, his arms resting on the barrel of his rifle, the butt on the ground between his legs. His head hung low, his chin on his chest, asleep.

So he hadn't left her to fend for herself! Delighted, she went to rise, her right hand scraping against a small rock.

Instantly, the gunman reacted, coming awake, sweeping the rifle up, searching for the source of the sound. His keen blue eyes fell on her.

"Oh. It's just you," Hickok grumbled, lowering his Navy Arms Henry Carbine, a reproduction of the original Henry used by pioneers in early America. Kurt Carpenter had stocked the Family armory with hundreds of firearms, the appropriate ammunition, other assorted weapons, and even a shop for reloading cartridges, repairing defective guns, and sharpening blades. The other Warriors could use whatever firearms they wanted, but the Colt Pythons and the Henry were Hickok's by virtue of his supreme skill with both, and his attachment to them bordered on the extreme.

"Thanks a lot," Sherry quipped. "You sure know how to make a girl feel flattered."

"Sorry I drifted off," Hickok apologized, standing and stretching.

"No need," Sherry said, following his example.

"Yes, there is," he stated seriously. "I'm trained not to fall asleep on the job. This is the first time I've ever done it. I hadn't slept for two days, but that's no excuse."

"It's good enough for me," Sherry stated.

"We could have been killed because of my laziness," Hickok remarked. "It won't happen again," he vowed.

"What are you plans?" Sherry asked him.

"Are you hungry?" Hickok responded.

"My stomach is growling loud enough to wake up the dead," she replied.

"Here." Hickok reached behind him and unfastened the flap on a leather pouch attached to the rear of his belt. He gripped a strip of dried meat and tossed it to her.

Sherry caught the meat and raised it to her nose. The aroma was incredibly appetizing. "What is it?"

"Smoked venison jerky," Hickok informed her. "It's all you'll get until I can take the time to kill some game."

"It will suffice," she said, biting into the tough jerky.

Hickok walked over and retrieved the Glenfield. He knelt and probed the dead Troll's tunic until he found a handful of bullets in a makeshift pocket.

"What are you doing?" Sherry inquired, savoring the tangy taste of the venison, her mouth watering.

"You know how to handle this?" Hickok waved the Glenfield at her.

"I can shoot," she told him.

"Good. It's yours." He handed the rifle to her and looked her up and down. Her dirty yellow blouse was torn in a dozen spots, and one of the short sleeves was missing. The faded jeans on her legs were in slightly better shape. "Are those pockets in one piece, ma'am?" Hickok asked her.

"Ma'am?" Sherry repeated, her mouth full of jerky.

"Are those pockets in one piece?" he demanded again.

"These?" She glanced down. "One of them is. The one on the left has a big hole in it, but the other one is . . ."

"Fine," he interrupted, shoving the bullets at her. "You'll need these to go with the rifle."

Sherry leaned the Glenfield against her right leg and took the bullets.

Hickok turned and began walking in an easterly direction.

"Wait a minute!" Sherry stuffed the bullets in her pocket and hastily caught up with him. "What's the rush?"

"While you were with those Trolls," Hickok ignored her query, "did you see anything of a guy dressed in black, totin' a six-shooter?"

"A what?"

"A revolver strapped to his right hip," Hickok replied, a bit impatiently. "To be specific, an Abilene Single Action in .44 Magnum. He's not much more than a kid, actually. Just turned sixteen."

"I haven't seen anyone answering your description," Sherry stated. "I've only seen one other person since the Trolls caught me, and he was a pitiful little man they tortured and killed. Kind of fitting, in a way."

"Why is that?" Hickok asked, still marching east. They were at the eastern edge of the town of Fox, the former Troll headquarters. The forest loomed ahead.

"The Trolls gouged his eyes out with a spear."

"Oh?"

"Yeah. The one you shot last did all the gouging."

Hickok nodded. "Fits."

"Fits?"

"I have a friend named Joshua," Hickok said. "He would call it the design of cosmic justice."

"Sounds like your friend is the brainy type," Sherry commented, taking another bite of the delicious venison.

"Where you from?" Hickok inquired, glancing at her face, amused at the sight of her full cheeks and mouth chewing furiously.

"Sundown."

"Beg pardon?"

"Sundown," she said again. "It's in Canada, just across the border from Minnesota. Dinky little place. Has a few dozen still living there. The Trolls caught me when I stepped out of my cabin to enjoy an evening stroll."

"Didn't the folks in Sundown evacuate to a larger city when the nuclear war broke out?" Hickok asked.

"Some did," she said, shrugging, "and some didn't. We heard horrible tales from our parents and our grandparents. There was a critical shortage of the necessities, of food and clothing and the like, right after the war. Governments collapsed. Our grandparents said they even heard reports of cannibalism from Winnipeg. Cannibalism! How terrible!"

"Winnipeg?" Hickok repeated, displaying his ignorance of Canadian geography.

"Winnipeg is the nearest major city to Sundown. No one has ventured there in years and years," Sherry explained.

"You got a family in Sundown?" Hickok questioned her.

"My mother and father." She smiled at the memory.

"No husband?"

"No." Sherry shook her head.

"Really?"

"You sound surprised," she said, amused.

"I am. How do you folks get by?"

"Oh, we grow a lot. We have livestock. Except for the damn Trolls, no one has bothered us in a long time. Guess Sundown is so far out in the middle of nowhere, no one knows we're there."

"You eager to get home?" Hickok asked.

They reached the forest, the tall trees and the dense underbrush confronting them with a dark wall of vegetation.

"It looks foreboding in there," Sherry remarked.

"It's your imagination," Hickok stated, and led the way along a worn trail. "The Trolls must have used this regularly. We'll follow it and see where we end up."

"What makes you think the Trolls came this way?"

Hickok knelt and pointed at the bare ground. "Look at all the scuff marks and heel prints. I have a friend named Geronimo, the best tracker there is, and if he were here right now he could tell you how many people had passed this way, how long ago it was, and even if they were right- or left-handed."

"You're kidding," Sherry commented.

"I'm telling the truth," Hickok said. "A competent tracker can determine from the depth of the imprint whether a person is right or left-handed. If a person is right-handed, the right heel digs in a bit deeper than the left. Or the other way around. Well, I'm not that good. But I am skilled enough to know a lot of Trolls passed this way some time back. I suspect the lousy varmints came this way when they moseyed out of Fox."

"Has anyone ever told you," Sherry noted, "that you talk funny sometimes?"

"You're kidding!" Hickok smiled.

"Why?" Sherry asked him.

Hickok rose and continued deeper into the woods. "I reckon it's because I like the Old West so much."

"The what?"

"The western frontier of America in the days of the gunfighters, the sheriffs, and the outlaws," Hickok answered.

"Never heard of it," Sherry admitted.

"You have a good vocabulary," Hickok observed. "You must be able to read."

"My parents taught me," she confided. "We have several hundred books, but none on this Old West."

"Too bad," Hickok stated. "We have a library where I come from, and it's filled with hundreds of thousands of books. Books on every conceivable subject. My favorites were always the westerns, and in particular any book on the life of James Butler Hickok."

"Who was he?" Sherry pushed a slim branch out of her path.

"One of the greatest Americans who ever lived. As a tribute to him, I took his name at my Naming."

"Your what?"

"My Naming. When we turn sixteen we're permitted to pick the name we want to be known by," Hickok told her.

"You're kidding!"

Hickok glanced over his left shoulder, frowning. "No. The man who built the place where I'm from wanted us to remember the past, to keep in touch with our historical roots, as he put it in his diary. So we're told to go through the history books, or any of the others for that matter, and select whatever name we like. It's as simple as that."

"Where are you from?" Sherry inquired.

"Somewhere," was his cryptic response.

"I told you where I'm from," she pointed out.

"Thank you."

"And you're not going to let me know where you're from?"

"I reckon not."

"Why?" Sherry asked, an edge to her tone. "Don't you trust me."

"Nope," he replied frankly.

"Why not?"

Hickok paused and stared into her eyes. "Trust is like love. You must earn it. Only an idiot trusts blindly."

Sherry followed on his heels as he resumed their trek. He certainly was a strange one. But then, all men were a bit on the weird side. Must be a quirk in their genes. She gazed at the trees overhead, watching a squirrel scamper from limb to limb. Funny, how she sensed she could trust this one right off the bat. There was something about him, a quality of confidence he tended to inspire in others. What was this "score" business? The chip on his shoulder must weigh tons!

The squirrel suddenly chattered like crazy and darted to the north.

Sherry detected a movement in the branches of a large tree ahead. The branches hung directly above the trail they were on. Was it the wind?

Hickok was strolling nonchalantly along the dirt trail, his Henry cradled in his arms.

Why should she worry? If Hickok wasn't concerned, if he didn't see anything wrong, then there probably wasn't. He gave the impression of being a proficient fighter. Surely his senses would alert him if anything were amiss?

Those branches moved again, sagging unnaturally, as if a great weight were on them, concealed by the leaves.

Should she say something? Sherry tensed as they neared the tree, her eyes focused on those lower branches. Maybe she should tell . . .

The leaves abruptly parted, and a hulking form hurtled from concealment, leaping at the gunman seven feet away.

"Hickok!" Sherry shouted, frozen in her tracks. "Look out!"

4

"Scavengers!" Geronimo yelled.

There were at least thirty, attired in filthy rags and armed with a variety of weapons.

Blade knew their type well. They traveled in groups, preying on anyone they found, stealing food and guns and lives with indiscriminate abandon. Thanks to the high walls encircling the Home, and the prowess of the Warriors, the Family was spared being ravaged by the bands of scavengers roaming the countryside.

"They're all around us!" Star screamed, awake and terrified, gripping her mother, the knuckles on her hands white.

Blade destested these human vultures. He saw one of them runnng up to his side of the SEAL, carrying a knife, apparently intending to thrust it through Blade's open window.

"Blade!" Rainbow needlessly cried a warning.

Blade slowly reached his right hand across his broad chest and drew the Dan Wesson .44 Magnum revolver from its leather shoulder holster. Like Geronimo, he had lost many of the weapons he'd taken to the Twin Cities. Before departing for Kalispell, they had paid the armory a visit and selected their arms for this run. He liked the feel of this revolver. The Dan Wesson .44 Magnum was a *big* handgun, but in his massive hand it felt just right. In addition to the revolver, an Auto-Ordnance Model 27 A-1 was on the console beside him. It reminded him of the Commando Arms Carbine he'd used before. Like the Commando, the Auto-Ordnance was modified by the Family gunsmiths so it could function on full automatic. The Auto-Ordnance was a re-creation of the Thompson Model 1927 used by gangsters during the early decades of the twentieth century.

"Blade!" Rainbow shouted.

Blade pointed the ten-inch barrel at the scavenger and squeezed the trigger. The boom of the .44 Magnum was deafening in the confines of the transport.

The scavenger reacted as though he'd slammed into a wall. His body was flung backward, sprawling in a heap at the side of the highway.

Blade aimed at a scavenger with a rifle and fired, the heavy slug taking the top of the scavenger's head off.

Geronimo entered the fray. He still carried an Arminius .357 Magnum under his right arm, and his remaining tomahawk was tucked under his belt. The new addition to his personal arsenal was a FNC Auto Rifle, and he swung it out his window as three of the scavengers closed in. The FNC burped and the three men tumbled to the ground, one of them shrieking in agony.

Bullets and arrows were striking the body of the SEAL, some of them whining as they were deflected by the bulletproof plastic.

"Hang on!" Blade yelled as he accelerated, flooring the pedal.

The SEAL surged ahead, plowing into one of the attackers and bowling him aside.

Blade and Geronimo rolled up their windows as the transport raced down the hill. The men in front parted, firing at the vehicle in a fruitless attempt to stop it.

"Mommy!" Star screamed, frightened by the shouting, gesticulating men and the projectiles colliding with the body of the transport.

One of the scavengers, braver or dumber than the rest, stood his ground, a shotgun leveled at the SEAL.

Blade deliberately mowed the shotgun-wielder over, ramming the scavenger at the same instant the man fired. Carpenter's scientists had performed their tasks, had met his rigid specifications, with remarkable precision; even at point-blank range, the shotgun pellets were unable to penetrate the impervious plastic shell comprising the SEAL's outer surface. The scavenger, however, was not as indestructible. The front grill of the transport caught him in the chest and caved it in, his ribs folding in upon themselves. For the fleetest moment, the scavenger was airborne, his face pressed against the windshield, his mouth gaping in silent horror at his untimely fate. Then his body slipped under the SEAL, his shoulders angling to the left, and the asphalt clutched his bouncing form and hurtled him under the front tire. His head was immediately pulverized in a spray of flesh and crimson.

"We made it!" Rainbow voiced her relief as the transport raced away from the scavengers.

Unexpectedly, Blade wrenched on the steering wheel, slewing the vehicle to a stop, its sleek structure positioned across the highway.

"What are you doing?" Rainbow demanded.

"What's he doing?" Star echoed her mother.

The scavengers, elated at this turn of events, charged the SEAL en masse.

Blade glanced at Rainbow and Star. "Nobody," he growled, "attacks us with impunity." He looked at Geronimo and grinned.

The scavengers were running toward the transport,

giddy at the prospect of its impending capture.

"Ready?" Blade asked Geronimo.

Geronimo nodded, his eyes twinkling. "Too bad Hickok couldn't be here. He'd appreciate this."

"What the hell are you doing?" Rainbow angrily inquired.

Blade hastily rolled down his window, scooped up the Auto-Ordnance, and pointed it at the approaching scavengers.

The scavengers in the front rows of the pack saw what was coming and tried to slow, to stop, to get out of the way, but the ones behind them pushed forward, oblivious to the danger.

Blade, smiling, let them have it.

The Auto-Ordnance bucked as the first rounds ripped into the scavengers, the slugs decimating the front rows, the scavengers tripping over one another as legs became entangled in falling bodies and limbs flew every which way.

Geronimo flung his door open and stood, his feet on the sideboard, the FNC supported by the roof for a better aim. He fired into the rear ranks of the scavengers, venting his war whoop.

The scavengers broke. Those still alive and able fled, disappearing into the forest. The road was covered with dead or dying scavengers, moaning and groaning and pleading for assistance.

Blade and Geronimo ceased firing.

"With a hundred like you two," Rainbow commented, "my people could easily defeat the Citadel army."

Blade placed his Auto-Ordnance on the console and wheeled the SEAL on its westward course, slowly picking up speed.

Geronimo slid into his seat and closed the door, keeping his eyes to their rear. "No sign of pursuit," he mentioned.

"I don't expect any," Blade remarked.

"When you think about it," Geronimo commented, "we've been pretty lucky so far."

"How so?" Blade asked.

"That was the first time we were attacked on this trip," Geronimo noted. "We've been keeping on the highway too, right out in the open."

"Not too surprising," Blade said. "The wild animals shy away from the SEAL for some reason. Even the mutates, like that one we spotted yesterday afternoon, seem to sense the transport is not a living thing and avoid it. As for the Watchers, they prefer to congregate near inhabited areas and maintain their outposts in the larger towns. If we can avoid a Watcher patrol, we will probably reach Kalispell in one piece."

"Probably?" Rainbow questioned.

"You never know," Blade stated fatalistically.

"I'm hungry," Star announced.

Blade glanced at Rainbow. "Why don't you give her some jerky. Take some for yourself too. We won't stop until it's almost dark. I want to go as far as we can today." Because, he reflected, the sooner we reach Kalispell, the faster I can return to my darling Jenny.

Rainbow nodded and turned to her rear. A glass jar, filled with venison jerky, was on top of a pile of supplies in the rear section of the vehicle. She picked up the jar, unscrewed the lid, and handed a strip of meat to her daughter.

"Thanks, Mom," Star said, dutifully expressing her gratitude.

Rainbow removed another piece of jerky and bit into it. "Do either of you want some?" she inquired of Blade and Geronimo, her mouth full of venison.

The two Warriors shook their heads.

"But I would like to ask you some questions," Blade

said.

"What's on your mind?" Rainbow replaced the jar in the back of the transport.

"What's life been like for your people" Blade queried her. "Since the Big Blast, I mean?"

"Since the war?" Rainbow thought a moment. "My parents told me it was real rough right after the war. There were shortages of everything. But then things changed."

"Changed?" Blade echoed. "How?"

"The white man was gone," Rainbow elaborated. "Evacuated from all the towns and cities by the Government and moved south."

"Why weren't your people evacuated?" Blade interrupted.

Rainbow shrugged. "Beats me. We were left to fend for ourselves. After the tribal leaders organized, after the initial shock passed, we discovered we could do a lot better on our own, better than we did under white rule. Western Montana was not hit by any of the nuclear missiles, except for Great Falls, hundreds of miles to the southeast of Kalispell and the Reservation. The prevailing winds blew the Great Falls fallout to the east, away from us. My people found themselves exactly as they had been before the white man arrived in this country: living in fertile land teeming with game and abundant water. We reverted to a simpler lifestyle, living as the Indian had for centuries before the coming of the whites. My people became hunters and tillers of the soil. We rediscovered our heritage and our dignity. Within a generation after the war, alcoholism, once a rampant problem, was almost eliminated." She paused, then stared at the passing scenery. "My people discovered they were better off without the whites. Of course," she stressed, "all of this happened before I was born, but my parents and grandparents told me all about it. We are a free people now, and we will never submit to the white man's rule again!'"

"Your people have stayed on the Reservation?" Blade inquired.

"We spread out some," Rainbow replied. Many moved north and east and settled around Flathead Lake."

"You said before," Blade pointed out, "that Kalispell has been deserted all these years. Why didn't your people just move into Kalispell or one of the other towns?"

"Because they belonged to the white man," Rainbow said distastefully, "and we want nothing to do with anything belonging to our former masters."

"You sound bitter," Blade observed.

"Can you blame me? I know our history. The whites lied to us, murdered us, stole our land, and then forced us to live on a small parcel they so graciously offered. My people were little more than slaves! What hypocrites the whites were! They proudly claimed they released the black man from bondage, while at the same time they kept the red man confined to the reservations. No, my people want nothing to do with the white man or anything belonging to the white man! Be thankful we're the way we are. It's the only reason the hospital in Kalispell went untouched all these years."

"What about this Cheyenne Citadel?" Blade questioned her. "Are all the people living there white? Do you have any idea who these people are, and why they've sent an army to attack you?"

Rainbow glanced down at her daughter. Star was asleep again, curled up on the seat, her head resting on Rainbow's lap. "We know very little. The Cheyenne Citadel is a fortress. We believe the people living in the Citadel, and those south of it, in what was once called Colorado, are the descendants of the ones the Government evacuated at the outset of World War Three. Once, years ago, before I was born, one of these people, a fugitive, came to live with my tribe. He told us about his life. . . ."

"Your tribe didn't kill him?" Blade interjected.

"No. Why should we?" Rainbow responded, puzzled.

"He was white, wasn't he?"

"You've misunderstood," Rainbow stated. "We don't hate individual whites. I don't hate you. We can't blame you for what happened centuries ago. It's the bastards who were running your Government—the crooked politicians, as they were called—and the bigots and the greedy fleecers. It's their memory we despise. So long as one Flathead remains to tell the story to our children, my people will remember. And, remembering, we will never become slaves again!"

"What did this man tell your people?" Blade wanted to know. He looked at Geronimo, wondering why his friend wasn't contributing to their conversation.

Geronimo was gazing out the windshield, apparently uninterested.

"He said the city of Denver, Colorado, is now the capital of the United States Government. He told my parents the Government was oppressive, and he left because he couldn't tolerate being completely controlled and told what to do and when to do it. About a month after this man came to live with my tribe, he was found dead one morning, still in his sleeping blankets."

"What did he die from?"

"No one knew. They couldn't find a mark on him. Anyway, we haven't had anything to do with the Citadel or the people living there. We kept to ourselves. They kept to themselves. At least, that's the way it was until several years ago. Then they began sending patrols into our country, and these patrols fired at us whenever they saw us. Our warriors usually chased them off. Nothing

else happened until this army marched from the Citadel
and attacked us, forcing us into Kalispell and surrounding us. We know they intend to wipe us out, but we have
no idea why. They're better armed than we are, and it's
only a matter of time before my people run out of food in
Kalispell."

"So why are you going back?" Blade asked.

"I must," Rainbow said. "We should never have
left."

"So why did you?"

Rainbow stretched and yawned. "I'm getting tired.
Do you mind if I take a nap? We can talk some more
later."

"Fine by me," Blade said, watching her close her eyes
and lean her head on the seat. Why was she avoiding his
question? Did she know more than she was telling? Who
was she, really? After all, three soldiers had followed
Star and her over a thousand miles, intent on killing
them. Why?

The terrain was hilly and covered with brush, the
highway winding across the landscape like a giant black
snake.

Blade glanced at Geronimo.

"You okay?"

"Sure. Why?"

"You're not saying much."

Geronimo sighed and faced Blade. "I thought I was
the last Indian."

"I know."

"It's been quite a surprise to learn differently,"
Geronimo stated.

"I can imagine," Blade commiserated with him.

"Can you?" Geronimo asked doubtfully. "I've read
every book in our library on Indians. I know our history
as well as she does." He pointed at Rainbow. "I'm
proud to be an Indian. That's one of the reasons I

selected the name Geronimo at my own Naming. Geronimo inspired me in my youth. He refused to abandon the Indian ways, and fought against being dominated and domesticated. Geronimo is a symbol of me, a reminder I must never lose sight of my Indian heritage. Now, I learn an entire tribe feels the way I do. Now, I'm not so sure. . . ."

"About what?"

"About where I belong."

"What do you mean?"

Geronimo stared at Rainbow and Star. "I'm not so sure I should stay with the Family."

Blade struggled to prevent his shock from showing. "What?"

"Maybe I should be living with the Flathead Indians," Geronimo stated.

"You can't be serious!"

"I am," Geronimo declared. "I've never been more serious in my life. The Flatheads and I share a common heritage. I've always felt slightly different from the rest of the Family. . . ."

"Because you're the only Indian in the Family?" Blade asked.

"That's part of it," Geronimo admitted. "I've talked with Rainbow about it, and she says her people would welcome me into their tribe. She wants me to come live with them."

"She does, does she?" Blade remarked, his tone tinged with anger.

"Yes." Geronimo turned and watched a hawk high overhead. "In fact, she was the one who first suggested the idea."

"Really." Out of the corner of his eyes, reflected in the rear-view mirror, Blade caught sight of Rainbow's face.

She was still leaning her head on the seat, still lying with her eyes closed, still taking her nap.

But she was grinning in smug satisfaction.

5

Hickok's reflexes were panther quick. The barrel of the Henry swept around and the long gun boomed, the slug catching his assailant in the chest and flipping him backward, arresting his momentum, causing him to fall to the ground at Hickok's feet. Another figure sprang from the leafy tree, and Hickok smoothly danced to one side. The gunman rammed the barrel of the Henry into the stomach of his attacker while the man was still in midair.

The second assailant grunted and tumbled to the grass at the side of the trail. He was armed with a knife, and he clutched it in his right fist as he went to rise and renew his assault.

The barrel of the Henry was jammed into his left cheek. "Make one move, pard, and you'll have a lot of trouble eating your food from now on. Drop that knife!"

The man froze in a sitting up position. He dropped the knife.

Hickok stepped in front of his prisoner. "Any more of you hereabouts?"

The man vigorously shook his head.

"I hope so, for your sake," Hickok informed him. "If I hear so much as a twig snap, I'll blow your brains out."

The man was gaping in horror at the barrel of the Henry, now positioned at the tip of his bullbous nose.

Hickok studied the captive. He was in his thirties and had brown hair and brown eyes. His narrow face was clean shaven, but dirty. In fact, his entire body was covered with a fine layer of dust. He wore shabby clothes, crudely patched together at the seams, black pants, and a grimy gray shirt missing all the buttons.

"This one is dead," Sherry announced. She was kneeling next to the first attacker, holding his limp left wrist in her right hand. "I can't find a pulse."

"You want to wind up like your friend here?" Hickok asked, tapping the Henry barrel against the man's nose.

The captive gulped. "Sure don't, mister!"

"Good. Roll over and lie on your stomach, your hands above your head, and cross your legs. Do it!"

The prisoner immediately obeyed.

"Good." Hickok scanned the area, but the woods were quiet and peaceful. He relaxed slightly, knowing the man on the ground could not possibly reach him before receiving a bullet in the brain. "I'm going to ask you some questions," he stated. "You will answer right away, without taking time to think. If you hesitate, I'll shoot you in the head. Do you understand?"

"Yes, sir!"

"If you move your arms or legs, I'll shoot you in the head. Do you understand?"

"Yes, sir!"

"If I get the impression you're lying, guess what happens?"

"You shoot me in the head!" the prisoner said in a high, squeaky voice.

"Good. We have a mutual understanding. According to this wise man I know, name of Plato, that's the best kind of relationship to have. Don't you agree?"

"Yes, sir!"

"You don't have the slightest damn idea of what I'm talking about, do you?"

"No, sir!"

Hickok heard Sherry laugh.

"What's your name?" Hickok asked.

"Silvester."

"Where you from, Silvester?"

"I'm from the Mound, sir."

Hickok squatted on his haunches. "Look at me," he ordered.

Silvester complied, his eyes wide and fearful.

"What's the Mound?" Hickok inquired.

"It's where we live."

"We?"

"My people. The others call us the Moles."

Hickok glanced at Sherry. She shrugged and shook her head, indicating she was also confused.

"What were you doing here?" Hickok continued his interrogation.

"Wolfe sent us to see where the Trolls came from," Silvester answered.

"The Trolls? You're friends of the Trolls?"

"Friends?" Despite his situation, Silvester chuckled. "No, not friends. We were sent to see if any were still alive."

Hickok tensed. "Explain. Tell me everything."

"We ambushed the Trolls and killed most of them," Silvester went on, unaware of the impact his words were having on the gunman. "We took some prisoners. They told us about Fox, the town they came from. They said they were getting out of this area, trying to get away from some fierce people called the Family, I think. The Trolls were looking for a new home when our scouts found their camp. We snuck up on them during the night, because no one can see in the dark like us. They never knew what hit them!"

"And you slaughtered most of them?" Hickok probed, uncertain whether he should feel relieved the Trolls were dead or mad because his revenge was being denied.

"Most of them, yes," Silvester acknowledged. "Like I said, we took some prisoners. About fifteen, I think. Eleven Trolls, three women, and the strange one."

"Strange one? Who's the strange one?" Hickok questioned the Mole.

"We don't know," Silvester responded. "He won't tell us his name, no matter what we do to him. He was captured by the Trolls first. We found him when we sacked their camp. The Trolls told us he was one of the Family."

Hickok reacted as if jolted by an electric current. He grabbed Silvester and lifted his shoulders several inches off the ground. "Describe him to me," he growled.

Silvester cringed. "He's not much more than a kid. Can't even be twenty yet. Wears black clothes. I don't know much else! Honest!" He detected a gleam in Hickok's eyes and tried to pull away. "Honest! Wolfe is holding him in the cells. That's all I know!"

"Who is this Wolfe?" Hickok asked harshly.

"Wolfe is our leader."

"Where is this Mound of yours?" Hickok demanded.

"About fifty miles southeast of here," Silvester replied. "Why?"

Hickok slowly stood, his brow creased. Shane probably dogged the Trolls, trying to learn where they would settle next, and was captured. Then, when these Moles almost wiped out the Trolls, Shane fell into their hands. Terrific! He walked over to Sherry.

"The one in black he talked about," Sherry commented. "Isn't he the one you're looking for?"

"Sure is." Hickok nodded at Silvester. "I'm going to this Mound and free Shane. . . ."

"Just like that?" Sherry interrupted.

"Just like that. There's no need for you to go along, though. Could be dangerous. You've got the Glenfield. Think you could find your way to Sundown?"

"I don't know," Sherry answered. "I might be able to do it."

"Well, you can either head for Sundown," Hickok said, detailing her options, "or you can travel due west until you run into the Family. Tell them I sent you and they'll make you welcome. Or, if you want, you can stay in Fox until I return. It's up to you."

"You've overlooked one choice," Sherry said.

"What's that?"

"I can come with you."

"No way," Hickok disagreed. "Sorry."

"Why not?"

"I told you. It could be dangerous. I'll be traveling hard and fast. . . ."

"I can keep up," she promised.

". . . and I might not be able to protect you if we have a scrape or two."

"I can take care of myself," Sherry stated. "And you'll need someone to cover your back."

"I don't need anyone to cover my back," Hickok retorted.

"Is that right?" she asked, grinning.

"That's right," Hickok confirmed.

"The male ego!" Sherry laughed. "Well, Mr. High and Mighty, if you don't need anyone to cover your back, I guess you don't need me to tell you your prisoner is getting away."

"What?" Hickok spun, bringing the Henry level. Sure enough. Silvester was ten yards away and crawling for all he was worth. "One more inch," Hickok warned him, "and you'll be growing roots in your chest!"

Silvester stopped and glanced sheepishly over his right shoulder.

"Back here, now!" Hickok barked.

Silvester turned and crawled to his original position.

Sherry was snickering. "Still think you don't need me?"

Hickok glared at the Mole. "Sneeze, and you're dead!" He looked at Sherry. "You know, I asked you once before if you were eager to return to Sundown and you never answered me. Now you've got a rifle and ammunition, enough to see you safely home. And yet you seem reluctant to go. Why?"

Sherry avoided his riveting gaze. "Maybe," she said softly, "I was bored to tears in Sundown. Maybe this is the most excitement I've ever had. Maybe I think I've found something here worth sticking around for."

"Just like that?" Hickok marveled at her honesty.

"Just like that!" Sherry threw his earlier response back at him.

"Women!" Hickok said in exasperation. "And you talk about the male ego!"

"I'm going with you," Sherry vowed.

"What about the Trolls?" Hickok inquired.

"What about them?"

"For crying out loud, woman, they raped you!" he snapped savagely.

Sherry recoiled from the violence in his tone, stunned. "Hey, don't worry about me. I'm okay. Really. I hated what they did to me. I loathed it! I wanted to kill them if I could! I'll probably bear the emotional scar the remainder of my life. But except for some bruises, they didn't hurt me physically. They were saving me for more fun. At least, they were until right before you arrived. I heard them say they were going to kill me."

"I'm glad I killed them," Hickok declared.

"So am I." Sherry smiled hopefully. "So the argument is over and I'm going with you, right?"

"I don't know," Hickok hedged.

"I can help you," she stated. "I'm a good shot. I won't get in your way. You can trust me."

"I don't trust very many people," Hickok admitted.

"Give me a chance," Sherry urged him.

"You sure are spunky. I'll give you that," Hickok conceded.

"Is that good?" Sherry queried him.

"I like spunk in a woman," Hickok revealed.

Sherry smiled and gently placed her right hand on his arm. "Then that's the best news I've heard in a long time. Let's hear it for spunk!"

Hickok realized Silvester was staring at them, grinning. He aimed the Henry at the Mole. "And just what are you looking at?"

Silvester buried his face in the grass.

"You still haven't answered me," Sherry pointed out.

Hickok frowned and sighed. "I hope I don't live to regret my decision, but . . ."

Sherry squealed in delight and twirled completely around.

"Wait a minute before you get all excited," Hickok said. "There are some conditions."

"Such as?"

"You do what I tell you," Hickok informed her, "when I tell you. Agreed?"

"Yes, master!"

"Don't be smart! If I tell you to stay put, you'll obey me?"

"Till death do us part," she pledged, giggling.

"Be serious! We could face life-and-death situations, and I want to minimize the risks. I need complete compliance with any order I give. . . ."

"That could be fun!"

". . . with no questions asked," he finished.

"May I ask a question?" she inquired.

Hickok lowered his head and sighed. "What?"

"Does this compliance include after we make camp for the night?"

Hickok impatiently began tapping his right toe. "There you go again!"

"I'm spunky, remember?" she reminded him.

Hickok walked over to the prone Mole. "I think I've bitten off more than I can chew," he mumbled.

"If you don't mind me saying so," Silvester commented, his voice muffled because his face was pressed against the grass, "I think you're right!"

6

As it turned out, the initial mileage estimates on the distance between the Family's Home in Minnesota and Kalispell, Montana, were overestimated. Blade kept a meticulous log of each run the SEAL made, and according to the odometer the actual mileage was slightly less than eleven hundred miles. "One thousand and thirty-three miles," Blade announced as he braked the transport on a low rise two miles northeast of Kalispell, just past Evergreen.

"I can't believe we made the trip so quickly," Rainbow commented.

It was the morning of the fifth day after their departure from the Home. Blade silently thanked the Spirit that the trip, except for the incident with the scavengers, had been trouble free. By carefully detouring around the larger towns, driving cautiously during the day and maintaining an average speed of only fifty miles per hour, and hiding the transport in dense brush at night, they had reached the vicinity of Kalispell with surprising ease. The area, as Rainbow foretold, was unscathed by the nuclear war, the flora and fauna evident in prolific profusion, a natural paradise.

Only one element was absent.

"Where are all the Citadel men?" Star asked her mother.

"That's a real good question," Blade remarked.

Rainbow was leaning forward, searching in every direction, her expression one of intense bewilderment. "I don't understand it," she said softly. "There's no sign of the army from the Citadel, and we should have encountered them by now."

Geronimo, his window rolled down, poked his head outside and felt a cool breeze caress his brow. "There's no sign of anyone," he noted. "I did spot tire tracks and, from the appearance of that field over there, the one with the crushed vegetation and the fresh ruts, a large body of men was here. But they're gone now."

"I don't understand," Rainbow reiterated.

"Geronimo," Blade directed, "see if you can determine how recent those tracks are."

Geronimo nodded, grabbed the FNC, and jumped from the SEAL. He ran to the field and knelt, studying the earth and running a handful of dirt through his fingers.

Blade glimpsed Rainbow in the mirror, unconcealed resentment distorting her features. "Something wrong?" he inquired.

"You like bossing him around, don't you?" Rainbow asked.

"What?"

"Don't think I haven't noticed," Rainbow stated. "You treat him like he's your slave."

"You're nuts, lady!" Blade snapped. "I'm Alpha Triad leader, and Geronimo is one of the Warriors in my Triad. It's my job to give orders. It's what I was trained for. Geronimo's never complained."

"He wouldn't!" Rainbow retorted.

Blade twisted in his seat and faced her. "What's with you, Rainbow? I've seen how you treat Geronimo.

You're trying to wrap him around your little finger, play on his sympathy and his affinity for his Indian heritage. Why?"

"Maybe," Rainbow said, her tone bitter, "I think Geronimo will be better off with my tribe than with your Family."

"Why?"

"He belongs with his own people," she said.

"The Family are his people," Blade told her.

"The Family are mainly whites!" Rainbow hissed.

Blade, startled by the venom in her voice, nodded. "I think I've finally figured you out."

"Oh?"

"Yep. You remember that neat speech you gave several days ago, about how you didn't hate me personally for the crimes the white race inflicted on your people?"

"What about it?" Rainbow asked testily.

"You were lying through your teeth, Rainbow. The real reason you want Geronimo to live with your tribe is because you can't tolerate the thought of any Indian living in harmony with the whites. You're a bigot, Rainbow. Nothing more, nothing less than a disgusting, spiteful bigot!" Blade sadly shook his head. "I pity you, woman."

Rainbow's face reddened, her lips quivered in silent rage, and she was about to explode when she abruptly stiffened, relaxed, and smiled. "That's quite interesting, Blade. Thank you for bringing it to my attention."

Geronimo opened his door and climbed into the SEAL.

"What's the verdict?" Blade asked him.

"My guess would be about a hundred men bivouacked in that field for three months or so, judging from the volume of traffic. There are a number of fire pits and a latrine trench."

"How long ago did they leave?" Blade questioned.

"Oh—" Geronimo glanced at the field again. "I'd estimate at least four weeks. Not much less. The ground reveals two heavy rains since their departure, and an exact time frame is difficult to gauge."

"Four weeks!" Rainbow exclaimed. "That can't be!"

"If Geronimo says it has been four weeks," Blade said, "it has been four weeks."

"Close to it," Geronimo affirmed.

"But where did they go?" Rainbow questioned. "Why did they leave?"

"That's what we're going to find out," Blade stated. He started the transport toward Kalispell.

Geronimo saw the confusion and worry Rainbow was experiencing and attempted to soothe her. "Anything could have happened," he mentioned. "The army from the Cheyenne Citadel might have run out of supplies and returned to their fortress. Or maybe they simply grew tired of trying to starve your tribe out of Kalispell. Your people could have launched an assault of their own and driven the army off, couldn't they?"

"I suppose," Rainbow said doubtfully.

"There is another possibility," Blade interjected, knowing he shouldn't, but unable to control his simmering anger over Rainbow's attitude toward the Family.

"What's that?" Geronimo asked.

"The Citadel army defeated the Flatheads and left the area."

"Mom?" Star inquired in alarm. "Do you think Blade is right? Did the Citadel army kill our people?"

Blade felt a twinge of regret for baiting Rainbow at the child's expense.

"No, honey. Don't worry!" Rainbow comforted her daughter. "I'm sure our people are okay."

"We'll soon know," Blade said.

The SEAL was still a mile from the outskirts of Kalispell. The highway was not severely damaged and clear of obstructions, enabling Blade to keep the transport in the center of the road, his senses alert for any threat or indication of an ambush.

"I hope my people don't fire on us before they realize who we are," Rainbow voiced her concern.

Blade slowed, proceeding at a snail's pace, just in case.

"I still haven't seen a sign of anyone," Geronimo observed.

"What's that?" Star suddenly cried, pointing straight ahead.

The road at the edge of town was littered with debris, old wooden crates and rusted metal drums, ancient furniture and useless appliances, and various other items, all scattered over the ground on either side of the highway.

"It's one of the roadblocks we constructed," Rainbow explained.

"Or was," Blade amended. "It looks like something broke through."

"Oh, no!" Rainbow said, fearfully clasping Star. "No!"

Blade scanned the buildings they passed, detecting evidence of a recent battle; some of the structures displayed gaping holes in the walls, many of the windows were shattered or riddled with bullet holes, and discarded cartridges of various calibers littered the ground. The Flatheads had put up a terrific fight before their defeat. It was odd, though, there weren't any bodies. Would the Citadel army take the time to cart off all the corpses and provide a proper burial? Highly unlikely.

The SEAL eased along the streets, Blade turning at random, first right, then left, and everywhere it was the same.

Kalispell was deserted.

"Which way?" Blade asked Geronimo, nodding at the map on the console.

"Your guess is as good as mine," Geronimo replied. "The map is of the state of Montana. It includes inserts of Great Falls, Billings, Butte, and Missoula, but not Kalispell. Pick any direction you want."

"Rainbow?" Blade glanced over his right shoulder.

Rainbow was absently staring into the distance, her mouth slightly open, her gaze blank.

"I have a suggestion," Star offered.

"What?" Blade queried her.

"I have an uncle living on the shore of Flathead Lake. Maybe he's still there."

"Wasn't he in Kalispell with the others?" Blade inquired.

"Nope." Star shook her head, her long hair flying. "He refused to leave his cabin. He probably hid until the army left. He's real good at hide-and-seek."

"Flathead Lake is south of Kalispell," Geronimo mentioned, grinning.

A rusted street sign, leaning at an acute angle to the pavement, appeared ahead.

"Let's see where we're at," Blade said, stopping the SEAL. The letters on the sign were faded, but legible. "We're at the corner of West Montana and North Main," he informed the others. He swung the SEAL right onto Main, heading south.

"I hope my uncle is home," Star stated hopefully.

Rainbow was still lost in her own little world, traumatized by the disappearance of her tribe.

The SEAL crossed railroad tracks and entered the downtown district.

"This building over here," Blade said, reading a faint sign on a wall, "was the Flathead Community College."

"A lot of stores over here," Geronimo remarked. "It

doesn't look like this part of town was damaged very much."

The transport was in the intersection of Main and Fifth when Star suddenly pointed to their left. "What's that?" she asked excitedly.

Blade had seen it too. A shadow flitting across the wall of a nearby building. He braked the SEAL.

"What was it?" Geronimo questioned.

Blade shrugged. "I better investigate. You stay here with Rainbow and Star, and keep the doors locked. I'll leave the SEAL running. You might need to take off, fast."

"I won't leave without you," Geronimo asserted.

"Do whatever is necessary to protect the SEAL," Blade directed. "Don't worry about me."

"I wish Hickok was here to watch over you," Geronimo said, smiling.

"Since when do I need a baby-sitter?" Blade demanded in mock irritation.

"According to Hickok," Geronimo rejoined, "from the moment you wake up in the morning until you go to sleep at night. Otherwise, you're fine."

Blade laughed. "Thanks." He opened his door and slid to the street, gripping the Auto-Ordnance Model 27 A-1 in his right hand.

"I don't understand why Plato didn't send one of the other Warriors with us to compensate for Hickok's absence," Geronimo commented.

"He wanted to send Rikki," Blade related, "but I vetoed the idea."

"What? Why?"

"I'll explain later," Blade promised, closing the door and moving away from the SEAL. He recalled his argument with Plato over a suspected power-monger in the Family, someone who wanted to oust Plato and assume the mantle of leadership without Family approval.

Before Alpha Triad departed for the Twin Cities, Plato had pledged he would reveal the identity of the culprit after they returned. In a rare violation of his word, still peeved because Alpha Triad had failed in its mission to the Twin Cities, Plato had refused to give Blade the power-monger's identity when Blade had returned. He had cited as his reason a need for additional proof. Partly out of petty spite, Blade had then declined to take Rikki-Tikki-Tavi with them to Kalispell. Outside of Hickok and Geronimo, Blade trusted Rikki the most. Rikki, as Beta Triad leader, would be in charge of the Family Warriors with Blade gone, and if the power-monger were stupid enough to instigate a rebellion while Blade was away, thinking it might be easier, Rikki would promptly prove him wrong and slice him into teensy-weensy pieces with his katana.

I did right, Blade told himself, by leaving Rikki with the Family.

He was fifteen yards from the transport, standing in the center of Fifth Street, the wind ruffling his hair.

Someone . . . or something . . . was watching him.

Blade felt the short hairs at the base of his neck tingle as he searched the nearest buildings. A century of neglect had taken its toll. Windows were cracked, dust covered everything, and the stores were in abject disrepair.

Dust?

What about tracks?

Blade moved to his left, scanning the sidewalk.

Nothing. A few leaves, rusted cans, and other trash.

From somewhere ahead came a distant scratching noise.

So! Someone was playing games.

Blade cautiously walked east on Fifth Street, his gray eyes constantly surveying his surroundings, the A-1 at the ready.

Something rattled for a few seconds, then abruptly ceased.

Keep it up, sucker! Blade grinned. Someone was in for a big surprise!

The wind was picking up, blowing the dust into the air.

Blade reached the intersection of Fifth and First Avenue East, according to a street sign.

A loud knock sounded to his left, north on First Avenue East.

Blade hesitated. If he continued, he would lose sight of the SEAL. But what choice did he have?

As an added incentive, the knock was repeated.

Blade walked to the middle of the street, his finger on the trigger of the A-1.

Where are you?

Doors and windows on this street were intact, and most of them were closed, except for a large window on the second floor of a building to his right. It was conspicuously open.

Accident or design?

Blade edged toward the building with the open window. Was one of the Flatheads still in Kalispell, hiding in fear? Or had the Citadel army left someone behind to ensure any stragglers were disposed of? Or was it a trap to . . .

A slight click came from the vicinity of the open window.

Blade aimed the A-1 at the shadowy aperture.

A tiny pebble fell to the sidewalk below the window.

Damn!

Blade whirled, knowing he'd fallen for one of the oldest tricks in the book. The pebble had been tossed at the brick wall near the window to distract him, to divert his attention from the real attack. He was still trying to turn when powerful arms encircled him from behind, pinning his arms to his side and rendering the A-1 ineffective.

Something growled in his left ear.

Blade dropped the A-1 and surged, his mighty muscles straining, against the restricting arms. His face reddened and his veins bulged as he applied his full strength, calling on all the resources of his massive, superb physique.

No go.

The thing still held him fast.

Hot breath was tingling the nape of his neck.

Blade realized the thing's face must be directly behind his head. He relaxed for a moment and dropped his chin onto his chest.

From behind him came a low, unnatural, sibilant voice. "What you do?"

Dear Spirit! What in the world had a hold of him?

Blade suddenly attempted to break free again, every fiber of his being stretched to the limit. At the same instant he drove his head backward and felt his cranium connect with his assailant's face.

The thing released him.

Blade ducked aside and crouched, instinctively drawing his right Bowie, turning to confront his enemy, prepared for anything.

Or so he thought.

Blade hesitated, gaping in astonishment at his attacker. It was the size of an average man, on the lean side, and essentially humanoid, being bipedal and possessing two arms and a face, but after that any human resemblance ended. Its skin was light gray and leathery, its nose narrow and pointed, and its ears tiny circles of flesh on either side of a bald, hawk-like skull. The mouth was a thin slit, and the eyes endowed with a bizarre hypnotic effect because of bright red pupils. The creature was naked except for a brown loin cloth covering its genitals and a metal collar around its squat neck.

In the second Blade delayed, overcome by amazement, the thing pounced, slamming into the Warrior and driving him back. One of its bony hands clamped on Blade's neck and the other grabbed his right wrist to prevent him from using the Bowie.

Move!

Blade allowed the force of the creature's impact to work in his favor. He rolled onto his back, drove his feet into the thing's stomach, and kicked.

The creature flew over Blade's head and landed on its back in the street, recovering immediately and leaping to its feet.

Blade followed suit, extending his Bowie, mentally debating if he should kill this thing or try to capture it alive.

The creature grinned at the Warrior. "You good one, no? Not be easy, yes?"

Blade couldn't believe the thing was actually speaking to him. What *was* it?

The thing held its hands out, palms up. "Surrender, no? Not hurt you, yes?"

Why did it talk the way it did? "If you expect me to give up, bozo," he told it, "you've got another think coming."

The creature cocked its head and stared at him, puzzled. "What mean you? Not bozo, no! Gremlin, yes."

"Why did you attack me?" Blade demanded, straightening.

"Doktor's orders."

"I don't understand," Blade admitted, still wary, suspecting a trick.

"Must take you, no? Come along, yes?" The creature pointed at the Bowies and the .44 Magnum under

Blade's left arm. "Drop, please."

"You're nuts," Blade retorted.

"Incorrect. Not want to hurt, yes? Please," the thing pleaded with him.

"Who are you?" Blade ignored the entreaty. "Better yet, what are you?" Despite its ferocious visage, the creature apparently didn't desire to continue their fight.

"Please!" the thing repeated, and abruptly gripped the metal collar it wore with both hands, trembling.

Blade noticed a small indicator light in the middle of the collar. Until now the light had been unlit, but it unexpectedly glowed a brilliant blue hue.

The creature reacted as if it were in pain. "No, Doktor! Will do bidding, yes! Stop! Stop!"

The blue light went out.

What the hell was going on here?

The thing was quaking and whining, doubled over.

"What's going on?" Blade asked. "Is there anything I can do to help you?"

The creature looked up, its face contorted in sheer rage. "NOOOOOOO!" it shrieked, and charged.

Blade was caught off guard. The thing barreled into him, incredibly strong, unbelievably fast, and rammed him to the ground. His right Bowie clattered to the asphalt as his right wrist hit the pavement.

"NOOOOOOO!" the creature wailed again.

Blade swung his left fist, clipping the thing on the chin. The creature swayed, but stayed astride his chest. It seized his neck in both hands and squeezed. Blade felt a constricting sensation in his throat as he placed his hands together and, using his arms as a single, steely mallet, struck the creature on the left ear.

Snarling in fury, the thing rolled to the street and jumped erect.

Blade was trying to rise when he caught a fleeting glimpse of a foot coming at his head. Pain exploded in the right side of his skull, and he staggered, still game, attempting to focus on the creature. Vaguely, he experienced the sensation of two more blows striking his head.

Damn!

The thing was so astoundingly quick!

So . . .

7

Silvester the Mole was grabbed from behind, wrenched around, and compelled to appreciate the craftsmanship of a Henry barrel from a distance of two inches.

"You know, pard," Hickok rudely informed him, "I get the distinct impression you are jerking me around by my G-string, and I'm here to tell you it's a decidedly unhealthy practice."

Silvester's eyes widened in abject terror. "Wh . . . Wh . . . What do you mean?" he fearfully stammered.

Hickok swept his right hand in an arc. "We've been waltzing around this forest for a day and a half looking for this Mound of yours. You said it was in this area. By my reckoning, we're over fifty miles southeast of Fox. So where the blazes is the Mound?"

"I'm . . . I'm not sure," Silvester mumbled.

Hickok stared into the Mole's eyes. "Are you tryin' to stall me, pard?"

"No, sir," Silvester promptly replied.

"Then explain to me why you can't find where you live," Hickok gruffly demanded.

"I'm not much good in the woods," Silvester replied sheepishly.

"You can say that again," Hickok agreed. "I can't

afford these delays!" he snapped. "I need to find Shane and return to my Home."

"Maybe we should spread out?" Sherry suggested. They were standing in the sunlit center of a small clearing in the forest.

"No way," Hickok disagreed. "The way my luck's been running, you'd get lost and I'd lose more time findin' you. It took us two days to reach this part of the country, and now we've wasted all this time looking for this jerk's Mound. I'm here to tell you," he said, glaring at the Mole, "I'm beginning to get a mite ticked off!"

"I know it's around here somewhere!" Silvester stated.

"From what I've seen of you," the gunman commented, "you're a lousy fighter, a rotten tracker, and about as useful in the woods as a fish out of water. So why did this Wolfe send you to check on Fox?"

"Two reasons," Silvester said.

"I'm listening."

"First, if anyone was still living there, we could raid it," the Mole said.

"Raid it? You mean to tell me you raid other communities and towns?" Hickok queried him.

"How else could we get by?" Silvester said, protesting Hickok's angry tone.

"You could grow your own crops and hunt your game, for starters," the Warrior proposed.

"No one knows how to do that stuff," Silvester retorted. "Oh, we grow some food, but not much. Mostly, we take what we want."

"You're no better than the scavengers," Hickok muttered.

Silvester, embarrassed, stared at the ground. "It ain't my idea, you know," he said. "It's just the way we do things."

"You're no better than the Trolls even!" Hickok

rebuffed him. "They made slaves of all the women they found, and killed any men they encountered. What do you do with the people in the places you raid?"

Silvester mumbled a few words, unintelligible to the other two.

"Speak up," Hickok ordered. "We can't hear you."

"We . . . we . . ." Silvester began in a low voice. "We make slaves of the men."

"And the women?" Hickok pressed him.

"They're auctioned off to the highest bidder," Silvester explained.

"Sounds like the kind of place I'd want to avoid like the plague," Sherry noted.

Hickok grabbed Silvester by the front of his gray shirt. "I was right. You're no better than the Trolls!" He stopped, struck by a thought. "I'm surprised the Moles and the Trolls didn't run into each other long before this. Too bad you didn't! You could have killed each other off and made the world a better place in which to live."

"The Trolls are too far north of us," Silvester mentioned. "Or, at least they were too far north. We don't usually send out patrols to the north. We send them south."

"Why?" Hickok asked.

"Because a lot of people still live south of us, on the other side of the lakes."

"What lakes?" Sherry inquired.

"The Upper Red Lake and the Lower Red Lake. On the other side of the lakes are some towns with people still in them," Silvester responded. "There are a lot of people in the Bemidji area," he added.

"And the Trolls seldom conducted their pillage and plunder tactics to the south," Hickok said thoughtfully. "So that explains it."

"There's just too much forest between Fox and the Mound," Silvester threw in. "Too many wild animals, and the mutant monsters.''

"The mutant monsters?" Hickok repeated.

"Yeah. You must know about them. The things with all the pus. They'll eat you alive if they catch you." Silvester shuddered at the prospect.

"We call them mutates," Hickok revealed.

"What are you talking about?" Sherry questioned them.

"You don't know?" Hickok replied.

"Nope. What kind of animal is it?"

Hickok studied her closely. "You mean to tell me you don't have mutates in Canada?"

"Doesn't sound like anything I've ever heard of," Sherry confirmed.

"But that's impossible," Hickok declared. "Mutates are all over the place around these parts."

"That's right," Silvester concurred. "They're ugly things! All brown, and smelly, and dripping pus from their bodies."

"They'll attack you the moment they see you," Hickok elaborated.

"That one isn't attacking," Sherry said calmly, and pointed to their right.

Hickok spun, bringing up the Henry, hoping she was joking.

She wasn't.

The mutate, a former badger, was crouched at the edge of the clearing, glaring at them, wheezing and drooling. Mounds of slimy pus covered its nostrils and coated its ears. It was at least three feet long and weighed in the vicinity of thirty pounds.

"Kill it!" Silvester screamed, panic-stricken.

The mutate's beady eyes focused on the Mole, it snarled and charged.

Five yards separated the monstrosity from its intended meal.

Hickok levered the Henry as fast as he could, firing one shot after another. Two, three, four times, the 44-40 slugs ripping into the mutate and spraying pus and a greenish fluid in every direction.

On the fifth shot the mutate slowed, growling and hissing, and stumbled.

Hickok planted the sixth shot between the beady eyes.

A gaping hole blossomed in the mutate's forehead and the badger collapsed in a heap at Silvester's feet, only inches from his toes.

Silvester was gawking at the mutate in petrified terror, unable to move.

Hickok warily approached the mutate and peered at its body, ensuring the thing was truly dead.

It was.

Hickok sighed and glanced at Sherry. "The next time a mutate tries to eat us for lunch," he quipped, "I'd appreciate it if you wouldn't be quite so nonchalant about the whole deal."

"I had no idea," she blurted, gaping at the mutate. "I'd never seen one before."

Silvester was trying to speak, but only muted, choking sounds emanated from his throat.

"Mutate got your tongue?" Hickok cracked, grinning at the sight of Silvester's pale complexion and perspiring brow.

"Th . . . tha . . . than . . . thanks," the Mole managed to croak, "for saving my life."

"I couldn't let you die, pard," Hickok told him. "Not before you show me where the Mound is, anyway."

Silvester smiled weakly and began weaving.

"You okay?" Hickok asked.

Silvester nodded twice. "Thanks, again," he said, his voice barely audible.

"Piece of cake," Hickok stated. "Are you sure you're okay?"

Silvester nodded again, then fainted, toppling over backward onto the grass.

"The Moles must be a bunch of wimps," Hickok opined.

"Poor baby!" Sherry commented, walking to Silvester and lightly slapping his cheeks. "Come on, handsome. Snap out of it!"

Silvester slowly roused to a sitting position.

"Are you still dizzy?" Sherry inquired solicitously.

"I'm fine," he replied. "Really. Give me a second to catch my breath."

"I still can't see why you were sent to Fox," Hickok mentioned. "You're lucky to still be in one piece." He abruptly remembered their conversation before the mutate appeared. "Say, you never told us the second reason Wolfe sent you to Fox."

"Because of my sister," Silvester responded, still catching his breath.

"Your sister? What's she got to do with it?" Hickok queried.

"Wolfe wants my sister, Gloria. She doesn't want him. So, he decided to get even with her by sending me out with Doug. . . ."

"Doug is the one I shot?" Hickok interrupted.

"Yes. Wolfe figured Gloria would change her mind about sleeping with him. He thought she would give in to save me, to prevent me from leaving the Mound." Silvester sadly shook his head. "He doesn't know my sister very well. She thinks I'm a creep and could care less what happens to me."

"I see your family is real strong on love and loyalty," Hickok sarcastically commented.

"I wish we were," Silvester said longingly. He gazed at the Warrior. "I owe you for saving my life."

"Piece of cake. It was no big deal."

"It was to me," Silvester disagreed. "No one has ever

saved my life before."

"Silvester," Sherry caught his attention. "What do you do at this Mound? What are you good at?"

"I empty the pails," Silvester replied forlornly.

"The pails?" Sherry's brow creased. "What pails?"

"I don't want to talk about it," Silvester rudely announced, and rose to his feet. "We better be going."

Hickok went to speak, to order the Mole to answer, when Sherry caught his eye and shook her head. The gunman shrugged and followed the Mole.

Silvester entered the forest and forged ahead. They were fifteen yards from the clearing when they intersected a wide, fequently used trail.

"I think I know this!" Silvester exclaimed, delighted at the discovery. He glanced both ways, grinning. "I do know it! It's one of ours!"

"So how far to the Mound?" Hickok questioned him.

"Just a few miles," Silvester answered happily. He pointed to the south. "Not far."

"It better not be," Hickok warned ominously.

"Silvester," Sherry spoke up from the rear, "would you answer some questions for me?"

"If I can," the Mole promised.

"Who built the Mound? What's it like?" Sherry inquired.

Silvester looked over his right shoulder at Sherry and tripped on a protruding root. He managed to regain his balance before he fell on his face.

"Keep your eyes on the trail," Hickok advised. "What a klutz!"

Silvester resumed walking. "My parents told me," he responded to Sherry's query, "the Mound was built by a man named Carter a long, long time ago."

"Why?" Sherry asked.

"It was right before the big war," Silvester said, sorting his facts, striving to recall the stories he'd been told. "Carter and some others were sure the war was going to break out. They felt they didn't have much time, so they packed up their families and things and hiked to the Red Lake Wildlife Management Area," Silvester said slowly, uncertain if he had remembered the correct name.

"That's what we're in now?" Sherry guessed.

"Right. It was real far from everything and Carter thought the bombs would miss it. He was pretty smart," Silvester said appreciatively.

"How did he build the Mound?" Sherry probed curiously.

"He started digging," Silvester replied.

"Digging?"

"You'll see!" Silvester stated. "Of course, the Mound has been added to a lot since Carter first began it," he added.

"Enough talk," Hickok directed. "We're getting close to this Mound and they may have guards or patrols."

"We do have guards," Silvester informed him, "but we don't have many patrols. Just some scouts who go out from time to time. Not many people come to this area. It's too far out of the way."

"You can say that again," Hickok retorted. He stopped and gazed ahead. "Hold it, Silvester."

The Mole paused and looked back. "What's the matter? Did I say something wrong? Are you mad at me?"

"Don't pee your pants!" Hickok grinned. "I want you to get behind me and stay there." He strolled past the Mole and touched the Henry barrel against Silvester's chin. "And remember, if you make one little peep, do anything to give us away, you'll be the first one I send to the worlds on high."

"The what?"

"Just do as I tell you," Hickok said, jerking his right

thumb backward.

"Yes, sir," Silvester replied, meekly complying.

Hickok warily took the lead, listening for any unusual sounds, searching for any unnatural movement, his finger on the trigger of the Henry. If they were close to the Mound, even a few miles distant, silence was called for. He wanted to approach the Mound undetected and study the layout before he made his move. Was Shane still alive? The fool kid! What a stupid stunt! And all to impress him! Unbelievable. Until Shane had told him, he had had no idea the younger Family members considered him a hero. A hero! Him? They wouldn't say that if they knew him better. Maybe it was the exciting allure of becoming a Warrior. Maybe that accounted for the hero worship. If they only knew what being a Warrior was really like! Your life was on the line every day. You never knew when the next threat would appear.

Hickok rounded a curve in the trail.

Who could blame the younger ones? he reflected. Look at the life they lived. Raised in the sheltered environment of the Home, they attended the Family school, were indoctrinated with Family teachings, lived a quiet existence as a Carpenter, or Tiller of the soil, or a Healer, or Weaver, or whatever, married another Family member, settled into one of the cabins in the center of the thirty-acre compound, and devoted their lives to having children, to raising another generation, to perpetuating the cycle decade after decade. Tranquil. Quaint. Pleasant even.

But utterly boring!

Wasn't that the reason, Hickok asked himself, he had become a Warrior? Dissatisfaction with the dull, repetitive routine, the same thing day after day after day after day? Maybe, Hickok reasoned, he shouldn't be so hard on Shane when he found him. After all, the youth merely felt the same way Hickok had felt at his age.

Ironic, Hickok noted, he should be rescuing a younger version of himself, a youth who was longing for action and excitement at a time when he, Hickok, was becoming slightly weary of the constant fighting and killing. How many men had he killed in recent months? He'd lost count. Trolls. Watchers. Porns. All of them, it was true, were trying to kill him. But did that justify the killing? Hickok shook his head, clearing his mind. It wouldn't do for a Warrior to entertain such thoughts. That blasted Joshua was having an affect on . . .

Hickok abruptly stopped, motioning for the others to halt.

The woods ended, and the trail crossed a wide field and re-entered the forest on the other side.

No good, Hickok noted. They'd be exposed, vulnerable. Should they go around the field? It would take longer, but be safer.

"What's wrong?" Sherry whispered.

"I don't like it," Hickok replied softly.

"There's nothing to worry about," Silvester said. "We're still a long ways from the Mound."

Hickok glanced at him. "You sure?"

"Pretty sure."

"Terrific." Hickok scanned the field for signs of life. The weeds and brush were waist high, and there were few hiding places. Near the center of the field were some huge boulders and rocks. The trail passed between them.

"Oh, go ahead," Sherry goaded him. "We'll make it."

Despite his better judgment, Hickok nodded and started across. He saw a field mouse scamper from their path, and a rabbit bounded away to their right. Nothing out of the ordinary, though. That was a good sign.

The trio reached the section littered with the rocks and boulders and Hickok followed the trail between two of the larger ones. He hoped rescuing Shane would be a relatively easy task. Break into this Mound, bust out again with Shane, and head for their Home. One, two, three. That was the ideal scenario, the way he wanted the events to unfold.

It wasn't what he got.

As Hickok passed between the two large boulders, something scraped above him and he idly glanced upward, not expecting trouble.

A lean Mole with a net was perched on the boulder above his head.

Hickok crouched and ducked as the Mole dropped the net. He swept the Henry up and fired, the 44-40 blasting, the noise deafening in the narrow confines between the boulders. The slug struck the Mole in the forehead and propelled him backward, out of sight.

"Hickok!" Sherry screamed as the first net missed him.

Hickok heard the swish of the descending net before it enveloped him and knew there was another Mole on top of the other boulder. He tried to dodge, to no avail. The heavy net, comprised of knotted rope, cord, and nylon, draped over his shoulders and pinned his arms to his sides.

Blast!

The Glenfield boomed and the Mole on top of the second boulder shrieked and pitched from view.

Good for Sherry, Hickok mentally elated as he struggled against the net. The damn thing was clinging to him like a bear to honey. He couldn't shake it off, and he was unable to reach his Pythons and bring them into play.

Moles swarmed from everywhere.

Silvester was leaning against one of the boulders, his face a frozen mask.

Sherry aimed the Glenfield as several Moles closed on

her. She shot, hitting a husky Mole in the left shoulder and spinning him around. Before she could shoot again, two Moles pounced on her and bore her to the ground, kicking and fighting. They succeeded in wresting the rifle from her grip and restraining her as each man grasped one of her arms in a sturdy hold.

Hickok glanced around.

Six Moles faced him, three on either side, each with a firearm pointed in his general direction. There wasn't sufficient space for all of them to crowd between the two large boulders, but they were able to cover him effectively with their weapons.

"Slip your rifle through one of the holes in the net," one of the Moles ordered, a tall, bearded man with sandy hair and green eyes. "Do it slowly! One false move and we'll blow you away!"

"I sure can't say much for your hospitality." Hickok grinned. He complied, slowly feeding the Henry through an opening in the net.

One of the Moles took possession of the rifle.

"Now the short guns," the same Mole directed. "Same as before. Nice and easy, pal!"

One of the other Moles reached over and eased the slack on the net.

Hickok carefully drew his right Colt and passed it through the net. The Mole with his Henry took the Python.

"Now the other shot gun!" commanded Sandy Hair.

Hickok reluctantly obeyed, realizing his refusal meant instant death.

"Good! Now stand still like a good little boy and we'll have you out of there in a jiffy."

Hickok pondered his next move. The Moles had his Henry and the Colts, but they were unaware he carried two backup pieces: a Mitchell's Derringer strapped to his right wrist, under his buckskin sleeve, and a four-shot C.O.P. in .357 caliber tied to his left leg above the ankle. Should he make a move after the net was lifted over his head? Sherry was being firmly held by the pair of goons, and they were outnumbered four times over.

Nope.

He would have to wait.

The net was pulled off him and he smiled at the Moles.

"You find something funny about all this?" Sandy Hair demanded.

"I was just thinking about how good a job you guys did hiding behind these boulders and rocks," Hickok commented. "It was real professional, pard."

"That surprises you?" asked their apparent leader.

"Relieves me," Hickok replied.

Sandy Hair was puzzled. "What do you mean, it relieves you?"

Hickok nodded at Silvester, still plastered against the boulder. "Well, if Wimpy here was any indication, I figured all the Moles must be miserable cowards who couldn't find their butts in broad daylight."

Sandy Hair walked up to Hickok and smirked. "Is that what you thought?"

"Yep."

Sandy Hair was holding a Winchester, and he savagely rammed the barrel into Hickok's stomach, doubling the gunman over.

"Leave him alone!" Sherry yelled.

Silvester finally came to life. "Goldman," he said to the sandy-haired Mole, "it's good to see you again."

Goldman ignored both the entreaty and the greeting and hauled Hickok erect by the front of his buckskin shirt. "I can tell you're a real smart mouth," Goldman snapped. "By the time I'm done with you, you'll wish you never learned to talk!"

Hickok, resisting an intense pain in his abdomen,

managed to force a smile. "There is one thing I wish, pard," he stated.

"Oh?" Goldman took the bait. "What's that?"

Hickok snickered, anticipating the reaction he would get and proceeding anyway. Submitting meekly was not his style. "I wish you would do something about your breath! It's enough to gag a skunk!"

There was the flashing gleam of the Winchester barrel, a moment before it collided with the gunman's head.

Hickok sagged and dropped to his knees.

Goldman cocked the Winchester and aimed it at Hickok's heart. "If breath bothers you so much," he growled, "let's see how well you do without yours!"

8

Her name was Cindy, and she was happier than she could ever recall being. She was standing on a small rise in the northeast corner of her new home, *the* Home occupied by the group known as the Family. The Home was a thirty-acre compound located in northwestern Minnesota, near Lake Bronson State Park. From her vantage point, Cindy could view most of the compound. She could plainly see the encircling brick wall, twenty feet high and topped with barbed wire. Portions of the moat were also visible, the stream entering the property under the northwest corner of the wall. It branched due east and due south and reformed at the southeast corner before flowing under the outer wall. The moat, thanks to the huge trench the builder of the Home had dug, was an effective second line of defense in case of a concerted enemy assault.

Cindy caught a glimpse of the drawbridge in the center of the western wall, the only means of entry and the solitary exit. A few of the concrete blocks were partially discernible, the reinforced structures the Family utilized for various purposes. There were six of them, arranged in a triangular formation in the western section of the Home. A Block was the southern point of the triangle, and was the Family armory. One hundred yards northwest was B Block, used as the sleeping facility for unwed Family members. Another one hundred yards further northwest was C Block, the infirmary. D Block was one hundred yards east of C Block, and was utilized as the carpentry and construction shop. The same distance east of D Block and E Block, the library stocked with hundreds of thousands of books by Kurt Carpenter, the Family's revered Founder, himself. Southwest of E Block was the Block used for preserving and preparing the Family food and storing its agricultural supplies, F Block. Finally, another hundred yards southwest of F Block, A Block completed the formation.

The central area of the compound was devoted to the cabins inhabited by the married couples and their children. In the remainder of the Home, in the eastern sector, the fields were cultivated for agricultural purposes or, like the rise on which Cindy stood, preserved in pristine splendor.

Cindy contentedly watched a flight of birds winging their way westward. She walked to a felled tree, a mighty oak toppled by age and the fury of the elements, and sat with her back against the trunk, facing the eastern wall. The moat, a watery ribbon lazily meandering along the base of the eastern wall, was in full view.

Funny, she wondered, that the Founder didn't position the moat outside the wall. Why put it inside? She imagined the surprise any attacker would feel after scaling the outer wall only to find another obstacle ahead. If a hostile force did manage to breech the brick wall, the time it would require them to cross the moat would enable the defenders to rake them with devastating gunfire. Kurt Carpenter certainly knew what he was doing.

Cindy relaxed, enjoying the morning sun on her face.

She considered herself the luckiest woman alive. Thank God Alpha Triad had found her and her brother Tyson and brought them to live at the Home! Blade, Geronimo, and Hickok had been on their way to the Troll headquarters, located in the town of Fox, when the Warriors had run into the ambush Cindy's father had planned, mistakenly believing the Warriors might be Trolls. Cindy laughed at the memory, her blue eyes twinkling and her brown hair bobbing. Her father, Clyde, an elderly farmer, had wanted revenge on the Trolls for the abduction of his wife. Cindy's youthful features clouded. Now they were both gone. Her mother had been taken by the Trolls and never heard from again, not even after the Warriors had defeated the Trolls. And unfortunately, during the battle, Clyde had been killed.

Cindy's eyes filled with tears. Why did her father have to die? It wasn't fair! The poor man had tried so hard to be a good parent. All those years of wandering the landscape, living from hand to mouth, her father did the best he could to provide them with all the things they needed, especially love. If only Clyde were alive today! After all the scrounging, the scraping to stay alive, he would have been delighted at the conditions in the Home. Here, life was so peaceful, so wonderful. There wasn't someone trying to murder you every other day. You didn't have to constantly be alert for the wild animals, or the pus horrors, or any scavengers. You could enjoy life! How long had she been here now? Around three months! And she had loved every minute of it.

But what about Tyson? She was worried about him. He displayed a disturbing tendency toward restlessness. On the surface, he conveyed the impression of being happy. She, though, knew her brother better than anyone, and she suspected something was troubling him. But he refused to confide in her, which was highly unusual.

Cindy gazed at the flowing water in the moat. How could anyone in their right mind be dissatisfied here? You were protected from attack, you ate regularly and well, and your clothing was the proper fit and clean. She looked at her brown blouse and green pants, both provided by Jenny, Blade's fiancee. The people here, the members of the Family, were so nice, so receptive to strangers. Outside, it was a different story. You never knew whom you could trust. The survival of the fittest was the rule of the day. What could . . .

Her thoughts were interrupted by the sounds of several people approaching the rise, coming from the west.

Who could it be? Not many Family members came out this far on a regular basis. Joshua did, sometimes, to worship. And Rikki too, to do whatever he did. Could it be one of them?

Cindy twisted and glanced over her right shoulder.

Three men crested the top of the rise and paused, scanning their surroundings.

Cindy recognized them.

Gamma Triad, consisting of three Warriors.

Napoleon was the leader of Gamma Triad. He was in the lead, his balding head glistening with sweat.

Cindy was about to greet them, to announce her presence, when her intuition stopped her. There was something about the manner in which Napoleon carefully glanced in every direction, something furtive in the way he appeared slightly nervous, causing her to freeze with her mouth partly open.

"There's no one else here," Napoleon informed the other two men, and walked nearer to the fallen tree. He was wearing his customary garb, consisting of an old Air Force uniform with the holes patched and the seams resewn. Napoleon had added a personal touch, bright silver buttons and a red sash around his stocky waist.

Cindy crouched lower behind the tree. The three men were on the other side of the trunk, unaware she was so close.

"The sentry on the west wall can see us," commented the second man, a tall Warrior with light, closely cropped hair and sparkling blue eyes. He wore buckskin pants and a brown shirt, the shirt pieced together from several discarded pillowcases. Strapped to his waist was a long broadsword.

"So what if he does, Spartacus?" Napoleon said. "He'll assume we're conducting a training session, or holding a private meeting. It's not against Family rules to have private meetings," he added bitterly. "Yet."

"I just don't like it," Spartacus stated.

"Where else can we talk?" Napoleon asked harshly. "There are very few places in the entire Home where a person can go to be truly alone. It's just another of the many reasons I detest this place!"

Cindy eased her body to a prone position.

"We know how you feel," the third Warrior threw in, his tone conveying a slight impatience. "We've listened to you often enough."

Napoleon glared at the third member of Gamma Triad. "If I didn't know better, Seiko," he said icily, "I'd swear you'd lost your enthusiasm for our little enterprise." His right hand drifted to the revolver he wore on his right hip.

Seiko laughed. He was one of the half dozen Family members with an Oriental lineage. His complete wardrobe—his shirt, pants, and even his shoes—was black, fabricated from a soft, yet durable, material. He did not appear to be bearing any weaponry. "You know I could care less about your little enterprise," Seiko said to Napoleon.

"Ahhh, yes." Napoleon smiled sardonically. "You have loftier motives. You simply want Rikki dead."

Rikki-Tikki-Tavi dead? What was going on here? Cindy knew she would be in serious trouble if they caught her. Why did Seiko want Rikki dead? Rikk-Tikki-Tavi was the head of Beta Triad, and in Blade's absence he was also the chief of all the Warriors. Cindy liked Rikki. He was friendly and supportive to everyone he met, and well liked by the entire Family. Well, almost the entire Family. Rikki took his name from a creature called a mongoose in one of the books in the library. Strange name, but she had asked him about it once and he had told her it was fitting for his role as a guardian of the Home and the Family. He had suggested she read the book. She never had.

The Gamma Triad was another story. Cindy hardly knew them. Napoleon was courteous, but distant, although she did observe him on several occasions conversing with her brother Tyson.

Spartacus was an unknown entity. She'd seen him plenty of times as he went about his business, and once he had even said hello to her. Beyond that, he was a virtual stranger.

Seiko she knew only by reputation. He was one of the better martial artists in the Family, almost as skilled as Rikki. Nine years ago, so the story went, Rikki and Seiko had fought in a friendly contest to see who would have the honor of owning the only genuine katana the Family possessed. The katana was one of the many unusual weapons Kurt Carpenter had stocked in the Family armory. In addition to hundreds of firearms, and the ammunition to go with them, Carpenter had included weapons from around the world in the collection.

"I don't want Rikki dead," Seiko was saying.

"No," Napoleon replied. "You just want the katana, and the only way you will get your hands on it is if Rikki is dead."

Seiko crossed his arms and stared thoughtfully at the ground. "It is unfortunate, but true," he said regretfully. "I wish there was another way, but there isn't. The Elders bestowed the katana on Rikki after our bout. They ignored my protests. They disregarded the fact he won by a fluke. And to this day, they refuse to permit another match. Plato insists the matter was decided years ago, but it wasn't! I should have won! I was shamed before the whole Family! Honor dictates a rematch."

"You will get your chance to claim the katana," Napoleon promised.

"All well and good," Spartacus interjected. "Seiko is in this for his dignity, and gets the stupid sword. . . ."

"The katana is not merely a stupid sword!" Seiko angrily countered. "In the Code of Bushido, the katana is an extension of the samurai, as essential to the samurai as the air you breathe is to your very life."

"Give me a break!" Spartacus mocked Seiko. "You're about as much a samurai as I am a gladiator. It's just a concept you picked up from one of the books in the library."

Seiko took a step toward Spartacus, his face clouded in anger. "You are mistaken! I am samurai!"

"Grow up!" Spartacus cracked.

Seiko crouched, his legs bent, his stance firm, and raised his hands to chest level, his fingers formed into rigid claws. "I am samurai!" he stressed menacingly.

Spartacus gripped the hilt of his broadsword. "If it's a fight you're looking for . . ."

Napoleon stepped between the two. "Both of you, stop it! We are allies, remember? We have more important considerations than your petty squabbles."

"No one insults the way of the samauri," Seiko said, glaring at Spartacus.

Napoleon smiled broadly. "No one is insulting you.

Spartacus meant no offense. You know very few Family members take the way of the samauri as seriously as you do, or give it the respect it is due. Don't take his comments personally."

"You're too touchy," Spartacus stated, grinning at Seiko. "How long have we been together? Don't you know me by now?"

Seiko relaxed and straightened. "You are right. I apologize for my behavior."

"There you go again," Spartacus pointed out. "Relax! You take life too damn seriously!"

"I know no other way," Seiko replied.

"Well, now that that's settled," Napoleon sighed, "maybe we can get to why we came here today."

"Before we do that," Spartacus interrupted, "I still have something I need to get off my chest."

"What is it?" Napoleon asked.

"Seiko is in this for the katana," Spartacus noted. "You want to be Family Leader. But what's in this for me? For years now, you've been trying to win us over, to persuade us to join you. At one time, I even thought of turning you in to Plato as a power-monger. But I kept my mouth shut. We're a Triad, after all, and we should stick together through thick and thin. So you've finally won Seiko over, but I'm still not completely convinced. What's in this for me?"

Napoleon draped his left arm across the gladiator's broad shoulders. "You, dear Spartacus," he said, "I can promise a prize more precious than any sword, a treasure comparable to the fabled Helen of Troy."

"What are you talking about?" Spartacus demanded.

Napoleon's grin seemed to stretch from ear to ear. "I am referring to Jenny."

Spartacus appeared stunned.

Napleon laughed. "What? You thought I wouldn't recall how you vied for her affection? How you tried to persuade her to like you instead of Blade?" Napoleon paused. "Let's see. Wasn't it when you were in your late teens? I never did understand why you wasted your time on her. Everyone knew she loved Blade, and had loved him since childhood. And, like me, everyone saw how she rudely rejected your sincere devotion and preferred that musclebound lout. I must confess, women have always been something of a mystery to me. They are so illogical, so . . . strange. Don't you agree?"

"How could Jenny love me?" Spartacus finally found his voice.

"Ahhhh. I never promised she would love you." Napoleon shook his head. "I simply emphasize, with Blade out of the way, Jenny would be, shall we say, available to the first man wanting to claim her. Do you get my drift?"

Spartacus stroked his square chin, pondering the implications of Napoleon's words. "Jenny. Mine?"

"If you want her." Napoleon beamed.

"You mean," Spartacus said slowly, comprehension dawning, "just take her?"

"With Blade dead," Napoleon responded, "who could stop you?"

"You think the Family will just stand by and do nothing?" Seiko interjected.

"The Family are sheep!" Napoleon snapped contemptuously. "Except for the Warriors, of course."

"And what about the Warriors?" Seiko inquired. "What about Omega Triad and Beta Triad?"

"Follow me on this," Napoleon said. "If we remove Plato from his position of leadership, the Elders will have lost their authority figure, their conduit of command. By eliminating Blade, Geronimo, and Hickok, we have disposed of our primary opposition, Alpha Triad."

"Hickok won't be easy," Spartacus mentioned.

"Let me finish," Napoleon urged. "After Seiko disposes of Rikki, Beta Triad will be leaderless. Omega Triad will be the only other Triad still intact, and like the majority of the Family they'll be confused by our takeover, uncertain of what to do. Remember, in the century since Kurt Carpenter founded the Home, this has never happened before. The Family will be like headless birds, flopping around with no sense of direction. We'll tell them there was a plot, that Plato, with the complicity of Alpha Triad, planned to turn the Home over to the Watchers. . . ."

Spartacus waved his hands in the air. "Hold the fort! Are you crazy, or what? The Family may be sheep, but they're not stupid. They'd never buy that bull in a million years!"

"I agree," Seiko chipped in. "I'm surprised you would concoct such a stupid plan."

Napoleon sighed and turned away from them, gazing at the distant western wall. He didn't want them to see the look of triumph on his face. The fools! Seiko and Spartacus were as gullible as the rest of the Family, and so easy to manipulate. Of course he told them an idiotic scheme! He wanted them to reject it, so they would the more readily embrace his real scenario. A true leader of men knew how best to utilize psychology to its maximum advantage. He faced them, frowning, his shoulders slumped. "Well, if you feel that way about it, let me propose another idea. Tell me if you like this one."

"Just so it's better than the first," Spartacus remarked.

"Okay. Point out any flaws," Napoleon told them. "The entire Family knows about the saboteur, the one who tried to blow up the SEAL."

"The one Blade killed," Seiko elaborated. "Right before Alpha Triad departed for the Twin Cities."

"Exactly. No one knows where the saboteur came

from, but the speculation is he was a Watcher, sent to destroy the Family's only mode of transportation. Correct?"

"That's what everyone thinks," Spartacus acknowledged.

"So," Napoleon said, winking at them, "what's to prevent these same Watchers from sending an assassin into the Home?"

"An assassin?" Spartacus repeated.

"Of course! An assassin sent to murder our leaders in the dark of the night." Napoleon grinned.

"I get it!" Seiko exclaimed. "If Plato and Rikki are killed in their sleep, we could blame an assassin seen escaping over the wall. Everyone would assume the Watchers did it, and we would be off the hook."

"Precisely," Napoleon nodded. "Now, according to the instructions Kurt Carpenter left us, who assumes leadership of the Family in an emergency, in a time of crisis?"

"The Warriors," Spartacus answered.

"Specifically?" Napoleon goaded him.

"The head of the Warriors," Spartacus clarified.

Napoleon rubbed his palms together, a devilish gleam in his eyes. "And, if Plato and Rikki are murdered by the assassin, and with Alpha Triad absent, who is next in line to become leader in a crisis?"

Spartacus extended the fingers on his left hand as he listed the chain of command. "Let's see. Plato comes first, and if something happens to him, Alpha Triad is in charge in emergencies, and if they were put out of commission, Rikki, as Beta Triad head, would be next. . . ."

"And if something happened to Rikki?" Napoleon goaded him.

"Then the next in line would be . . ." Spartacus glanced up, smiling. "You."

"All nice and legal. What do you think?" Napoleon asked them.

"It's brilliant," Seiko commented.

"With Alpha Triad gone," Spartacus detailed, "and if we—sorry, I meant the assassin—kills Plato and Rikki, you would have every right to become official Family Leader."

"Official Family Leader," Napoleon nodded, savoring the sound of his new title.

"This proposal has merit," Seiko said, complimenting Napoleon.

"Will you go along with me on this?" Napoleon earnestly asked.

"It would enable me to settle my score with Rikki-Tikki-Tavi," Seiko mentioned. "At the same time, I would finally acquire the katana, the only legitimate weapon for a true samauri." He paused, mulling his decision.

Come on, you buffoon! Napoleon was on the verge of achieving a victory years in the shaping, and he could scarcely contain his impatience.

"You can rely on me," Seiko finally stated.

"Good!" Napoleon stepped over to Seiko and gave him a friendly pat on the back. "I am delighted!"

"But what about Spartacus?" Seiko asked.

"Yes indeed." Napoleon faced the third member of Gamma Triad. "What about you, Spartacus? Will you join us?"

Spartacus, his hands hooked in his belt, idly poked a small bush with his right foot. "I don't know. . . ." He was wavering.

Damn your bones! Not now! Napoleon inwardly seethed at this seeming reversal of his master plan. Outwardly, he smiled. "You don't want Jenny?" he inquired politely.

"You know I do," Spartacus replied.

"Then what's the problem?" Napoleon queried him.

"It's a big step. If we're caught . . ."

"We won't be caught," Napoleon hastily interrupted.

"You can't guarantee that," Spartacus noted.

"Spartacus, Spartacus, Spartacus," Napoleon said in a paternal tone. "What am I to do with you?" He placed his arms behind his back and began pacing, talking as he walked. "For years I have tried to convince you that I could do a better job of leading the Family than Plato, bless his poor, inept soul. I have tried to reason with you, to explain the necessity for the Family to reach out, to attain broader horizons. The Family can't stay cooped up in the Home for its entire existence. We are at a critical point in Family history. A new form of leadership is called for. Bold, imaginative, aggressive leadership such as you well know I can supply." Napoleon shook his head and sighed. "And still you refuse, still you balk. Why? Don't you want to see the Family assumes its rightful position of dominance in the world today? Don't you want to be a part of all this?"

"Of course I do," Spartacus responded.

"Then what's the problem?" Napoleon demanded again.

"I feel guilty," Spartacus admitted, "like I'm betraying my trust, betraying the Family."

"How can you be betraying the Family if you are helping to lead them to bigger and better things?" Napoleon asked, pressing him.

"But what about Plato and Rikki?" Spartacus asked.

Napoleon stopped his pacing. "Progress," he stated somberly, "demands sacrifice. Study your history."

"Rikki won't be easy," Spartacus said, nitpicking.

"You said the same thing about Hickok," Napoleon noted. "Believe me, they're only men, just like us. They're no harder to kill than anyone else. Don't worry about Rikki. We're going to get some assistance there.

We may not even need the assassin alibi."

"What type of assistance?" Seiko curiously inquired.

"The newcomer Tyson," Napoleon answered. "I'll explain once I'm certain we can count on him."

Tyson? Involved with this horrible plot? Cindy couldn't believe her own ears! She wanted to jump up and run, to race to Rikki and reveal all the sordid details, but she held herself in check. Napoleon would probably murder her on the spot. Besides, if Tyson were somehow caught up in this scheme, she had to learn to what extent and how best to extricate him before he found himself in serious trouble.

"I guess I'll just have to trust you," Spartacus was stating. "You can count me in."

"Good!" Napoleon almost leaped for joy. At long, long last! The fruition of his cherished ambition was within his grasp! To become Family Leader was a necessary goal, but it was only the first step in his grand design. Thanks to the information supplied by the Alpha Triad, he knew the Family possessed more raw firepower than most other groups and occupied communities. If directed by a capable military mind, the Family's arsenal could be utilized most effectively in subduing any opposition. The Watchers might pose a problem, but Napoleon suspected they might be amenable to a mutually beneficial truce. If the Watchers hadn't wiped out the Family by now, there could only be one logical reason; they simply weren't strong enough to conquer the Family in pitched warfare. The Watchers would welcome a treaty of peace, and leave him free to prosecute his strategy for reorganizing the pitiful remnants of society still functioning in a world scarred by a nuclear holocaust. What the world needed was someone with vision, someone capable of recharting the course human destiny should take.

Someone, Napoleon knew, like himself.

As he so often did, Napoleon grinned at the thought of his pet motto, one conceived during his turbulent teen years after he had repeatedly approached the Family Elders with his concepts for improving Family life and after his grandoise ideas had been constantly rejected. Today the Family, tomorrow the world!

9

He abruptly became conscious, wishing he hadn't. His head was sore, his temples throbbing. He had the impression of being carried. And, somewhere close, someone was whistling.

Whistling?

Blade opened his eyes and squinted in the morning sun. He realized his arms were tied behind his back.

"Welcome back, yes? Sleep good, no?"

His assailant was effortlessly toting him across a barren field, one arm under his knees and the other around his shoulders.

"Put me down!" Blade ordered.

The creature chuckled. "You make Gremlin laugh."

Blade took stock of his situation. His weapons were gone. "Where are my Bowies?" he demanded. "And my revolver and the Auto-Ordnance?"

"Not needed, no. Left behind," the thing replied.

Damn! Unarmed, in hostile territory, and a prisoner. This day was definitely not getting off to a good start. "What if we are attacked?" Blade questioned his captor.

"Not worry, no. Gremlin protect," the creature responded.

"I take it your name is Gremlin?" Blade probed.

The thing actually grinned. "You smart, yes?"

Blade realized the creature had a sense of humor. What else? It was incredibly strong and fast, obviously intelligent. So many questions flashed through his mind. Where to begin? "Why do you talk the way you do?"

"Know brain, yes?" Gremlin countered Blade's query with one of his own.

"Do I know the brain?" Blade repeated. "A little bit. Anatomy wasn't my primary study, but we had to learn the nervous system, pressure points, kill zones, and the like. Why?"

Gremlin glanced at Blade and frowned. "Warrior training, yes?"

Blade involuntarily attempted to straighten, surprised at the creature's knowledge of his Family status.

Gremlin stopped and looked around. A patch of grass to their right arrested his attention, and he crossed to the roughly circular area and gently deposited Blade on the ground. "We stop, yes? Walked all night." He remained standing, alert for any potential threats.

"How do you know I'm a Warrior?" Blade demanded, perplexed.

"Doktor tell, yes?" Gremlin answered.

'Who is this Doktor? You mentioned him before," Blade noted.

"You meet soon, yes?" Gremlin chuckled. "Wish you hadn't."

"Well," Blade pressed the creature, "how does this Doktor know so much about me?"

"Doktor know everything," Gremlin informed him.

"But how?" Blade asked.

"Learn soon, yes," Gremlin replied.

This was getting him nowhere! Blade returned to his original question. "You still haven't told me why you talk the way you do. Does it have something to do with the brain?"

Gremlin's features seemed to soften, to sadden. He nodded. "Brain control words, yes? Part of brain kaput!"

"Part of your brain has been damaged?" Blade requested clarification.

Gremlin shook his head, one corner of his mouth slanted downward. "Damaged, no. Gone, yes."

"How could part of your brain be gone?" Blade asked skeptically.

Gremlin's jaw muscles tightened. "Doktor."

Blade struggled to a sitting position. "The Doktor removed part of your brain? Why?"

Gremlin avoided looking into Blade's eyes. "Experiment."

Blade's mind was racing. What was going on here? What type of physician experimented on the brains of . . . Wait a minute! Inspiration struck. "Gremlin, what are you? Where are you from?"

"From Doktor, yes? Understand, no?" Gremlin angrily glared at Blade. "Enough talk, yes? Rest!"

"Just answer one more thing for me," Blade said, taking advantage of the creature's loquacity and apparent friendliness. "You could have killed me and didn't. You said I would meet this Doktor soon. Is that where you're taking me? To the Doktor?"

Gremlin nodded. "Doktor say take alive, yes?"

"Where is the Doktor, Gremlin?"

The creature pointed to the southeast. "Citadel."

"You're taking me to the Cheyenne Citadel?"

Again, Gremlin nodded.

No! He couldn't allow it to happen! He had to get back to Geronimo and the SEAL.

"Rest!" Gremlin ordered.

"One more question," Blade said, refusing to comply. "You said this Doktor knows everything, that he knows I'm a Warrior. How could . . ." Blade paused, his

memory stirring. Deja vu. When Alpha Triad had made
the run to Thief River Falls and fought with the
mysterious Watchers, they had learned that the
Watchers evidently knew all about the Family and the
Warriors. For weeks afterward, they had engaged in
futile speculation, debating possible methods the
Watchers could have employed to gain their familiarity
with the Family. Was there a spy in the Family? Were
the Watchers mind-readers?

Was the answer staring him in the face? Was there a
connection, Blade wondered, between the good Doktor
and the Watchers? Only one way to find out.

"Gremlin." Blade nudged the creature's left ankle
with his right moccasin. "Have you ever heard of the
Watchers?"

Gremlin grinned at his prisoner. "Yes."

"Are the Watchers and the Doktor related in any
way?" Blade inquired hopefully.

"All the same, yes?"

"How do they know so much about everything?"

Gremlin gazed skyward. "Spy in the sky, yes?" He
glanced at Blade. "And parabolic ears, yes? Understand?"

Blade shook his head, confused.

"Rest!" Gremlin directed. "Talk more later."

"But . . ." Blade began.

"Rest!" Gremlin curtly cut him off. "Now!"

Blade shrugged and reclined on the grass. What was
he to make of all this new information? The Watchers
and the Doktor were related in some respect. Did the
Watchers hail from the Citadel? Was the Doktor the
head of the Watchers, or simply part of their organization? What in the world was a spy in the sky and a
parabolic ear? Was Gremlin deliberately speaking in
riddles? Each answer received created dozens of new
questions and only compounded the overall picture, pro-

ducing additional uncertainties.

Of *one* thing he could be certain, though.

He was positive his wrists were bound by stout rope, and no matter how firm a rope might be, if it was worked on long enough, pulled and stretched and tugged at every opportunity, any rope would eventually slacken. Surreptitiously, during his conversation with the creature, he'd applied his powerful arm muscles to work on the rope.

It was only a matter of time.

And then, Mr. Gremlin, Blade vowed, I'm returning to Kalispell whether you like it or not!

10

The noon sun was high overhead on the day after Blade vanished. Geronimo approached the SEAL from the east, having spent most of the morning searching for his friend. What, he wondered, could have happened? Ever since Blade had failed to come back the day before, he had been filled with apprehension. Geronimo stopped at the driver's door and glanced over his left shoulder. He'd gone to investigate and found the Auto-Ordnance, the Dan Wesson, and the Bowies in a pile in the center of First Avenue East, abandoned. Blade would never commit such a foolish act, so there was ony one, inescapable, conclusion: Blade was dead or captured. Geronimo had carried the weapons to the transport and left them in the rear section while he went hunting for some sign, any clues, to Blade's disappearance. Nothing.

With Star and Rainbow, Geronimo spent the night in the SEAL, protected from any dangers lurking in the dark. Despite Rainbow's urging, Geronimo refused to leave Kalispell until he discovered the reason for Blade's absence. Rainbow, recovered from her initial shock at finding her people gone, insisted on seeking her tribe immediately. Geronimo stubbornly balked.

"I will not leave Kalispell," he told her, "until I know beyond a shadow of a doubt that Blade is dead. Until then, we stay right where we are!"

Rainbow, annoyed, sulked until she fell asleep.

Star was strangely quiet all night, although she slept fitfully.

At daybreak, Geronimo was up and out, hoping to find a trail, some tracks, anything indicating Blade's plight. Now, hungry, tired, and disgusted by his failure, Geronimo opened the door and climbed into the SEAL.

"Let me guess," Rainbow said as Geronimo wearily reclined in his seat. She was in the front row, using the bucket seat on the passenger side. Star was lying across the back seat.

"I couldn't find a trace of him," Geronimo acknowledged.

"Why don't you face facts?" Rainbow demanded. "Blade is dead. It's useless for us to stay here. We should be looking for my tribe."

Geronimo fixed her with a probing stare. "You're awful eager to write Blade off. Why?"

"I am not," Rainbow protested. "I'm just realistic. Blade is only one person. My tribe numbers about three thousand. I am sorry for Blade, but we have a greater problem to solve. Namely, what has happened to my people? We must find out!"

Geronimo stared out the windshield, reflecting. In all fairness, he couldn't fault her for wanting to locate the Flatheads. How would he react if he returned to the Home and discovered the Family missing? The same way, no doubt. But he just couldn't bring himself to leave Kalispell. Not yet, anyway. He also wasn't willing to tolerate Rainbow's constant harping on the fate of her tribe. Maybe he could kill three birds with one stone: stay in Kalispell, take Rainbow's mind off the Flatheads for a while, and achieve the task Plato sent them to perform.

"Where's this hospital you told us about?" he asked her.

"The hospital?" Rainbow seemed surprised by the question.

"You do recall telling us about a hospital in Kalispell," he reminded her. "The one where we might find the items Plato is looking for, remember?" His tone was slightly sarcastic.

"I know which hospital," Rainbow replied. "I didn't expect you to be thinking about it at a time like this."

"I think about it all the time," Geronimo informed her. "It's always in the back of my mind. The future of the Family is at stake. Alpha Triad was sent out twice after the medical equipment and supplies Plato needs, and each time we were unsuccessful. We won't strike out a third time, not if I can help it. I'm getting whatever we find back to the Home, even if I have to lug it on my back."

"I see." Rainbow slowly nodded. "Okay. The Kalispell Regional Hospital is north of here. We've got to take Highway 93 north to Sunnyview Lane, then head east. It's not far."

"Fine." Geronimo reached into his right front pocket and extracted the keys. He hesitated before inserting the ignition key. This was risky. He'd never driven the SEAL before. What if he wrecked it? He'd studiously observed Blade and Hickok when they drove, and he'd studied the Operations Manual. Was it enough, he wondered, to enable him to drive the transport to the hospital and back?

There was only one way to find out.

Geronimo placed the key in the ignition and held his breath. He'd remembered to throw the red lever located under the dashboard to the right first thing in the morning. This lever activated the solar collector system. On a sunny day, the batteries required about an hour to reach full charge. A gauge above the red lever indicated when energization was complete, and the red lever was then replaced in the straight-down position.

"Something wrong?" Star asked. She rose to a sitting position and leaned foward between the bucket seats.

"I've never driven the SEAL before," Geronimo revealed.

"You haven't?" Star asked.

"What?" Rainbow interjected. "You're kidding."

"Nope," Geronimo shook his head. "Wish I were. Blade and Hickok did all the driving. Frankly, I didn't want the responsibility."

"Just great!" Rainbow snapped. "Do you think you can get us to the hospital in one piece?"

"I'll do my best," Geronimo promised.

"I hope so," Rainbow muttered.

Brother, was she in a crabby mood! "If you think you can do any better," Geronimo proposed, "you're welcome to try."

"No, thanks," Rainbow declined. "I wouldn't know the first thing about driving this vehicle. The cars and trucks my people owned wore out long ago. We had no idea working vehicles still existed until the army from the Citadel attacked. They had a lot of jeeps, I think they were called, some trucks, and three things called tanks."

"How many soldiers were there in this army?" Geronimo inquired.

"My best guess would be a couple of thousand," Rainbow replied.

"Well, here goes nothing." Exactly as he'd seen Blade and Hickok do on dozens of occasions, Geronimo twisted the ignition key. The engine turned over, purring softly, producing a muted whine. So far, so good. Mentally enumerating the steps, Geronimo carefully followed the correct procedure. Place right foot on the brake, shift the lever on the steering column from PARK to DRIVE, place the right foot on the acceleration pedal and gently depress.

The SEAL creeped forward.

"You did it!" Star exclaimed, delighted, clapping her hands.

Geronimo forced his tense muscles to relax. He wheeled the transport in a tight U-turn, heading north on Main.

"What are those for?" Star inquisitively inquired, pointing at a row of toggle switches in the center of the dash. There were four of them, each with a single lever below it. M, S, F, and R.

"No one knows," Geronimo said. "They're not mentioned in the Operations Manual for the SEAL. Everyone's been afraid to touch them until we discover their purpose."

"Let's find out," Star declared, reaching for one of the toggle switches.

"No!" Geronimo lunged and caught her wrist in his right hand. "Don't ever touch them! Or anything else in here, for that matter. We can't afford to damage the transport through ignorance or negligence."

"I'm sorry," Star said sheepishly.

"She didn't mean any harm," Rainbow offered.

Geronimo gripped the steering wheel with both hands, his knuckles white.

"I'm sorry," Star said again.

"No problem," Geronimo lied, smiling to reassure her. He drove at five miles an hour until they reached the intersection of Main and Sunset Boulevard.

"Take a left here," Rainbow directed. "Sunset Boulevard turns into Highway 93."

Geronimo followed her instructions. After several minutes, a faded sign read HIGHWAY 93 NORTH.

Perfect.

The junction with Sunnyview Lane appeared in a few minutes more.

"Take a right," Rainbow guided him.

Geronimo slowly turned onto Sunnyview.

"The Kalispell Regional Hospital is that big building up ahead on the right," Rainbow said, pointing.

The area surrounding the hospital, like the rest of Kalispell, was deserted. Several rusted hulks, former cars and trucks, lined Sunnyview Lane. The hospital parking lot contained three antiquated cars parked near the main entrance.

Geronimo braked the SEAL at the curb near the front entrance. The transport jerked a bit as he stopped.

"Sorry," he said, apologizing for the bumpy motion. "These brakes are touchy."

"It looks dark in there," Star noted.

The child was correct. Dark and foreboding. Geronimo glanced upward, counting the stories. Five. A sign to his left, still legible in sections, proudly proclaimed the completion of the Kalispell Regional Hospital expansion project.

"Let's go!" Star eagerly urged him.

"You're staying here," Geronimo told her, "with the doors locked."

"I want to go!" Star protested.

"He has a point," Rainbow informed her daughter. "You'll be safe in here. We won't be too long."

"I don't want to stay here alone!" Star disputed her mother.

"You'll be safe in here," Geronimo stressed. "Keep the doors locked, like I showed you, and nothing can get inside."

"You don't have any choice," Rainbow added.

"You're staying in here whether you like it or not."

Star pouted and sat back in the seat.

"How well do you know the inside of this hospital?" Geronimo asked Rainbow.

"I've only been inside it two times," Rainbow replied, "and I never really memorized the interior."

"Well, I guess it doesn't matter all that much," Geronimo stated. He picked the FNC up from the console and reached into his left front pocket with his other hand to ensure the list Plato had given them was still there.

It was.

"Okay," Geronimo announced. "Let's get to it."

Rainbow and Geronimo exited the transport and waited for Star to lock both doors from the inside.

"She's done it," Geronimo commented. He led the way up the front steps to the door, a shattered, gaping aperture, framing a shadowy hallway.

"Think anyone is in here?" Rainbow whispered.

"Never know," Geronimo stated. "Stay alert, just in case."

The Kalispell Regional Hospital was deathly quiet, the air stale and musty, the floors and the furnishings covered with the dust of decades of neglect.

"It's spooky in here," Rainbow nervously noted.

Geronimo, vividly recalling his harrowing experiences in the sewers of the Twin Cities, tightened his grip on the FNC. If anything so much as squeaked, he'd shoot first and ascertain its identity later!

The light filtering in from outside provided only marginal illumination, sufficient to reveal the interior but not with any clarity.

"How will you find what you're looking for?" Rainbow inquired.

Geronimo, proceeding from door to door, glanced over his shoulder. "Most of the plates on the doors are still attached and legible. I'm looking for the laboratory."

"Why?" Rainbow questioned.

"Because of all the rooms in a hospital," Geronimo responded, "the lab is most likely to contain what we need."

"What exactly is it you're looking for?" Rainbow queried, staying right on his heels.

"A number of things," Geronimo answered. "We already have the generator Plato wanted. We confiscated it from the Watcher outpost in Thief River Falls. Now we need a microscope. . . ."

"What's that do?" Rainbow interrupted.

"Makes little things big," Geronimo said. "Plato said he needs one to examine our blood." He paused. "That reminds me. I must find test tubes and a blood-testing machine, among other items."

"I'm surprised," Rainbow mentioned, "you don't have all of this stuff already. The Home impressed me as being well stocked by your Founder, Carpenter."

"We have a few test tubes," Geronimo confirmed. "The Family owned a microscope at one time too, but some dummy broke it years ago."

They were nearing the end of the hallway.

"Is this what you're looking for?" Rainbow pointed at a sign on the wall.

Geronimo crossed to the sign and studied the white lettering. "This may be it," he said excitedly. The sign, faint and barely legible in the gloom, read LAB. Below the single word was a small arrow pointing at a nearby door.

"I'll help you carry out whatever you find," Rainbow offered.

"Thanks." Geronimo walked to the door and tried the knob. "It isn't locked!" He cautiously pushed the door open, the hallway filling with the eerie creaking of hinges unused for a century.

The Lab was spacious and filled with a variety of medical equipment and scientific apparatus. Wide windows permitted radiant sunshine to fill the room. Cobwebs and dust overspread everything.

Rainbow leaned against the door jamb as Geronimo anxiously went from one piece of equipment to another. "How will you know what you're looking for?" she asked him. "I wouldn't know a microscope if I was sitting on one."

"Plato showed us photographs of the things he wants," Geronimo explained as he examined a white box with six silver switches and a row of colored buttons. "Many of them were in the encyclopedi or our medical reference volumes. He also provided each of us with a copy of his list."

"Your Plato thinks of everything," Rainbow commented.

Geronimo frowned. "Believe it or not, as sharp as Plato's mind is now, he was once even sharper. Did I ever tell you he has the senility?"

Rainbow slowly shook her head, her long black hair swaying. "No, I don't believe so. You said the Family was affected by the premature senility, but you never mentioned names."

"Well, Plato has it," Geronimo said sadly. "And, between you and me, it's beginning to affect him visibly, to the point where others have noticed. Plato is not quite fifty years old, and already he has the appearance of someone over seventy before the nuclear war. His brown hair turned completely gray in the space of nine months' time. Once he was robust and energetic, but now his body is stooped and frail. It's pathetic."

"How many Family members did you say have the disease?" Rainbow inquired.

"Only five of the oldest," Geronimo replied. "But

when you only have a population of seventy or eighty to start with, five is a lot."

Rainbow stepped into the hallway and looked at the front doorway. "I'm not too thrilled at leaving Star alone this long."

"I'll hurry as best I can," Geronimo promised. A table near the center window drew his interest. He peered at a thing with a glass tray at the bottom, four knobs above the tray, and a metallic tube extended beyond the knobs. "Thank the Spirit!"

"What is it?" Rainbow walked inside the lab.

"Found a microscope!" Geronimo elated. "And here's a rack of vials and test tubes!"

"Keep searching," Rainbow urged, eager to return to the SEAL.

"I'm on a roll now," Geronimo stated enthusistically.

"Say," Rainbow mentioned, "I've been meaning to ask you something."

"What is it?" Geronimo kept scanning the tables.

"You told me you picked the name Geronimo," Rainbow said. "I know all about the Family practice of selecting any name you want to use on your sixteenth birthday, about how seriously you view your Naming."

"Yeah. So?"

"So why did you choose the name of Geronimo? Our tribe has some books, and many of us were taught to read by our parents. I know who Geronimo was. Why did you pick him?" Rainbow watched Geronimo move from table to table.

"It was my Indian heritage," Geronimo revealed as he sought the items on his list.

Rainbow smiled knowingly. "I can imagine how proud you feel, being an Indian."

Geronimo glanced at her. "That's part of it. My parents departed this sphere to join the Great Spirit on high, leaving me as the sole Indian in the Family. For all

I knew, I was also the only Indian left alive in the country. This was before we discovered the members of the Family weren't the only survivors of the Big Blast."

"But why Geronimo?"

"I admired his indomitable courage. No matter how many hardships befell him, Geronimo refused to give up. He persevered against insurmountable odds. True, he ended his days an alcoholic wreck, but he was essentially a survivor. I could identify with him."

"That's it?" Her voice reflected her disappointment.

"What did you expect? Geronimo's life story?" Geronimo asked, puzzled by her disapproving expression.

"I thought maybe you admired him for another reason," Rainbow said.

"Like what?"

"Like," she began, walking toward him, "his intense hatred of the white man and everything the white man stood for."

"Geronimo?" He stopped searching and stared at her.

"Of course!" Rainbow exclaimed. "He recognized the true character of the whites! They're deceitful, conniving liars and hypocrites, all of them! The whites mistreated our forefathers and cheated them at every opportunity. You must know all of this, what with all the books in your Family library."

Geronimo concealed his reaction to her fiery words and flushed features. Why was she getting so worked up over events long past?

"The Flatheads know the whites can't be trusted," Rainbow continued proudly. "We learned from our history. We know what the whites did to the world. After all, it was predominantly white races responsible for starting World War Three, wasn't it?"

"I never thought of it that way," Geronimo admitted.

"We are a free people now," Rainbow said. "And we

will never let the whites control us again! If the army from the Citadel has taken my people prisoner, we shall find a way to free them. Did I ever tell you one of my favorite sayings?" she asked, grinning.

"No." Geronimo was startled by the almost fanatical gleam in her eyes when she talked about the white race.

"Yes," she giggled. "The only good white is a dead white."

Geronimo, appalled, leaned against one of the tables. "You can't be serious!"

"I most certainly am," Rainbow affirmed.

"But not all whites are bad," Geronimo objected. "I have close friends who are white. . . ."

"So I noticed," she said archly.

"But surely all of the Flatheads don't feel the way you do?" Geronimo inquired.

"Of course they do," Rainbow said with conviction.

"But your tribe took in that white man from the Citadel," Geronimo reminded her. "The one who came to live with your people before you were born."

"Him!" Rainbow snapped, sheer hatred twisting her lovely face. "I didn't quite tell the whole truth there." She smiled shyly. "I didn't want to antagonize Blade."

"What do you mean?"

"He wasn't a fugitive." Rainbow laughed. "He was part of a Citadel patrol we ambushed. We killed all of them, except for one. We took him to an old cabin and locked him in, but he escaped during the night. He was fleeing when he stumbled across some of our women bathing in a stream." She savagely pounded the nearest table. "There the bastard was, in our territory, un-armed, running for his life, and he still found the time to rape one of our maidens!"

Geronimo watched her tremble with the intensity of her emotions. He realized her aversion to the whites was all consuming.

"The irony of it all," Rainbow was saying harshly, "was he raped one of my cousins. My own cousin!" She paused and her muscles hardened. "The fool should have kept going! Our warriors caught up with him and returned him to our meeting hall."

"What did you do to him?" Geronimo questioned her.

"We tortured the son of a bitch!" Rainbow declared proudly. "We made him tell us everything we wanted to know about the Citadel, and then we peeled his skin from his body while he screamed and pleaded for mercy. We castrated him," she said with relish, "and forced him to eat his own genitals. Finally, we slit his throat."

Geronimo was speechless with horror.

"Our warriors wrapped the body in a blanket and carried it far to the south," Rainbow continued. "They deposited it in the middle of a heavily traveled road near the Citadel in the dead of night, leaving it as a warning. That was my idea." She beamed.

And this was the woman who wanted him to come live with her tribe? Geronimo silently shook his head.

"Is something the matter?" Rainbow demanded.

"I had no idea," he told her, "you were so bloodthirsty."

"And I," she said stiffly, "had no idea you were so weak."

Geronimo went to speak, but thought better of it. Her hatred was too ingrained to be influenced by mere words. "I have found several pieces of equipment on the list. Would you give me a hand loading this stuff into the back of the SEAL?"

"Dropping the subject, eh?" she taunted him.

"For now," he replied.

Working together in strained silence, they quickly loaded the microscope, the test tubes and vials, and other items into the transport. On each trip from the laboratory Star would unlock the doors at their approach, wait while they deposited their burdens in the rear section of the SEAL, and relock the doors when they re-entered the hospital. On their final trip to the laboratory, as they were lifting a heavy machine designed to evaluate and diagnose hemoglobin properties, they heard a loud thump sound somewhere upstairs.

"What was that?" Rainbow nervously whispered.

"Don't know," Geronimo responded softly. "Don't like it either. Let's get this to the SEAL."

They hastily loaded the last piece of equipment into the vehicle.

"I saw someone," Star announced as Geronimo walked around to the driver's side and prepared to climb up to the driver's seat.

"What did you see?" Rainbow asked.

"Faces," Star informed them. "At a window on the second floor. At least two or three."

"Were they soldiers from the Citadel?" Rainbow questioned, glancing up at the windows.

"Couldn't tell," Star stated.

Geronimo hefted the FNC, debating his course of action.

Rainbow noticed his thoughtful expression. "You're not thinking what I think you're thinking!"

"Stay in the SEAL," Geronimo ordered. "I'll be back as soon as I can."

"Why?" Rainbow demanded. "You have the stuff from the lab. Why risk going back in there?"

"Whoever is in there," Geronimo reasoned, "may know something about Blade's disappearance. I've got to find out."

"But what if something happens to you?" Rainbow objected.

"Stay in the SEAL. Keep the doors locked. You'll be safe inside the transport, and no one can see inside, remember. So wait for your chance and slip away. There may still be some of your tribe in the vicinity of Kalispell." Geronimo detected the vague outlines of a face peering from a tinted second-floor window. The face withdrew a second later. "Find your tribesmen," Geronimo advised. "There's bound to be a few who escaped the Citadel army."

"This is stupid!" Rainbow groused.

"Be careful, Geronimo," Star urged him.

"Keep the doors locked." Geronimo ran to the front entrance, paused to ensure mother and daughter were safely tucked inside the SEAL, and ducked into the ominous interior.

11

"Hickok! Wake up!"

The urgent voice was besieging his pounding head, assaulting his sluggish, returning senses with a nagging insistency. "Hold the fort!" he said, his lips and tongue feeling thick and awkward. "Not so loud."

"Wake up, damn you!"

The gunman slowly opened his eyes. He was lying on the ground, his head cradled in Sherry's lap. The sun was high in the sky. "My aching head!" he muttered. "What hit me? A two-ton meteorite?"

"Goldman," Sherry answered, smiling. "Thank God you're alive! I was beginning to think you'd never come around."

"How long have I been out?" Hickok asked her.

"You were out almost a full day," Sherry answered.

"What?" Hickok abruptly sat up and promptly regretted the motion as another searing pain lanced his head.

"He knocked you out yesterday afternoon," Sherry explained, "about this same time."

"Goldman did this to me?" Hickok gingerly rubbed a nasty bump on his right temple.

"Sure did," Sherry confirmed. "He hit you,

remember? And said he wanted to learn if you could do without breathing?"

"I vaguely recall it," Hickok said, struggling to clarify his fuzzy memory.

"I couldn't believe what you did next." Sherry grinned. "Why did you do it?"

"What did I do?"

"You looked at him and said you could do as well without breathing as he was able to do without any brains," Sherry replied.

"And that's when he slugged me?" Hickok asked.

"Sure did. As hard as he possibly could. I thought you were dead," she stated, concern reflected in her green eyes.

"This noggin of mine is as hard as granite," Hickok boasted.

"Lucky for you," Sherry mentioned. She reached out and gently stroked his injured temple. "It must hurt like crazy."

"That's an understatement," Hickok muttered. "Looks like I owe Goldman," he growled.

"First the Trolls, now Goldman." Sherry frowned. "You're real keen on revenge, aren't you?"

Hickok simply nodded, flinching as he did so, squinting at her.

"Did you ever hear of forgive and forget?" Sherry asked him.

"I have a friend," Hickok told her. "Name of Joshua. Old Josh is real big on the forgiveness stick. He's always trying to convince me to forgive my enemies, to love them as I would have them love me. Nice ideal, but I wouldn't be sitting here right now if I'd followed his advice. To answer your question, nope, I ain't much for forgiveness. I prefer to do it to them before they do it to me, and if they do it to me first and leave me alive, I aim to ensure they never do it to anybody else again. Savvy?"

"What?"

"Do you understand?" Hickok inquired.

"Unfortunately, all too well," Sherry responded.

Hickok opted to redirect their conversation. "Where the blazes are we, anyway?" For the first time he glanced around.

"We're at the Mound," Sherry informed him.

Hickok's eyes widened in disbelief.

They were at the northern edge of a huge clearing, surrounded by a dozen Moles standing ten yards away. The clearing itself was several hundred yards in circumference and dominated by a massive structure in the center of the clearing, a gigantic mound.

"Isn't it amazing?" Sherry queried him.

"Incredible," Hickok acknowledged.

The Mound was at least seventy feet high and one hundred wide, constructed of a dark, heavy clay, packed into a tight, cohesive, sturdy dome. Windows dotted the outer surface, and entrance was gained through doorways imbedded in the base of the Mound at thirty foot intervals.

"How . . . ?" Hickok began, glancing at Sherry.

"Silvester told me a little while you were out," Sherry said. "The Moles have been working on this thing since the war. They get their clay from near the Upper Red Lake, about three miles south of here. Remember that man Silvester told us about, the one named Carter? Well, he started the whole thing when he came out here to escape the nuclear exchange. Apparently, Carter and his followers didn't have the material needed to build a genuine shelter, so they improvised by digging some tunnels and piling tons of dirt and clay on top of the tunnels for protection and insulation. The Moles have been expanding it ever since."

"Speaking of Silvester," Hickok said, glancing around, "where is our klutzy pard?"

"Goldman and Silvester went into the Mound this morning," Sherry revealed. "Goldman said they were going to bring a man here to check us out."

"What did he mean by that?"

"Beats me." Sherry shrugged. She gazed at the Mound and pointed. "Look! Here they come now."

Hickok spotted them. There were a number of Moles, primarily women, outside the Mound. Some were tending to children, others hanging clothes on ropes tied between two poles, and still others idly engaged in animated discussion. Except for the presence of armed guards ringing the Mound, the scene was tranquil and pleasant.

Almost reminds me of the Home, Hickok mentally noted.

Goldman, Silvester, and another Mole were approaching, still one hundred yards distant.

"How did I get here?" Hickok asked Sherry.

"A pair of Moles carried you," Sherry replied.

Carried? Had they found his backups? Hickok pretended to pat dust from his buckskins as he felt for the Mitchell's Derringer under his right sleeve and the C.O.P. under his pants, above his left ankle. Both were still there. Thank the Spirit!

"You preening for Goldman?" Sherry asked innocently.

"Anyone ever tell you," Hickok rejoined, "you have a warped sense of humor."

"Just everybody." She grinned.

"How did they carry me?" Hickok asked her.

"What?" Sherry seemed surprised by the question.

"I'm curious," Hickok stated. "How?"

"One of them grabbed you by the armpits, the other by the knees, and they brought you here. Why?"

"Never mind." Hickok kept his eyes on the trio heading their way. "Listen up. We don't have much time. If we get separated, I'll come for you as soon as I can."

"What can you do against so many?" Sherry asked doubtfully.

"You let me worry about that," Hickok answered. "Just have faith. I'm going to get us out of this mess, and Shane too, if they haven't killed him yet."

"I have faith in you," Sherry declared affectionately. "I'll be waiting."

Hickok smiled at her, noting the lovely contours of her features and admiring her strength and courage. She was some woman! If they managed to get out of this mess in one piece, he resolved to indulge in some heavy courting. His thoughts strayed to Bertha, awaiting his return to the Twin Cities, and he frowned. What in the blazes was he going to do about her? He knew she liked him; she flagrantly displayed her fondness for the whole world to see! But how did he feel about her? He cared for her, sure, but more as a close friend than a lover. Would Bertha understand if he became attached to Sherry? Knowing Bertha, she'd probably beat Sherry to a pulp.

"Is something the matter?" Sherry inquired.

"No. Why?"

"You look upset," she said.

"It's nothing I can't handle," Hickok promised. Yep. The only way to confront Bertha would be with complete honesty. Lay all his cards on the table, and pray she understood.

"You never did tell me much about where you come from," Sherry commented ruefully.

"Don't worry," Hickok said. "You'll see for yourself soon enough."

"I will?" she asked hopefully.

"You can count on it," Hickok vowed.

Sherry smiled. "That bump on the head has done you some good."

"If he likes it so much," someone sarcastically interjected, "I can put another one there, real easy."

Hickok stood and turned, facing Goldman, Silvester, and the third Mole, a thin man dressed in clean clothes, a brown shirt, and blue pants and carrying a black-leather bag similar to the type used by the Family Healers.

"I'd like to see you try." Hickok glared at Goldman.

Goldman took a menacing step forward. "Don't think I wouldn't love to cram this Winchester down your arrogant throat, but I have other orders."

"Don't let that stop you," Hickok goaded him.

The skinny Mole walked up to Hickok and extended his right hand, smiling. "My name is Watson. I'm pleased to meet you."

Hickok took the proffered hand and shook. "The name is Hickok."

"I know." Watson nodded. "Silvester told me about you and the charming lady you're with."

"You're a bit out of place here, aren't you?" Hickok commented.

"I don't follow you," Watson stated.

"You act almost human."

Watson laughed. "Let's just say I don't necessarily appreciate the rougher element in our cloistered society."

"You must read a lot," Hickok reasoned.

"How did you know?"

"I'm psychic."

"Really?" Watson took the claim seriously.

"No."

Watson glanced at Sherry, uncertain whether to accept Hickok's statements at face value. She was grinning from ear to ear. "I'm something of a physician," he informed them. "I must check you over before you can enter the Mound."

"How come?" Sherry inquired.

Watson placed his black bag on the ground and opened a worn flap. "Some time ago," he explained as he sorted the contents, "a prisoner entered the Mound and was sentenced to a tunnel crew. Unknown to us, he carried a new type of virus, a particularly deadly viral organism. We lost four dozen before the contagion stopped as mysteriously as it spread. Shortly thereafter, Wolfe decided all prisoners would be checked before they entered the Mound. That's why I'm here."

"Where did you learn to be a physician?" Sherry questioned, watching as he extracted a stethoscope.

"From my father," Watson replied. "He taught me what he could. He learned from his father, a member of the original Carter group."

"You any good?" Hickok bluntly demanded.

"I do my best," Watson said. He fidgeted, hesitating.

"Get on with it!" Goldman ordered.

"I'm afraid," Watson said, somewhat embarrassed, "you will need to remove your clothes."

"What?" Hickok snapped.

"Right out here in the open?" Sherry asked. "You can't be serious!"

"I am sorry," Watson apologized.

"With all these men watching?" Sherry stressed her objection to the requirement.

"You're not hiding anything I won't see eventually," Goldman declared. "Strip."

Hickok moved in front of Sherry, protectively placing his body between the Moles and his newfound romantic interest. "No way," he said, looking directly at Goldman, challenging him.

Goldman aimed the Winchester at Hickok's chest. "You'll do as you're told!"

"What about your orders?" Hickok defied him. "You think your boss is going to like it if you blow me away before he has a chance to interrogate us?"

Goldman paused, lowering the rifle. "Think you know everything, don't you, smart ass? I was told you're to be checked, and you will be whether you like it or not!" He nodded at the encircling guards and they began closing in.

Hickok tensed. What should he do? If they stripped, the Moles wound find his hideouts and he would lose his edge. If he drew the Derringer, he might be able to catch them off guard, break free, and reach the nearby forest. But if he did escape, it would minimize their chances of rescuing Shane. He had only seconds to decide.

"I have a solution," Watson proposed.

"Who cares?" Goldman snapped impatiently.

"Would you prefer it if I tell it to Wolfe?" Watson countered.

Goldman glanced at Watson, chewing on his lower lip, debating. "No," he said finally. "You're one of his favorites. He might become angry, and I wouldn't want that."

"I bet you wouldn't." Watson beamed, relishing his verbal victory.

Hickok noted the friction between the two and filed it for future reference.

"So what's your bright idea?" Goldman asked in an annoyed tone.

"See those bushes?" Watson pointed at a thick stand of tall bushes fifteen yards away, at the perimeter of the forest.

"Yeah. So?"

"So I take one of them over there at a time. They undress, I examine them, and they put their clothes back on. This way, we avoid bloodshed."

Goldman snickered. "What a dumb idea!"

"Why?" Watson patiently inquired.

"What's to stop them from taking off once they're in

the bushes?" Goldman demanded.

Watson frowned and sighed. "With the guards so close? How far do you think they would get? Besides," he added, "I doubt one of them would run if you keep the other one here."

Goldman stroked his hairy chin. "I guess you're right. Go ahead. But you're responsible."

"Fine." Watson faced Hickok and Sherry. "Which one of you wants to be first?"

"I'll go," Hickok volunteered. He smiled reassuringly at Sherry and followed Watson to the forest. They found a small open space in the center of the bushes, wide enough to accommodate two people and shielded from prying eyes in the clearing. "Turn your back," Hickok directed.

Watson's eyebrows raised, but he complied with the request.

Hickok quickly removed his clothes and the backups, hiding them in the pile of buckskins at his feet. "You can examine me now."

Watson performed his examination in silence. As he replaced his instruments in the black bag, he glanced at Hickok. "I wish everyone in the Mound was as healthy as you are. There's no evidence of malnutrition, a common malady these days. Except for a few bumps and bruises, and a lot of scars, you're one of the fittest specimens I've ever seen."

"You think I'm fit?" Hickok motioned for the physician to turn around. "You should see a friend of mine named Blade. He has so many muscles, he makes me look like a ninety-eight-pound weakling."

Watson, absently staring at the vegetation, shook his head. "I wish everyone here would follow the dietary advice and hygienics guidelines I've established. It would drastically reduce many of our health problems."

Hickok, his eyes on Watson's back, dressed, reattach-

ing the Derringer and the C.O.P. and their respective
holsters and leather straps. Satisfied the hideouts were
safely concealed, he patted Watson on the right
shoulder. "I'm ready."

"Funny. I didn't take you for the bashful type," the
Mole observed as they moved through the bushes to the
clearing.

Hickok declined to comment, wonderfing if Watson's
suspicions were aroused.

Goldman was visibly relieved when they appeared.
"Okay," he barked at Sherry. "Get it over with."

Hickok winked and grinned at Sherry as he passed
her.

"Take a good look around," Goldman gloated as
Hickok stopped near Silvester. "It's the last daylight
you're ever going to see!"

12

In the middle of the afternoon, with the sun high overhead, she finally found him standing on the bank of the moat, all alone, in the southwestern corner of the Home. His long brown hair, the same shade as his eyes, was blowing in a stiff breeze. Although, at sixteen, he was two years her junior, since the death of their father he had adopted a paternal attitude toward her, an unexpected protectiveness and intense loyalty. She suspected the realization they were the last members of their family left alive had something to do with the change in his behavior.

"Hi, Tyson," Cindy greeted him. "What are you doing?"

Tyson, startled, glanced around until he saw her approaching from his rear. "Oh. Hi, Cindy. I didn't hear you," he said.

"I asked what you're doing out here," she repeated.

Tyson stared into her deep blue eyes. "Just thinking."

"About what?" Cindy leaned against a tree and watched his face as he spoke, striving to detect signs of possible stress.

"About us," Tyson responded.

"What about us?"

Tyson faced her, placing his hands into the pockets of his camouflage pants. The pants and the matching shirt he wore were gifts from Nadine, Plato's wife. Both garments were worn and faded, but after Nadine had hemmed them and patched the holes and rips, repaired the frayed sections and completely cleaned them, they were almost as good as new and the best clothes Tyson had ever owned. He frowned as he gazed at the moat. "Are you happy here, Sis?"

"Of course I am," Cindy affirmed. "What kind of dumb question is that to ask?"

"Are you sure?" Tyson pressed her. "I mean, is there anything about this place you don't like? Would you like to leave the Home?"

"Leave the Home?" Cindy straightened, shocked by the query. "Be serious!"

"I am," Tyson emphasized.

"Why would I want to leave the Home?" Cindy demanded. "The safest, happiest place we've ever been! Of course I want to stay right here, dummy!"

"Even with all the things that've happened to you?" Tyson inquired, his expression somber.

"What's happened to me?" Cindy countered, perplexed by his conduct.

"You tell me."

"What is that supposed to mean?" Cindy could tell something was really bothering him, eating at her brother's insides. But what?

"Has anyone been bothering you?" Tyson asked, confronting her.

"Bothering me? In the Home?" Cindy shook her head. "Of course not."

"These people aren't the angels they like you to think they are," Tyson said bitterly.

"The Family members are the nicest people we've ever run into, Ty," Cindy said, disagreeing. "How can you make such a claim?"

"And you're sure no one has been bothering you?" Tyson asked.

"No." Cindy laughed, finding the suggestion ludicrous. The Family members were moral to a fault, and most of their energy was devoted to loving their Maker and one another as perfectly as possible. "Who would bother me?"

Tyson sighed and crouched, absently plucking blades of grass and tossing them aside.

"Answer me," Cindy ordered him. "Who would bother me?"

"Drop it," Tyson said. "I didn't think you'd tell me."

"Tell you what?" Exasperated, Cindy moved away from the tree and positioned herself directly in front of her brother, forcing his eyes to meet hers. "Tyson, I want you to tell me what's bothering you."

"Why should I?" Tyson snapped. "You won't tell me who's bothering you."

"No one is bothering me!" Cindy exploded.

"He said you wouldn't tell me," Tyson muttered.

"Who said . . ." Cindy began, then stopped, insight dawning. "Was it Napoleon? Did he tell you something about me?"

"Napoleon is our friend," Tyson stated.

"Tyson . . ." Cindy crouched and gently took his rough hands in hers. "I want you to listen closely to what I'm about to say. We are brother and sister, the last of our family. You know I love you and would never lie to you, don't you?"

"Yeah," Tyson grudgingly admitted. "I guess so."

"Then believe me when I tell you Napoleon isn't our friend."

Tyson went to protest, but Cindy quickly placed her left hand over his mouth.

"Don't interrupt!" she directed. "Just listen. I overheard Napoleon plotting a rebellion. He mentioned your name. How do you fit into his scheme?"

"What do you mean, a rebellion?" Tyson asked after she removed her hand.

"Napoleon is planning to kill Plato and Rikki-Tikki-Tavi and take over the Family," Cindy explained.

Tyson grinned. "You must have misunderstood. The only one Napoleon wants to kill is Rikki, that bastard."

"What?"

Tyson's face clouded with anger. "Napoleon told me how Rikki has been bothering you! Why wouldn't you confide in me? I can help you, you know. I won't let the son of a bitch get his hands on you!"

"Ty, Rikki hasn't . . ."

"Napoleon told me all about it," Tyson said, cutting her off. "About how Rikki wants you to go to bed with him, how he's been pressuring you to give in or he'd kill me. Well, just let the prick try!"

Comprehension flooded her mind, and Cindy gripped him by the shoulders. "Ty, calm down. Listen. Napoleon lied to you. . . ."

"But . . ."

"He . . . *lied to you*," she reiterated, her voice rising. "He is using you to get at Rikki. I give you my word, Rikki-Tikki-Tavi is not trying to force me to have sex with him. He would never do a thing like that. And besides, don't you think I'd come to you if I really was in trouble? I'd tell you about it, and we would probably go to Blade or Hickok and let them know. They're our friends. What do you think Hickok would do to anyone trying to do what you said Rikki is supposed to be doing?"

"Put a bullet in his head," Tyson answered thoughtfully.

"Right. So there's no reason why I wouldn't confide in you, is there? Not when we both know we could count on Blade and Hickok to help us. Do you agree?"

"Yeah . . ." Tyson concurred, her logic making an impression.

"So when Napoleon claimed I wouldn't tell you," Cindy said, her features reflecting her affection, "why the hell did you believe him, Ty?"

Tyson seemed confused. He vigorously shook his head and held his hands out, palms up. "I . . . I don't know, Sis. It made me so mad when Napoleon told me, I wanted to kill Rikki. I wasn't thinking. Napoleon said you wouldn't tell me because you were afraid I'd do something rash and Rikki would kill me. I don't know Rikki that well. For all I knew, it could have been true."

"I bet Napoleon had a way you could do something about it," Cindy surmised.

"As a matter of fact," Tyson stated slowly, "he did."

"What was his plan?"

Tyson's anger was building again, only this time at the realization Napoleon duped him. "Napoleon said he knew this spot Rikki goes to sometimes to be alone. He said we should confront Rikki, and he offered to give me a gun for protection."

Cindy's mind raced as she tried to deduct Napoleon's true motive. "I'll bet Napoleon planned to shoot Rikki and lay the blame on you. He'd probably kill you too. He wouldn't want any witnesses."

Tyson rose, his eyes blazing. "That prick!" He looked at Cindy. "What do we do now, Sis?"

"One thing's for sure," Cindy said as she stood. "We can't afford to wait until Blade and Hickok come back. Napoleon is too dangerous. There's no telling what he may do."

"But how can we stop him?" Tyson asked.

"We can't," Cindy declared. "But I know someone who can."

"Who?"

"Rikki-Tikki-Tavi."

13

The first and second floors of the Kalispell Regional Hospital were uninhabited.

Geronimo, standing in the stairwell between the second and third floors, paused, debating his next move. He'd spent the better part of the afternoon painstakingly searching the first two floors of the hospital, and there was still no sign of whoever was lurking in the upper stories. Apparently, whoever it was knew they had been spotted and had seen him enter the hospital to investigate. He leaned over the ring and peered up the darkened stairwell. Either his quarry had used another exit, or they had gone higher, believing a lone man wouldn't be foolish enough to pursue them.

How he missed Blade and Hickok! As Alpha Triad, as a functional fighting unit, they relied on one another for support and assistance. You didn't worry about covering your back because you knew someone else was doing it, someone who would gladly give his life to defend your own.

Now, alone in hostile territory and probably outnumbered, he considered returning to the SEAL. The further he ascended, the more vulnerable he became.

He didn't like it one bit.

Something scraped against a metallic object above him, the slight noise the equivalent of a thunderclap in the deathly silence of the musty stairwell.

Someone was on the stairs above him!

Geronimo crouched and slowly climbed the steps, one at a time, his eyes alertly probing the shadows for movement.

The stealthy pad of a foot on concrete reached his ears.

They were close!

Geronimo leaned against the wall, blending his body into the stygian inkiness of a recessed corner.

Was it someone coming down to see if he was still in the building?

The waiting was nerve racking, the seconds seeming like hours. Geronimo pointed the FNC at a stretch of stairs descending from the third floor. If someone was coming, it would be his first . . .

A black form materialized on the stairs, the vague shape of a man in discernible contrast to the dusty paleness of the concrete steps.

"Don't move!" Geronimo shouted.

The figure above him snapped three shots in the direction of the yelled command. One of the bullets struck the wall inches from Geronimo's head.

Geronimo fired a short burst from the FNC, the slugs ripping into his target and flinging the man to the steps.

The man gasped once, then tumbled down the stairs. A pistol fell from his hand and clattered to the landing.

Geronimo cautiously moved to the body and knelt over it. He could hear the man wheezing.

Was he alone?

Geronimo patiently waited for any reaction to the gunfire: voices, footsteps, anything.

Nothing.

Good.

Geronimo reached into his left front pocket and

removed a pack of matches, part of the booty taken from the Watchers in Thief River Falls. He struck a match and held it over his fallen foe.

The man was a Flathead Indian, in his early or mid-thirties. He wore buckskins and carried a knife and a pouch on a belt around his waist. The slugs from the FNC had perforated his chest and lungs. Blood was oozing from the wounds and staining his shirt. He was still alive, but barely.

Geronimo frowned, unhappy with himself. Maybe he should have let the man come closer and tried to knock him out, to somehow subdue him without using the FNC. A commendable idea, he noted, but not very practical. The Flathead might have seen him, or sensed him, or simply resisted, and at close range one of his shots was bound to find a target.

There was no other way.

Geronimo leaned back on his heels, relieving a slight cramp in his lower left leg, and the motion saved his life.

The blast of the shotgun was deafening in the confines of the stairwell, coming from the landing above.

Geronimo felt a stinging sensation in the hand holding the match, and the wall exploded in a shower of cement and brick.

Unexpectedly, the Flathead Geronimo had shot abruptly opened his eyes and sat up, just as another deafening discharge of the shotgun filled the stairwell.

Geronimo saw the Indian's face blown apart, the eyes and nose and mouth erupting in a crimson spray of flesh.

The match flickered out, plunging the stairwell into complete gloom.

Geronimo rolled to his feet and ran, pressing his left hand tightly against his side. He had the impression his hand was bleeding, and he didn't want to leave a trail of blood for his opponents to follow.

"I got him!" someone shouted, elated, from the floor above.

Geronimo reached the door to the second floor and pushed it open, holding it with his right hand so it wouldn't bang when it swung closed. He heard feet pounding on the stairs and saw the faint beam of a light.

"You asshole!" another voice snapped. "You shot Spotted Elk!"

Geronimo raced down the hallway, carefully avoiding furniture and equipment left abandoned along the hall. He knew it was only a matter of moments before they came after him. If he could get to the SEAL, he'd be safe inside its protective bulletproof body. He was almost at the end of the hall, yards away from a door leading to another flight of stairs to the first floor, when the men after him, hot on his heels, came through the first door, the one he'd used to reach this floor. The door forcefully crashed into the wall behind it.

At the sound, Geronimo glanced over his right shoulder, taking his eyes from the hallway ahead. He failed to see the discarded wheelchair in his path, and he flinched as his knees smashed into the wheelchair, his momentum carrying him forward and lifting him from the floor. He frantically tried to correct his balance, but it was too late. The wheelchair toppled over, Geronimo on top. He landed hard, one arm on the wheelchair gouging him in the ribs.

"Down here!" someone shouted.

His pursuers didn't seem much concerned with stealth any more.

Geronimo twisted and aimed the FNC at several figures hurrying toward him. He fired and watched them dive for cover.

Keep moving!

Geronimo scrambled to his feet and reached the door. He shoved his way through it and hastened down the stairs, limping now, his left knee throbbing. He could hear a commotion on the floor above him.

They were still coming.

He was three steps from the bottom and the door to the first-floor hall, when the door suddenly opened, framing an armed Flathead with a rifle in his hands.

Geronimo didn't hesitate. He went for a head shot, as Hickok constantly advocated, the slugs rupturing the Indian's forehead. The Flathead fell to one side and Geronimo jumped over his body and raced toward the front entrance, a beacon of hope at the far end of the hall. He was going to make it! There was no way they could stop him now!

The bright sunlight caused him to squint as he exited the hospital, and it took him a moment to adjust before he spotted Rainbow.

She was standing at the bottom of the steps in a wide stance, holding the Dan Wesson .44 Magnum, Blade's revolver, in her hands.

Geronimo started down the stairs, surmising she was there to aid him, that she'd heard the gunfire and grabbed the revolver to help. He was on the third step when a thought struck him. How could she have heard the shooting if she had the windows rolled up as he'd instructed? He glanced at her and noticed her peculiar smile.

"Rainbow . . . ?" he began.

She fired, the .44 Magnum bucking in her slender hands.

Geronimo felt the impact of the slug as it penetrated his left shoulder and jerked him from his feet. He was dimly aware of falling onto the concrete steps, the brutal contact jarring his entire body. In shock, his senses reeling, he raised his head and tried to focus on Rainbow.

She was slowly walking toward him, smiling in triumph.

Geronimo wanted to speak, but couldn't. His lips twitched and his head dropped, and as his eyes closed his mind was filled with one burning question: *Why?*

14

"Don't you ever get tired?"

"You ask too many questions, yes? Stop, yes?"

"My teacher once told me you only learn things if you're curious, if you constantly thirst for answers. He told us to always ask questions."

"That would be Plato, yes? The Family Leader, no?"

Blade angrily squirmed in the creature's grasp. "Damnit! How the hell do you know so much about the Family?"

Gremlin, carrying the Warrior south on Highway 35, grinned. "Told you before, yes? For one who asks so many questions, you don't listen to answers!" This struck him as hilarious and he laughed in genuine delight.

Blade grit his teeth and fumed. He looked to their right, to the west, noting the sun sinking toward the far horizon, the fiery star reflected on the surface of Flathead Lake. The beautiful lake was placid, its blue waters fringed by dense conifer forests. He recalled Geronimo mentioning the lake on their trip to Kalispell. What was it Geronimo said? Something about Flathead Lake being the largest freshwater lake west of the Mississippi River, almost forty miles long with one hundred and eighty miles of shoreline. According to a paragraph at the bottom of the map, Flathead Lake had been a popular tourist resort before the Big Blast. Now nature had reclaimed the lake and the surrounding shoreline and beaches. Disintegrating summer homes and crumbling docks lined the shore.

"Why so quiet? Mad, yes?" Gremlin snickered.

Blade glanced at his captor. "Why bother talking to you? You won't tell me what I need to know."

"Already did, yes?" Gremlin stated.

"You speak in riddles, Gremlin. I can't understand you."

"Sorry, but speak truth, yes?"

"If you say so," Blade mumbled.

"Don't believe Gremlin?" The creature seemed hurt by the insinuation he would lie.

"You expect me to trust you?" Blade asked, shaking his head.

"Why not, yes? Gremlin trustworthy."

"Well, excuse me for doubting your integrity," Blade said in a mocking tone.

Gremlin stopped and hissed. "No insults, yes? Not my fault Gremlin do this."

"Oh? Whose fault is it?" Blade asked sarcastically.

Gremlin resumed their trek, staring straight ahead. "Must do as told, yes? Not up to me, no?"

"If it's not up to you," Blade suggested, "why don't you let me go?"

"Can't."

"Why not? No one will ever know."

"Doktor know, yes? Hurt Gremlin, yes? Hurt him bad."

Blade was about to request an explanation when he remembered their fight in Kalispell. He'd had the impression Gremlin's heart wasn't in their struggle, and the creature had actually pleaded with him to drop his weapons to avoid hurting him. Hardly the trademark of a killer. But Gremlin's behavior had changed drastically after the blue light on the metal collar glowed; he had transformed into a rampaging demon. Why? How was the collar able to alter his conduct?

"Listen, Gremlin," Blade said, "I'm sorry if I offended you. But you can't blame me. How would you act if you were in my shoes?"

"Wouldn't fit, yes?" Gremlin grinned. "Your feet too big."

Blade smiled.

The road was hugging the shoreline. As they rounded a curve, a cluster of buildings appeared fifty yards ahead.

"Wonder where we are," Blade absently noted.

"Planet Earth, yes?"

Blade chuckled. "You missed your calling. You should be a comedian."

"Gremlin wa . . ." The creature froze, scanning the structures in front of them.

"What is it?" Blade asked.

"Quiet!"

Gremlin advanced warily. The buildings, several summer homes, were in decay, the windows gone, the wood rotting, and the shingles on one roof sagging.

Blade marveled at Gremlin's keen senses. What had the creature heard? Was there someone lying in wait for them? An ambush?

They were twenty yards from the first home when six men burst from cover, automatic rifles in their hands.

"Don't move!" one of the six shouted.

Blade recognized the men. They all wore green uniforms and carried M-16's, they all conveyed the professional air of a trained military man, and they all could only be one thing: Watchers.

The one who had ordered them to stop, an officer

judging by the insignia on his collar, advanced.

Gremlin snapped to attention. "Gremlin, G.R.D., serial number one-four-one-one, at your service, sir."

"At ease," the officer directed. He studied Blade. "I'm Lieutenant Angier. I see you have a prisoner."

"His name is Blade, yes? From the Family, no?"

"The Family?" Lieutenant Angier repeated, impressed. "I've seen the file. Isn't he one of their . . ." He paused, snapping his fingers. "What do they call themselves?"

"Warriors, yes?"

"Warriors! That's it!" Lieutenant Angier leaned forward, his face inches from Blade's. "I heard about the incident at Thief River Falls. You killed a lot of good men."

"I hope one of them was a relative," Blade cracked.

Angier swung the butt of his M-16, catching Blade on the chin and rocking his head.

Gremlin stepped back. "Not harm, please? Must keep intact, yes?"

"I'll take him from here," Angier stated gruffly.

"So sorry," Gremlin shook his head. "Will not, yes?"

Angier, annoyed, glared at Gremlin. "My patrol was ordered to establish a monitoring post here, to capture anyone passing this point, and escort them to the Citadel. I will take this prisoner off your hands."

"So sorry," Gremlin insisted. "Higher orders, yes? Must personally take this one to Citadel."

"Higher orders?" Angier challenged Gremlin. "From whom?"

Blade, recovering from the Watcher's blow, saw a thin smile on Gremlin's face.

"From the Doktor," the creature said, emphasizing the last word.

Angier visibly paled and swallowed hard. "My apologies. I had no idea. Of course, your orders supersede any I might have. Whatever the Doktor wants," he added nervously, "the Doktor gets."

"You've noticed that too, yes?" Gremlin said, grinning at Angier's subservient reaction to the mere mention of the Doktor.

"Is there any way we might assist you?" Lieutenant Angier inquired.

"You may, yes!" Gremlin nodded at Blade. "Need rest. Will you guard prisoner while Gremlin sleep?"

"Of course," Angier replied. "See that small building off to your right? The brown one by the lake? It was once an enclosed dock. I'll watch over the Warrior while you catch forty winks."

"Thanks. Appreciate it, yes?" Gremlin sauntered toward the designated structure.

Lieutenant Angier faced his patrol. "Resume your positions. Notify me if anyone comes along the road." He followed Gremlin.

The soldiers vanished from view.

Blade was carried through an open doorway into a well-lit boathouse. The building was constructed partly over the water, and waves rippled against the dock and splattered water on the moorings. Whatever vessel formerly occupied the boathouse was long gone.

"You behave, yes?" Gremlin deposited his captive on wooden planks to the left of the doorway.

Blade glanced up at the creature and grinned. "You know me."

"That's why I said it, no?" Gremlin surveyed the boathouse. "Smells like fish, yes?"

Blade realized Gremlin was right; the building did reek of a fishy odor.

"Watch carefully, yes?" Gremlin said to Angier, then left.

Blade's gray eyes fell on a boat hook mounted on a rack above his head.

Angier, standing in the doorway, his thumbs hooked in his webbed belt, watched Gremlin walk to a stand of trees forty yards away and disappear in the dense underbrush. "Those freaks give me the creeps!" he muttered.

"I'm sure Gremlin will be delighted to hear your description of him," Blade remarked, chuckling.

Angier turned and pointed his M-16 at Blade's chest. "One word from you and I'll cut you in half. Understand?"

"Perfectly."

"Good. Then shut your face until the freak comes back."

"Mind if we talk?"

Angier took a step toward Blade. "Didn't you hear me, asshole?"

"Perfectly."

"Then shut your mouth, jerk!"

"You haven't answered me. Mind if we talk?"

Angier raised the M-16, preparing to bash the prisoner with the rifle butt again.

"Your mother ever tell you about your nasty temper?" Blade asked, smiling broadly.

"You asked for it!" Angier tensed, about to swing the rifle.

"Look," Blade said quickly. "You can beat my brains in, if that's what you want. But I don't think Gremlin or the Doktor would like it much. Why don't we just talk?"

Angier warily lowered the M-16. "You may be right. The Doktor might not take it too kindly if I damage the merchandise."

"So why don't we talk?" Blade urged him, hoping at last to learn some of the answers to the questions he had.

"Why the hell should I talk to you?" Angier snapped.

"I can give you a few reasons," Blade told him. "How long have you been here? A month or so? You must be bored to tears. I thought you might find a little conversation a welcome break in the monotony."

Angier studied the Warrior, assessing his character. "We are bored shitless," he admitted.

"See?" Blade grinned. "So why don't we talk."

Angier walked to the doorway and leaned against the frame. "I guess it can't hurt. What do you want to talk about? The weather?" He laughed at his own joke.

"I'd rather talk about you," Blade said. "I have a million questions. . . ."

"I bet you do, at that," Angier agreed. He placed the M-16 down, reclining the automatic rifle against the wall.

"Are you guys Watchers?" Blade asked.

Angier stared into Blade's eyes. "No hard feelings over that bop on the chin?"

"No," Blade lied. "Why should there be? I provoked you."

"You certainly aren't anything like your reputation," Angier remarked.

"I have a reputation?"

"What else did you expect? Remember, four of our troops survived the firefight in Thief River Falls. I saw the report. It was included in one of our regular dispatches. Very impressive," he commented, extending a compliment from one fighting man to another.

"I had help," Blade reminded him.

"Ahh, yes," Angier nodded. "The Family gunfighter and the Indian."

"Hickok and Geronimo," Blade clarified.

"I'd like to meet this Hickok some day," Angier said. He rested his right hand on a holster attached to his belt above the right hip. A protective green flap covered an automatic pistol.

"No," Blade disagreed, "I don't think you would."

"Is it true?" Angier asked, looking at Blade. "Did

Hickok really take on all those troops with just a pair of revolvers?"

Blade nodded.

"I wish I had been there," Angier stated wistfully. "Instead I'm assigned to this lousy post."

"You guys must be Watchers," Blade deduced, prying.

"Some call us that," Angier said. "We're known by a lot of different names."

"But what are you really?"

Angier thoughtfully gazed at the surface of the lake. "Haven't you figured it out by now?"

"You tell me."

"We're what's left of the U.S. Army," Angier began. "Only now we're known as the Army of Samuel."

"I saw some coins in Thief River Falls," Blade interjected. "They were imprinted with the words *In the Name of Samuel*. Any connection?"

"Pretty shrewd, aren't you?" Angier nodded. "Yep. Those coins were probably minted during the reign of Samuel the First. The Denver Mint put out millions of them. Now his son, Samuel the Second, is running the Government."

"You mean to tell me your Government is headed by a king?"

"Worse." Angier frowned. "They don't tell us everything, not even in school. The curriculum is designed to discourage prying minds, but you can't help but be curious. I came across some banned books once in a house in South Dakota. We're under standing orders to destroy all unapproved material, but I couldn't resist the temptation to read a few of these books. From what I was able to piece together, I learned a lot about why things are the way they are. Very enlightening," he said bitterly.

"Enlighten me," Blade prompted him.

"The Third World War was a total mess," Angier stated. "Neither side came out of it as well as they thought they would, despite their anti-missile systems, both land based and the ones in space. None of the leaders on either side survived. The United States Government withdrew to Denver and reorganized under the direction of the Secretary of Health, Education, and Welfare. He was in Denver at the time the war broke out and was spared. His name was Samuel. Samuel Hyde. He implemented something called Executive Order 11490, an order signed into law long ago by a President named Nixon. Under this law, Samuel was able to exercise complete control. The Government evacuated as many citizens as possible into what is now known as the Civilized Zone. Samuel confiscated all firearms, seized control of all communications channels, nationalized all industry, took control of all forms of travel, began censoring all mail, and impressed whole segments of the population into enforced national service." Angier dolefully shook his head. "So much for the once-relatively-free country known as the United States of America," he said acidly.

"How could he get away with it?" Blade queried.

"It was all in the name of national security," Angier informed him. "That Executive Order gave him the power and the legal right. I don't think most Americans even knew it existed."

"Why didn't the people stop him?"

Angier snickered. "How were they supposed to do that? They'd just been through the worst war in the history of mankind. They weren't in much shape for resisting anything. Besides, Samuel had control of the Armed Forces and confiscated all privately owned fire-arms. How were they going to rebel? Stones and sticks aren't much good against tanks."

Blade was attempting to absorb the implications of

Angier's revelations. "How much territory does this Civilized Zone include?"

"Oh," Angier said, "the boundaries aren't clearly defined, but generally the Civilized Zone is made up of the former states of Kansas, Nebraska, Colorado, southern Wyoming, eastern Arizona, New Mexico, and the northern half of a state once called Texas."

Blade envisioned one of the maps from an atlas in the Family library. "What about the rest of the United States?"

"I've heard that the state of California refused to submit to Samuel's new federal organization. They're now calling themselves the Free State of California. Another state, one called Utah, was taken over by a religious group known as the Mormons. They told Samuel to get stuffed. I don't know much about the remainder of the states. East of the Mississippi is a complete mystery. We sent a few patrols there years ago, but none ever came back. All we have are rumors, and if they're true you wouldn't want to go east of that river."

"Why do you have outposts all over the place?" Blade asked. "Like the one in Thief River Falls, and the others ringing the Twin Cities?"

"We're keeping an eye on everybody." Angier grinned. "Biding our time. Waiting and watching. That's why the people in the Twin Cities call us the Watchers. Catchy name, isn't it?"

"What are you waiting for?"

"Until we're strong enough to reconquer the country."

"What?"

Angier laughed at Blade's surprised expression. "What else did you expect, dummy? Samuel has a grand plan to retake control of the entire country within fifteen years. If he had enough troops and hardware he'd do it tomorrow. As it is, we send out patrols. When they discover inhabited communities, like yours, we set up monitoring posts to learn as much as we possibly can about their numbers and strength. We keep a file on every populated spot we find."

Blade leaned forward. "But how do you learn so much? You seem to know all about the Family, even to knowing some of our names and whether we're Warriors or not. How could you learn all that?"

"It's easy," Angier replied, "with the technology we have at our disposal."

Blade recalled a comment made by Gremlin. "Spy in the sky and parabolic ears," he stated.

Angier nodded. "Then you know what I'm talking about?"

"Not quite," Blade admitted. "What are they?"

"A spy in the sky is a satellite. Do you know what a satellite is?"

"I've read about them."

"We have several still in operation. They're used for taking high-altitude photographs, and you wouldn't believe the resolution on these babies! They can pick up something the size of your hand from way, way up there."

Blade remembered an incident on the run to the Twin Cities. "What would one of these satellites look like if you saw it?"

"Saw it? They're hard to spot with the naked eye, but if you did see one it would look like a dot of light moving across the sky. Why?"

"I saw one once," Blade told him. All the time, so many of the answers were right in front of his face and he failed to realize it. "What's a parabolic ear?"

"A parabolic microphone."

"A microphone?" Blade repeated.

"Yeah. They can hear sounds at great distances. I've used one that would detect a whisper at five hundred yards."

"So that's how you did it," Blade said. "You set up one of your listening posts in the forest surrounding the Home. And we never knew!"

"How were you to know?" Angier remarked. "Like I said, I've seen the file on your Family. We've been monitoring you for years. That wall of yours presented a problem. . . ."

"Your microphones can't listen through brick?" Blade said, interrupting.

"Not very well, no. But I remember you people have a . . ." Angier paused, striving to recollect the word he wanted.

"A drawbridge," Blade finished for him. "And whenever we had the drawbridge down, like for working outside the Home clearing the perimeter or whatever, you simply aimed this parabolic thing at the opening in the wall."

"Exactly." Angier nodded. "We've recorded hours and hours of monitored conversations. You wouldn't believe how much we learned."

"Yes, I would," Blade commented.

"Hey! Don't take it so hard. Your group isn't the only one, you know. We have files on inhabited towns and communities in your state of Minnesota, in North and South Dakota, and Montana. Samuel intends to take them over first because they're the least populated. We'll do it one community at a time, until eventually we'll reconquer the entire United States," Angier said proudly.

"I take it you've already started?"

"You mean the Flatheads? Yes. They were the largest group in the target states. Samuel apparently plans to take the big fish first, then work our way down to the little minnows like your Family."

"You sound happy about it," Blade mentioned. "I thought you didn't like the guy."

"Don't get me wrong," Angier said. "I don't much like living under a dictator, but at least our society is orderly. It's progressive, unlike this mess you've got out here. I know my family is safe when I'm sent on field duty, and I also know the Government will take care of them if something should happen to me."

"Sounds to me like you've traded freedom for security," Blade observed.

Angier straightened, his jaw muscles clenching.

Blade knew he'd struck a nerve. He couldn't afford to antagonize the man now! He had to keep the conversation going. "I want to thank you for taking the time to explain all of this to me. It has really opened my eyes. But there are still some things I don't understand."

"Like what?"

"Like Gremlin and the Doktor," Blade said. "How do they fit in?"

Angier quickly glanced outside, ensuring Gremlin was still off sleeping.

"Why do you get so antsy around him?" Blade asked.

"I've got to be sure I'm out of range of that damn collar," Angier answered.

"The collar?"

"That's how the Doktor control his freaks, his creations. Gremlin is a G.R.D.," Angier stated, as if that would account for everything.

"What's a G.R.D.?"

"It stands for Genetic Research Division," Angier responded. "The Doktor's personal unit. They give me the creeps!" he reiterated.

"What does the Doktor use this Genetic Research Division for?" Blade inquired, eager to keep the momentum going, afraid Angier would decide he'd talked enough and clam up.

"Anything he wants," Angier answered. "He makes

'em, he can do whatever he wants with the damned things.''

"What do you mean, he makes them?"

"Just what I said. He creates them in his lab.''

"You're joking,'' Blade remarked. "No one can create life.''

Angier fixed Blade with a steady gaze. "Believe me, Warrior, you haven't the slightest idea of the Doktor's capabilities. You shouldn't doubt me. If memory serves, you and your friends are responsible for wasting four of the Doktor's pets in Thief River Falls.''

"What?'' Blade recalled the four hairy monstrosities Angier alluded to, one of which almost killed him. "You mean the Brutes?''

"We call them Rovers,'' the Lieutenant explained. "We use them for tracking and patrol duties. They're some of the Doktor's earlier handiwork. Not very bright, but loyal and obedient. Gremlin is a different story. He's one of the recent models. As you saw for yourself, the Doktor's made a lot of improvements.'' Angier's voice dropped to a horrified whisper. "The man is a devil, maybe *the* Devil! I'll never understand why Samuel took him into his confidence, into his inner circle of advisers.''

"Do others feel the same way about the Doktor as you do?''

"Some, yes,'' Angier said. "Not everyone. The man is an inhuman genius. He's the brains behind the chemical clouds.''

"The chemical clouds?''

Angier suddenly motioned for silence. "Did you just hear something?''

"No,'' Blade replied. "Like what?''

"Movement,'' Angier said, glancing outside and scanning the nearest vegetation, several trees and bushes, for signs of life. "If that freak transmits any of this, I'm as good as dead."

"Transmits? How?"

"I told you before. That damn collar!"

"The collar is a transmitter?"

"That metal collar is how the Doktor controls his freaks," Angier detailed. "His earlier creatures, like the Rovers, just wore leather collars. But the newer ones are intelligent, capable of thinking for themselves. To keep them in line, to ensure they'll always do his bidding, he fits them with special collars. The collars somehow carry an electronic impulse of some kind to the freaks from the Doktor's headquarters. I heard they can pick it up right through their skin. He tells them what to do, and if they don't do it the way he wants, he zaps them, causes intense pain and agony. The collars also transmit sound to the Doktor, so he can keep tabs on what's going on around his little pets. Of course, he's got almost fifteen hundred of the things, and he can't monitor them all at once, but you never know which ones he might be monitoring at any given moment. You never know if the Doktor is listening to you."

Blade took notice of the darkening evening sky. It was about time to make his move. "Why don't these creatures simply remove the collars?"

"Some tried. But they were killed by an electric shock. Now they all know better. They may want to make a break for it, to gain their freedom, but the collars contain a sensing device. If the collar senses someone is trying to take it off, there's a crackling and a burst of white light and the creature's head is fried to a crisp. I know. Saw it happen once." Angier shuddered at the repulsive memory.

Blade's arms were dripping sweat and his wrists felt bloody, but at long last his efforts were rewarded. "I want to thank you, again, for taking all this time to talk to me."

"It was nothing," Angier gruffly responded. "You guessed right. I was bored to tears. Now I want you to answer some questions for me."

"Sorry."

The Lieutenant faced Blade. "What the hell do you mean, you're sorry? I took the time. . . ."

"And I appreciate it," Blade interjected, "more than you'll ever know."

". . . so why aren't you going to give me the courtesy of answering my questions?"

"Because I have something else for you."

"Like what?"

"You see," Blade said, leaning forward, flexing his arm muscles to restore the circulation, "the whole time you were talking, I was working on this big surprise for you. I'd never have been able to do it without your help."

"What the hell are you babbling about? What surprise?" Angier demanded.

"This," Blade stated, bringing his torn and chafed hands around in front of his massive chest, the rope dangling from his left arm. "Surprise!" he grinned.

Angier lunged for his M-16.

15

"How far do you figure we've walked?" the gunman asked.

"I don't know," she replied. "Maybe five or six miles."

"I wonder how far underground we are?"

"If you don't shut up," Goldman snapped, "I'll plant you underground right here!"

"You know something, pard," Hickok said to Goldman, "you're all mouth!"

Goldman glared over his left shoulder at the Warrior, but he kept walking.

Hickok laughed, taunting him. They were in a well-lit tunnel, on their way to an audience with Wolfe, the Mole leader. Goldman led their column, followed by Watson, Silvester, Sherry, and himself. Behind him, ten armed Moles provided an escort.

"It seems like we've been down here for hours," Sherry wearily remarked.

"We're really not that far under the surface," Silvester mentioned. "Only a couple of dozen feet. We found if we dig too deep, our air shafts don't work too well."

"I'm still amazed at what you've accomplished," Sherry said.

Watson glanced back at her. "Remember, we've had about a hundred years to work on this."

"It shows," Sherry told him.

Hickok had to agree. It certainly did show. The area under the Mound, and apparently for miles in either direction, was a veritable maze of tunnels, an elaborate network of shafts. Each tunnel was named, indicated by signs at the junctions, exactly as the streets in any city or town. The ceilings and the floors of the tunnels were boarded over; sometimes the side walls would be, sometimes they wouldn't. Lighting was provided by crude candles placed in recessed receptacles at regular intervals. Hickok recognized the type of candle used; the Family employed a similar one, prepared by heating great, reeking gobs of animal fat until it liquified, then filtering the substance through dried grasses or reeds until you refined the pure tallow. Before the tallow hardened, you inserted a rope wick. Crude, yes, but effective. The candles did have one definite drawback; they stank to high heaven.

"Where do you get all this wood?" Sherry was asking.

"Do you realize how much forest there is in Minnesota?" Watson jokingly responded.

Rooms and larger chambers opened off the tunnels periodically. Some seemed to be public meeting places; others were apparently private domiciles. Children played in the tunnels, giggling and contented. Older Moles stared curiously at the newcomers as they marched to meet Wolfe.

Whatever he might think of their aggressive tactics and the sheer stupidity of living underground when there was abundant sunlight and fresh air up above, Hickok had to admit their system worked for them. As old Plato might say, the Moles had a viable social order, even if it was basically parasitical. He wondered how Plato was faring, whether the senility was continuing to debilitate the beloved Family Leader.

They reached a major intersection, four tunnels meeting at one point, and stopped. Huge wooden beams supported the arched roof.

"This way," Goldman announced, and led them to the right.

"How much farther is it?" Sherry complained. "I could use some rest."

"Not much farther," Goldman replied. He turned, grinning. "In fact, we're here."

Their forward path was completely blocked by a ponderous wooden wall. In the center of the wall, flanked by six armed Moles, was a door.

Watson glanced at Hickok and Sherry. "Whatever you do," he said, his voice low, "don't antagonize Wolfe. He may let you live."

"You got it backward, pard," Hickok stated.

"Hickok, please!" Sherry pleaded. "Don't pull another lame-brained stunt like you did with Goldman."

"Wouldn't think of it," the gunman remarked.

Goldman addressed one of the door guards, and the guard promptly opened the door and stood to one side, at attention.

Goldman motioned at the doorway. "After you," he directed.

Watson went first, followed by Hickok and Sherry. Silvester nervously hung back, reluctant to enter, until Goldman grabbed him by the right arm and shoved him through the doorway.

"Incredible!" Sherry exclaimed as they entered.

The chamber was immense, the walls, floor, and ceiling all constructed of smooth stone and mortar. A skylight fitted into the top of a vaulted roof served to adequately illuminate the audience room.

"Took us about two years to build this," Watson said to Sherry. "We found an abandoned quarry with a lime deposit, and mixed the lime with sand from a former highway-construction site. The water needed to achieve the bonding blend was easy to acquire." He proudly surveyed the chamber. "Yes, the mortar was easy compared to the arduous task of carting tons of stone here. We salvaged the skylight from a building in Bemidji."

Hickok estimated four dozen Moles occupied the audience room, most of them congregated at the foot of a series of cement stairs leading up to a circular dais. The exact middle of the dais was occupied by an enormous purple chair. But it was the man seated on the chair, scanning the chamber like a great, grim bird of prey, who drew Hickok's gaze.

Wolfe.

The Mole leader was exceptionally tall, a giant of a man, but as abnormally thin as he was tall. An unruly mane of red hair crowned a craggy countenance, resembling, more than anything else, the visage of a mighty eagle. His eyes were an intense blue hue, ever in motion, conveying the impression he saw everything going on around him. He wore clean clothes, both a purple shirt and purple slacks, and polished black leather boots. Strapped to his waist were a pair of pearl-handled revolvers, and leaning against the purple chair was a heavy-caliber rifle.

Hickok suppressed an impulse to charge up the steps and seize the revolvers and the rifle, *his* Pythons and the Henry. Well, at least he knew where to find them when the time came.

All eyes were on the prisoners as Goldman marched them to the base of the stairs. He bowed and smiled. "I have brought the new captives, as ordered."

"And they have been checked?" This question, spoken directly to Watson, came in an eerie, sibilant tone, remarkable in its uncanny projection and resonance.

Watson dutifully bowed. "They have, sir, and I can safely report they are clean."

"They better be."

"Your orders, sir?" Goldman requested.

Wolfe shot a stony stare at Goldman. "When I am ready."

Goldman bowed and averted his eyes.

"These are yours?" Wolfe looked at Hickok and patted the revolver on his right hip.

"You bet your ass," Hickok arrogantly replied, and Sherry abruptly groaned.

"I want to thank you," Wolfe said, ignoring the barb. "It isn't often we find weapons in such superb condition, of such excellent . . . caliber." The Mole leader snickered at his own joke.

"Enjoy 'em while you got 'em," Hickok advised. "You won't have them for long."

"Oh?" Wolfe's eyebrows arched upward. "Is that a fact?"

"It sure is," Hickok vowed. "The last son of a bitch who took my guns wound up as rat food. I don't like it when someone takes my guns," he added, speaking slowly, deliberately.

"You're scaring me to death," Wolfe commented drolly.

"You haven't seen anything yet," Hickok promised. He climbed the first step, then froze as guards materialized, ringing him, their weapons trained on his chest.

"No hasty moves, please," Wolfe directed. "My men might decide you pose a threat, and one of them might shoot before I could stop him. I wouldn't want that to happen. We have a lot to discuss."

"There's only one thing we have to talk about," Hickok disagreed.

"Indeed? And what is that?"

"I'm looking for a pard of mine, a kid wearing black clothes. I'm told he's here and I want him."

Wolfe, frowning, stood. "Goldman told me about your mouth, but I still can't believe anyone could be so inane." He walked to the edge of the dais and glared at Hickok. "No one talks to me the way you just did!" he growled. "No one!"

"Maybe you're hard of hearing," Hickok stated. "Want me to do it again?"

A deathly silence descended on the audience chamber as the assembled Moles awaited Wolfe's reaction to Hickok's taunt.

The Mole leader studied the gunman from head to toe. "You have courage, I'll grant you that. A remarkable lack of intellect, but courage. Just like the youth you seek. Very well!" He glanced at Goldman. "He wants to see his friend so much, we'll let him. Take him to the cells!"

"And the woman?" Goldman inquired.

Wolfe's blue eyes rested on Sherry's voluptuous body. "I see she is not without certain . . . talents," he announced, mentally undressing her. "I claim her for mine!"

"As you wish, sir," Goldman said, bowing, disguising his disappointment. He'd hoped Sherry would be offered on the public auction block, but among the special privileges enjoyed by the Mole leader was the prerogative of first rights to any new female.

Hickok quickly caught Sherry's eye and smiled reassuringly. "Hang in there," he urged her. "I'm coming for you soon."

Sherry bravely returned his smile and reached for his hand, but a guard grabbed her and spun her around.

Hickok leaped, diving from the first step, catching the guard across the lower legs and knocking him to the stone floor. He rolled past the guard and jumped to his feet, taking Sherry's hand in his. "Keep the faith, gorgeous!" he said, winking.

The stock of Goldman's Winchester slammed into Hickok's head from behind.

The Warrior dropped to his knees, weaving.

"Bastard!" Sherry angrily shouted, lunging at Goldman and clawing at his eyes. Her nails tore into the soft flesh above his left eye and ripped a chunk away, blood flowing from the wound and covering the eye as, enraged, he shoved her aside.

Goldman cursed and backed off as five of the guards swarmed on Sherry and wrestled her to the floor.

Wolfe held his right hand aloft. "Enough!" he bellowed. "Control them or else!" He motioned at one of the guards. "Take him to the cells as I ordered!" he snapped, pointing to Hickok.

A pair of guards gripped the gunman under the arms and hauled him from the audience chamber.

"And you," the Mole leader said, leering at Sherry, "will provide me with hours of amusement. I'm not afraid of your claws, witch! I like it when a woman fights me."

Goldman, his left hand pressed over his left eye, blood seeping between his fingers, moaned.

Wolfe glanced at his injured subject. "Take the woman to my private chambers," he ordered.

Goldman glared at Sherry with his good eye. "Get going, you bitch!" He pushed her so hard she stumbled and nearly fell.

"Goldman!" Wolfe barked.

Goldman looked up.

"If one hair on her beautiful head is damaged," Wolfe warned, "that little scratch will be the very least of your worries."

Goldman, furious, his face livid, bowed and nodded at

three of the guards. Two fell in on either side of Sherry and one brought up the rear as Goldman led them from the audience room.

Sherry searched for the men carrying Hickok, but they were out of sight and she had no idea which direction they'd taken.

Goldman turned at the intersection, his hand still over his eye. "You may be under Wolfe's protection now," he snarled. "But he'll tire of you soon enough, and then any man can bid for you. I intend to make sure I'm the one who gets you, and when I do, bitch, I'm going to make you pay for what you've done to me!"

Sherry, taking her cue from Hickok's example, mocked Goldman by saying sarcastically, "Should I tremble now or later?"

16

Cindy and Tyson located the one they sought after the Family's evening meal. Unfortunately, he wasn't alone.

"What do we do?" Tyson queried his sister as they paused twenty yards from the four people resting under a pine tree.

"We don't have any choice," Cindy replied. "We have to tell him now."

"But Plato, Jenny, and Joshua are with him," Tyson objected. "Should we involve them?"

"They're already involved," Cindy declared, "whether they know it or not."

"I hope we're doing the right thing," Tyson said apprehensively.

"Only one way to find out." Cindy mentally calmed her jittery nerves and boldly walked toward the seated quartet. How would they take the news of Napoleon's treachery? Would they even believe her? After all, she wasn't a legitimate Family member. Tyson and she were orphans, taken into the fold and, in a sense, adopted. They had only been in the Home several months. Would the others believe them?

Plato was leaning against the trunk of the tree, resting his head against the bark. His long gray hair and beard enhanced his aged appearance. He was talking to the trio encircling him, his features animated and his gentle blue eyes lively. His frail frame was attired in a brown shirt and pants.

Joshua, the youngest Family Empath, a devoutly spiritual man, wore a large Latin cross draped around his neck. His lengthy brown hair swayed in the cool breeze. He was leaning back on his elbows, heedless of the dirt smudging his faded green pants and blue shirt.

Jenny, Blade's intended, casually ran her right hand across her forehead, sweeping her blonde bangs aside. She was one of the Family Healers, and this evening she was wearing a yellow blouse and patched jeans.

It was the fourth person who spotted the approaching brother and sister first. A smallish, wiry man with black hair and dark, penetrating eyes, he wore baggy black pants and a loose-fitting blue shirt. Clutched in his right hand was a long black scabbard.

"He's seen us," Tyson stated.

"I know," Cindy confirmed.

Plato ceased talking as the duo joined his group. "Well, we have company," he announced. "Hello, Cindy. And Tyson."

Cindy couldn't take her eyes off the Warrior with the sword.

"Hi, Plato," Tyson said, returning his greeting. "Everybody." He nodded at the others.

"If you don't mind my saying so," Plato astutely observed, "I can't help but notice you both seem somewhat . . . troubled. Is anything wrong?"

"We came to talk to Rikki-Tikki-Tavi," Cindy explained.

"Oh? Would you prefer it if we leave you alone?" Plato asked.

Tyson looked at Cindy, letting her take the lead.

"No," Cindy responded. "That's not necessary. What

we have to say concerns all of you too."

Jenny was smiling. "You make it sound so serious."

"It is," Cindy affirmed gravely. "We have . . ." she began, then stopped as Tyson jerked her blouse. "What is it?" she demanded, annoyed at the interruption.

Tyson, his face pale, was pointing to their right.

"What . . ." Cindy followed the direction his finger indicated, her eyes widening in alarm.

"It's Napoleon!" Tyson whispered, frightened.

"Is something wrong?" Plato questioned them.

Napoleon was strolling toward them, his hand idly resting on the butt of his revolver.

"He knows!" Tyson, horrified, exclaimed. "He knows!"

"Look at me!"

Cindy and Tyson, openly stunned by Napoleon's appearance, turned at the command of the low, forceful voice.

"Close your eyes," Rikki-Tikki-Tavi calmly directed. "Now!"

They both hastily complied.

"Take deep breaths," Rikki advised. "Slowly. Relax. He is still a ways off. Don't open your eyes!" he ordered Tyson. "Slowly breathe in and out. Restore your balance. Good. Now open your eyes and smile."

Cindy and Tyson obeyed.

"Now act like nothing is the matter," Rikki said.

"What's going on?" Jenny asked, confused, glancing over her shoulder. "It's only Napoleon."

Plato, his brow furrowed, looked at Joshua. "Will you do something for me?"

Joshua eagerly nodded. "Anything. You know that."

"Devise a pretext and take Napoleon away from here."

"Why . . ." Joshua started to speak.

"There isn't time for explanations," Plato stated

hastily. "Please do as I ask and I will reveal my motives later."

They fell silent and a few moments later Napoleon reached them. "Mind if I join you?" he inquired, standing next to Cindy. "I have some time to kill before my next shift. A Warrior's work is never done," he joked, grinning.

"Whose is?" Plato rejoined in a friendly tone. "Why don't you have a seat. I'm attempting to elucidate the historical importance of philosophy in human culture."

"Oh, really?"

Joshua rose to his feet, dusting his clothes with his hands. "I've already heard Plato's views on the subject a dozen times. If you don't mind," he said, glancing at Napoleon, "I'd like to have some words with you."

"What about?" Napoleon asked defensively.

Joshua walked to Napoleon and placed his left arm around the Gamma Triad leader's shoulders. "As you well know, I make it my business to cultivate spiritual awareness in all of our brothers and sisters. I try to spend time with each of our brethren on a regular basis, answering questions and assisting them where necessary. More often than not, I learn more than I teach." He beamed at Napoleon. "And guess who I haven't talked with in quite a while?"

Napoleon, knowing the answer, shook his head. "There's no need to . . ."

"Ah!" Joshua cut him off. "But there is. Inner spiritual harmony, knowing we are sons or daughters of a Cosmic Creator, is essential to mental peace and physical well-being. Would you begrudge me the time until your shift, Napoleon?"

Napoleon, clearly uncomfortable, balked. "Look, Joshua. Can't we do this some other time?"

"Procrastination, my dear brother, is inimical to spiritual progress," Joshua said. "Haven't you heard?

Never put off until tomorrow what you can accomplish today."

"You better do it, Napoleon," Jenny prompted. "You know how Joshua is. He'll never give you a minute's rest until you give in."

Napoleon, resigned to the inevitable, sighed and nodded. "I know how Joshua is," he agreed. "When it comes to spiritual matters, he's as tenacious as they come." He looked at Joshua. "If you were a Warrior instead of an Empath, you'd be the toughest Warrior in the Family."

"That's an honor I could do without," Joshua stated. "My trips to Thief River Falls and the Twin Cities with Alpha Triad confirmed a conviction of mine. Violence is deplorable. It might be necessary on occasion, as I found out, but I wouldn't want violence to become a habitual experience in my earthly life. I don't see how you Warriors do it."

"Do what?" Napoleon asked.

"Confront violence on a daily basis and still retain some semblance of sanity." Joshua, reflecting on his slaying of a Brute in Thief River Falls, sadly shook his head. "Violence tears at the soul and destroys communion with our Maker and Shaper." He grinned at Napoleon. "Which, by the way, is one of the things I want to take up with you. Let's find someplace quiet."

Plato watched Joshua lead a reluctant Napoleon off. Interesting. Joshua had changed during his runs with Alpha Triad. He was still devoted to the Fatherhood of the Spirit and the Brotherhood of all men and women, but he was more . . . devious . . . since his return.

"Now will someone tell me what's going on?" Jenny demanded, her green eyes boring into Plato's.

"Bear with us," Plato said. He motioned for Tyson and Cindy to sit beside him. "Please, have a seat."

The brother and sister accepted his invitation, Cindy

sitting on his right and Tyson on his left.

"Now," Plato stated, smiling, "you can tell us what has you so frightened, although I believe I can speculate on the reason."

"You wouldn't believe it," Tyson spoke first. "You're in danger. One of the Family . . ."

". . . . wants to remove me from my position as Family Leader," Plato said, finishing the sentence for Tyson. "I know."

Cindy, startled, gaped at the elderly sage. "You mean you already know about Napoleon?"

"Napoleon?" Jenny repeated.

"I have known for some time," Plato informed them. "Napoleon feels he can do a better job than I of directing the affairs of the Family."

"What?" came from Jenny.

"But how do you know about it?" Cindy queried Plato.

"Many months ago," Plato began, "one of the Family was fishing in the moat, sitting on the bank under the stairs near the drawbridge. Napoleon and Spartacus were on guard duty on the wall above, and they never saw the man fishing. He overheard snatches of their conversation and later reported it to me. Napoleon was trying to convince Spartacus to join him in overthrowing myself and installing Napoleon as Family Leader. At the time, Spartacus refused."

"Who was it?" Tyson inquired. "Who heard them?"

"The information was supplied confidentially," Plato replied. "I promised I wouldn't reveal my source to anyone, and I must keep my word."

"Why didn't you do something about it?" Jenny interjected.

"What should I have done?" Plato retorted. "Confront Napoleon and have him deny the allegations? He would still crave power, but he would be more careful in the future. No, the wisest way was to allow Napoleon's scheming to achieve natural fruition. Besides, from what my informant overheard, Napoleon has been trying for years to persuade his Gamma Triad fellows to assist him in his rebellion. They have steadfastly declined."

"Until now," Cindy informed him.

"Oh?"

Cindy told them everything, every word as precisely as she could recall. Tyson then elaborated on Napoleon's deceit and his charges against Rikki-Tikki-Tavi.

Throughout their recital, Rikki sat motionless, cross-legged, his katana in his lap, listening.

". . . and, if you ask me," Tyson concluded, "you better do something, and do it quick."

Plato's facial features slumped in sorrow during Cindy's narration. To think! One of the Family, one of his beloved children, instigating a rebellion! In the one hundred years of Family history, not one member had rebelled against the prescribed order of things. And now? How could it be? What motivated Napoleon? A simple lust for power? The Family's Founder, Kurt Carpenter, had left specific instructions regarding many aspects of Family life. One of Carpenter's injunctions concerned power-mongers: they were to be unceremoniously ejected from the Home. If they refused to leave, and wouldn't recant, their fate was severe and final: execution. Plato vividly recalled a page from Carpenter's diary, in a section devoted to advice for future Family Leaders: "You must not permit a power-monger to flourish in the Home. Even if you suppress any overt rebellion, they will continue to sow discontent and spread unhappiness among the Family. You must not allow the Home to become a microcosmic reproduction of the sick society in which I find myself, a society in which arrogant, ignorant, and deluded individuals delight in assuming power over others. They relish being able to tell others how to live their lives, down to the smallest detail. Mark these words well. *There are those who crave power for the sheer sake of power.* They must be eliminated from the Family. This is imperative."

"Maybe we could wait until Blade returns?" Jenny suggested, shattering Plato's reverie.

"Who knows how long that will be?" Cindy countered. "We can't wait that long. You must do something now!"

Plato frowned and stared at the ground. "Regrettably, I concur. Napoleon has talked about insurrection for so long, I guess I hoped it would continue in the talking stage until I could formulate a method of dealing with him, some way of avoiding bloodshed."

"I don't see how you can," Cindy opined. "You weren't there. You should have heard him, seen the expression on his face. He wants to be Family Leader more than anything else in the world, and he doesn't care one bit how he reaches his goal."

"I can't believe Spartacus would agree to help Napoleon so he could have me," Jenny commented. "Blade is my man, and he's the only man I'll ever love. Spartacus knows that."

"I know what Blade and Hickok would do if they knew about this," Tyson said.

"Blade knows," Plato mentioned.

"What?" Jenny reached out and placed her right hand on Plato's leg. "Blade knows?"

"Oh, not all the details," Plato said. "I informed him there was a power-monger months ago, but I wouldn't tell him who it was. Like you," he said, glancing at Tyson, "I knew how Blade would react. You may not understand this, but I have a deep affection for each and every Family member, even Napoleon."

"Well, you'd best start thinking of the welfare of the whole Family and not just one man," Cindy declared.

Plato wearily nodded. "I know you're right. I apologize. My mental faculties seem to have atrophied with the advent of the premature senility. Perhaps Napoleon is correct. Maybe I should step aside."

"If you ever do," Jenny stated, "the Family wouldn't pick Napoleon as your successor. And stop worrying about your mental capabilities. Even with the damn senility, you are still sharper and smarter than anyone else in the Family."

"So what are you going to do?" Cindy asked, pressing Plato. "You've got to do something."

"We will . . . do . . . something." Rikki-Tikki-Tavi finally entered their discussion.

"What?" Tyson asked.

"To be precise," Rikki corrected himself, "I will do something."

"You'll need some help," Tyson offered.

Rikki shook his head. "No. Thank you. This is a matter I must deal with personally."

"Rikki," Plato said, drawing his attention, "will you permit me to talk to Napoleon first, to dissuade him from his foolishness?"

"No," Rikki answered, denying the request.

"What if I insist?"

Rikki thoughtfully stared at the katana in his lap. "Tell me if I'm wrong," he said, "but I do believe our Founder left certain guidelines concerning times of danger. Under normal conditions, in typical circumstances, the Family Leader has full charge of all affairs. But, in times of imminent danger, when the Family is being threatened, Family leadership is temporarily transferred to the Warriors. Specifically, the head of the Warriors. Am I right in this?"

"You are," Plato confirmed.

"And," Rikki said, continuing his reasoning, "since

Alpha Triad is gone, am I not in charge of the Warriors?"

"You are," Plato said, again affirming the obvious.

"Then I may decide how best to deal with Napoleon, may I not?" Rikki queried.

Plato sadly nodded.

"You're going to take them on all by yourself?" Tyson asked, his skepticism showing.

"I will do what is necessary to eliminate Napoleon's threat to the Family," Rikki said sternly.

"You could get some of the other Warriors to help you," Jenny recommended.

"No."

"What about your Triad?" Jenny suggested. "Yama and Teucer could back you up."

"No."

"Why not?" Jenny demanded, peeved. "It's stupid to face them all by yourself."

Rikki looked into Jenny's eyes. "The fewer who know about this, the better. We will keep this to ourselves."

"What do you want us to do?" Cindy inquired.

"You will go about your daily routine as if nothing out of the ordinary has transpired," Rikki quietly directed. "I will guard Plato tonight and ensure his safety. Tomorrow, the issue will be decided. Permanently."

"I think you're nuts," Tyson remarked.

Rikki disregarded the comment. "You must all leave now. Napoleon or one of the others may be watching us, and they might become suspicious if we spend too much time here. Remember," he warned them, "not a word to anyone else. This is strictly between ourselves. Agreed?"

"Agreed," Tyson said.

"Okay," said Cindy.

"Fine," Jenny stated.

They rose and departed, each walking off in a

different direction.

"You did not agree," Rikki commented, glancing at Plato.

"Was it necessary? You know I wouldn't tell another soul."

"Why are you so sad?" Rikki probed. "You know what must be done."

Plato sighed and gazed into the distance, his features mirroring his melancholy. "The knowing doesn't make the doing any easier to take. Do you realize the implications? If Napoleon is so dissatisfied with the status quo, there may be others. If not now, then later."

"I don't see how you can prevent it," Rikki observed.

"But don't you see?" Plato stared at the Warrior. "Perhaps the fault isn't in Napoleon, perhaps it's in our system. Kurt Carpenter meticulously established the Family organization and set forth our rules and regulations. His legacy has sufficed for one hundred years, maintaining harmony in the Family and ensuring our success as a functional unit. But what if there is a flaw in our system? What if we failed Napoleon in some way? Maybe we overlooked some aspect of his education or personal development. Maybe there is something we can do to prevent another Napoleon from arising in the future."

Rikki, touched by the Leader's distress, tried to reassure Plato with a broad smile. "There is nothing you could have done. Look at the Trolls. Some people can not be helped, no matter what you do. It was inevitable, I suppose, someone would come along to challenge the Family order. You should view it as a tribute to our Founder the challenge was a century in coming. It shows how well Carpenter did, the wisdom the man possessed."

Plato grinned slightly. "Looking at the positive side."

"Just as one of my teachers always advocated," Rikki said.

The Family school was taught by the Elders, and Plato was responsible for several of the classes.

"Will you come tell me when it's over?" Plato requested.

"Of course."

"I think I'll retire to my cabin," Plato remarked, slowly, painfully, rising to his feet. "Nadine will be worried if I stay out too late."

"I will follow shortly," Rikki promised. "You needn't fear for your safety. I will be outside, guarding you tonight. But lock your doors, just as an added precaution."

Plato fondly glanced at Rikki. "Thank you. I know I'm in good hands. Blade thinks very highly of your skill."

"He told me, you know."

Plato, about to leave, stopped in midturn. "What?"

"Blade told me about a power-monger in the Family. He didn't know who it was, because you hadn't told him."

"But I instructed him to keep the information to himself," Plato said, surprised. "And he told you?"

"He wanted someone aware of the situation," Rikki explained. "He needed me to keep an eye on things until he returned."

Plato absently nodded and walked away. Blade had deliberately disobeyed him! Incredible! It had never happened before. And yet, it made sense, didn't it? Blade was thinking of the welfare of the Family. Just as a future Leader should.

A sharp cramp rocked his left side and he stopped, waiting for the pain to subside.

His body was falling apart at the seams, and his mind

apparently wasn't faring much better. He'd jeopardized the entire Family because of an emotional reluctance to harm one Family member. What had happened to his judgment?

It was time to seriously consider retirement.

The spasm eased and Plato resumed his trek.

If Alpha Triad failed to return with the equipment they needed to isolate the cause of the senility, he would relinquish his command to Blade. Oh, the Family would need to vote their acceptance, but never in the Family's history had they refused to accept a Leader's chosen successor.

How much longer did he have?

Plato shuffled homeward, troubled by the question, one he'd avoided until now. The premature senility was a progressive disease, exhibiting distinct stages, and he knew he was entering the advanced state of senility. It was just a matter of time.

And the irony of it all!

After all those years of being alone, without his beloved Nadine!

And now, she was home, rescued by Alpha Triad from the Trolls. Together again, at last, for a few fleeting months before he passed on to the other side.

Plato paused and glanced up at the darkening sky, spotting several pinpoints of light, the first visible stars.

The Family records revealed Family members were living shorter and shorter lives with each passing generation. Not every member experienced a reduced lifespan and suffered the attendant premature senility, but in the past two decades the number had increased dramatically.

Why?

Why? Why? Why? *Why?*

For the umpteenth time, Plato mentally screamed at the heavens, berating their fate. To have survived the

Big Blast, to have perservered for a century despite the
constant threat from clouds and mutates and other
hostile forces, only to be gradually eliminated from the
face of the earth by a mysterious disease, was positively
frustrating, not to mention a profoundly inequitable
destiny.

There had to be an answer! Some element the Healers
had overlooked as they struggled to ascertain the cause
of the senility. But what?

Plato felt his eyes moisten. It couldn't end like this! It
simply couldn't! His precious Family, snuffed out with a
whimper from the pages of mortal history.

Everything depended on Alpha Triad. This time, they
had to return with the scientific and medical items the
Healers needed. Time was running out.

Please, O Spirit, he silently prayed, protect your
children, Blade and Geronimo, and see them safely back
to the Home.

Please!

17

As Lieutenant Angier dove for his M-16, Blade reached overhead and grabbed the boat hook.

Angier swept the M-16 up and around, his finger tightening on the trigger. He caught a motion out of the corner of his left eye, and agony exploded inside his head.

Blade swung the handle of the boat hook a second time, slamming it against the Watcher's ruptured left ear. Blood flowed down Angier's neck as the soldier slumped to his knees, then slid to the wooden planks. The M-16 slipped from his hands.

Perfect!

Blade retrieved the rifle and crouched beside the doorway. The coast seemed clear. The other Watchers were probably concentrating on the road, and Gremlin was fast asleep. If his luck held, he'd be able to sneak along the shoreline and return to Kalispell. Geronimo must be worried silly by now.

The bushes and trees nearest the boathouse were shrouded in the shadows of twilight.

Just the cover he needed.

Blade cautiously stepped from the boathouse and moved to his left, bearing north.

Just as a Watcher rounded the corner of a building twenty yards away, carrying a cup of juice and a tin of hash, bringing supper to Lieutenant Angier.

Damn!

Blade heard the man shout "Stop!" then the Watcher hastily dropped the food and clutched at his M-16, slung over his right shoulder.

Not now!

Blade raised the M-16 and fired, the slugs ripping into the Watcher's midsection and throwing him to the ground.

Another Watcher came into view from behind a tree, his rifle already pressed against his left shoulder, and he sighted on the giant Warrior and squeezed the trigger.

Blade flattened and rolled toward the doorway to the boathouse. He heard the bullets striking the boathouse wall and splinters stung his face.

Yet another Watcher joined the fray, opening up from a stand of bushes thirty yards to the northeast.

Blade crawled inside the boathouse, keeping low, as more and more slugs tore through the walls. He twisted, peered around the door jamb, and aimed at the Watcher alongside the tree. The M-16 burped, and the soldier crumpled.

The firing outside intensified, and the interior of the boathouse was filled with the buzzing of the slugs and the cracking and shattering of the wood.

All of them must be out there, Blade deduced.

Let's see.

Angier was out cold. He'd killed the one with the food and the one by the tree. There were six, originally.

That meant three to go.

And Gremlin, of course.

But how to do it? The Watchers had him pinned down, and their guns covered the only exit from the boathouse. If he attempted to dash into the underbrush, he'd be cut down before he got ten yards. They could wait him out, if need be. They had food, he didn't. He did have plenty of water, though, an entire lake at his . . .

Water?

The lake!

Blade grinned as he snaked to the edge of the wooden planks and glanced down. There was another exit from the boathouse, and one the Watchers couldn't possibly cover unless they had a boat. Which they didn't.

He hoped.

Blade eased over the edge and slid into the water, tentatively feeling for bottom with his feet. He touched small rocks and slowly stood, the water level coming to his waist.

The Watchers were still intent on whittling the boathouse to its foundation, chip by chip.

Blade moved deeper, the water rising to his chest as he reached the end of the boathouse and glanced around the corner.

No sign of anyone. Or anything.

He lowered his muscular body until only his head remained above the surface of the lake, holding the M-16 parallel to the surface and an inch in front of his nose. If the Watchers kept their attention on the boathouse, he'd be able to follow the shore until he was beyond their range.

The chorus of M-16's was continuing to perforate the boathouse.

Blade moved quickly now, knowing he would be at a tremendous disadvantage if they caught him in Flathead Lake. His body tensed as he crossed a stretch of open water, angling for a line of trees near the shore.

So far, so good.

He alertly scanned the trees as he approached the shoreline, the water level dropping to his waist, then his knees, and finally to his ankles as he hurried from the lake and ran to the trees.

The Watchers had stopped shooting at the boathouse.

Blade leaned against a trunk and assessed his situation. He was about twenty-five yards from the boat-house, north of the Watchers and hidden from their view by the trees. He could head for Kalispell again.

Only one thing bothered him.

Where the hell was Gremlin?

Surely the creature had heard the commotion. No one could sleep through all that racket. So where was he? With the Watchers outside the boathouse? Where?

Blade shook his head, watery droplets flying in every direction. Did it matter? There was no way Gremlin could stop him now.

Good riddance.

Blade cautiously weaved between the trees as he traveled away from the vicinity of the boathouse. The brief twilight was gone, replaced by the encroachment of nightfall. Must be careful, he warned himself. He could easily trip and sprain something, or worse. The vegetation was dense and clung to his damp clothing as he passed. He swerved to his left, struck by an idea. The shore near the lake was clear of growth; he could make better time.

Flathead Lake was reflecting the stars, the waves

lapping at his heels, as Blade ran northward, eating up the distance.

How long would it take him to reach Kalispell? He wasn't sure of the distance involved. The last sign he could recall was for a small town called Bigfork, and mileage wasn't printed on the sign. If he could maintain a steady pace, he knew he'd arrive in Kalispell by morning.

Something padded on the shore behind him.

Blade whirled, leveling the M-16, his eyes striving to pierce the darkness.

Nothing.

I must be getting jittery in my old age, he mentally joked, and resumed jogging northward.

The shoreline of Flathead Lake was a narrow band of rocky earth ringing the body of water. The pebbles and stones covering the shore gouged the soles of his moccasins. It would be easier, he reflected, if he crossed over to Highway 35 at first light.

The night was filled with sounds: the rhythmic lapping of the waves onto the shore, the breeze rustling the trees, a fish splashing in the water as it made a graceful arc, a bird twittering nervously in the pines, and footsteps from somewhere to his rear.

Blade dropped to his knees and stared along his back-trail.

There!

A lean form flattening on the ground.

Three guesses who.

Blade rose and ran at full speed, hoping Gremlin would fall for his gambit.

The creature did.

Blade could hear Gremlin pursuing him now, apparently throwing caution to the wind in an effort to overtake him. He could hear the pounding of Gremlin's feet and the creature's harsh breathing.

Timing was critical now.

Blade concentrated on speed, while gauging the space between them. He had to make his move at the right moment. Too soon, and Gremlin would have time to react and get out of the way. Too late, and the creature would be on him before he could defend himself.

Gremlin's labored breaths were close on his heels, just yards behind him.

Now!

Blade spun, the M-16 held waist high, and began firing before he completed his turn.

Gremlin, only four yards away, was caught by surprise. Several of the slugs caught him and lifted him off his feet. He fell to one side, landing partially in the cold waters of Flathead Lake.

Blade ceased firing and cautiously approached the creature. He felt a twinge of guilt at killing it. Gremlin wasn't responsible for his actions. They were controlled by the Doktor.

Was it really dead?

Blade paused, his moccasins inches from the water, and leaned over for a better look.

Gremlin surged out of the lake in a raging rush, hissing, his clawing hands grasping Blade's shoulders and pulling him off balance, toppling him forward into Flathead Lake.

Damn!

Blade released the useless M-16 and struggled against Gremlin's iron grip. Was the thing trying to drown him? The water closed over his head as Gremlin drew him under the surface.

Gremlin's clammy hands slid from his shoulders to his neck.

Blade thrashed and struck at the creature's face, to no avail. The water impaired his strength and reduced the effectiveness of his powerful blows.

They tossed and twisted and alternately rose above the surface as they rolled into ever deeper water.

Blade took a deep breath and went under for the fifth time, trying to dislodge Gremlin's hands from his throat. How could something so skinny be so strong? What could he do to hurt it? Angier's words came back to him. "If the collar senses someone is trying to take it off, there's a crackling and a burst of white light and the creature's head is fried to a crisp."

It was his only real chance.

Blade kneed Gremlin in the groin, gratified when he doubled over and his hold slackened slightly. In that instant, Blade clasped the collar in both of his brawny hands and exerted his formidable muscles, striving to pry the collar apart.

He was completely unprepared for what transpired next.

His hands and arms began tingling, and before he could release the collar, as Gremlin reached for his arms, there was a loud popping noise and the water in their immediate proximity was illuminated by a brilliant white flash.

Blade jerked as a tremendous shock jolted his body, propelling him away from Gremlin and toward the beach. His senses swirled as he staggered from the lake, gasping for air, and fell to his hands and knees.

Damn.

So much for his bright ideas.

He passed out on the rock-littered shore.

18

"Mommy, I think Geronimo is waking up."

"Good."

"Not good! You should have let me finish the creep off!"

Geronimo kept his eyes closed, listening to the conversation. A throbbing headache racked his forehead, and his left side was a pool of agony. He experienced the sensation of moving.

"All in good time." The voice was Rainbow's.

"Why not now?" an angry male demanded.

"I told you before," Rainbow responded impatiently, "we need him for now. He knows this vehicle better than we do. We might need some of his knowledge."

"But the bastard wasted Spotted Elk and Buffalo Grazing! We should kill him now! He deserves it!" the irate man urged.

"Are you disputing me?" Rainbow asked icily.

"No," the man hedged. "Of course not. It's just . . ." he said, and let the thought trail off.

Geronimo opened his brown eyes and slowly gazed around. He was inside the SEAL, propped in a corner of the back seat, behind the driver. His shirt was gone. It had been used to construct a crude bandage for his left

shoulder. Star was seated beside him, and a tall
Flathead sat on the other side of her. Another Indian,
the angry speaker, was in the passenger-side bucket seat.
Rainbow was behind the wheel.

"He's awake," Star announced, smiling at Geronimo.
Her features became downcast when he refused to
reciprocate.

"Welcome back to the land of the living," Rainbow
said, greeting him cheerily, glancing into the mirror.

Geronimo heard a scratching sound and twisted his
head.

Another Flathead was in the rear section of the
transport, lying amidst the equipment salvaged from the
Kalispell Regional Hospital. At least they hadn't tossed
it out. Yet.

"How are you feeling?" Rainbow inquired.

Geronimo watched the scenery pass by. From the
position of the sun, he knew they were bearing in a
southeasterly direction.

"I asked you how you're feeling?" Rainbow
reiterated.

"Do you make it a practice of specializing in stupidity,
or is a natural knack you have?" Geronimo said,
goading her.

"Let me smash him!" the one in the passenger seat
heatedly requested. He was short in stature and had a
ragged scar on his chin.

"Do you see what you've done?" Rainbow said to
Geronimo. "Now you've got Lone Cougar all upset."

"Pardon me all to hell," Geronimo retorted.

"Be nice," Rainbow warned, "or I'll let Lone Cougar
have you." She paused and tapped the steering wheel.
"What do you think of my driving?"

"I'm impressed," Geronimo admitted. "I had no idea
you could drive."

"I couldn't," Rainbow stated. "But I'm a fast

learner, and I had plenty of time to watch Blade on the trip to Kalispell. It's a lot easier than I expected."

"Mind if I ask where we're heading?" Geronimo queried.

"Not at all," Rainbow answered. "The Citadel."

Geronimo sat erect, forgetting his wound, the motion aggravating the discomfort. "You can't be serious!"

Rainbow laughed. "But I am."

"Why are you going there?" Geronimo demanded. "It's suicide."

"Oh, we'll take good care of your vehicle, if that's what you're worried about," Rainbow said. "I need to find out what happened to my people, and this is the fastest way to get us there."

"Is that the reason you shot me?" Geronimo needed to know.

"Of course." Rainbow slowly negotiated a curve. The road was sandwiched between rolling hills of pine forest. "Nothing personal, you understand." She grinned.

"I'm really sorry my mother shot you," Star chimed in sorrowfully. "I didn't want her to do it. I like you a lot, Geronimo."

"Don't get to liking him too much, little one," Lone Cougar told her. "He won't be with us much longer."

"That's enough!" Rainbow snapped. "I don't want you upsetting my daughter!"

"Your wish is my command," Lone Cougar stated, somewhat sarcastically.

"Be respectful when you talk to her!" the Flathead on the other side of Star barked.

Lone Cougar glanced at the speaker, amused. "Why, Tall Oak, you know I mean no disrespect. It is bad form to treat the wife of a chief with anything less than total sincerity."

"The wife of a chief?" Geronimo repeated, surprised.

"She didn't tell you?" Lone Cougar asked, feigning

amazement. "She's so proud of the fact, I thought she told everyone."

Geronimo saw Rainbow glare at Lone Cougar. If looks could kill, Lone Cougar would be Skewered Pussycat.

"Rainbow is the wife of Golden Bull, the chief of all the Flatheads," Lone Cougar was saying.

Golden Bull. Lone Cougar. Tall Oak. "I take it the Flatheads don't use names like George and Fred anymore?" Geronimo asked.

"We have reverted to the practice of our illustrious ancestors," Rainbow stated proudly. "Our parents name their children after natural things, or something they might see in a vision, or a special omen."

"I understand," Geronimo acknowledged. "So where is your husband now?"

Rainbow's shoulders slumped. "I don't know."

"He was with the others," Lone Cougar detailed, "in Kalispell, surrounded by the Citadel army. We slipped through their lines in search of game, but we had to go far afield to find anything. When we returned to Kalispell, our entire tribe had vanished."

"How many of you are left?" Geronimo inquired.

"There were five in our hunting party," Lone Cougar replied, "but you killed two of us, you son of a bitch!"

"Did any others escape?" Geronimo asked, refusing to become riled by the insult.

"Not that we know of," Tall Oak said, joining the discussion. "We saw your vehicle coming and thought you were some of the soldiers, so we hid in the hospital. When we saw you with Rainbow, we didn't know what to think. Spotted Elk went down to investigate. . . ."

"And you blew him away!" Lone Cougar snarled.

"It wasn't me," Geronimo corrected him. "Spotted Elk was still alive after I shot him. He sat up, and one of you got him with a shotgun."

"And we know who it was, don't we?" Tall Oak commented, deliberately looking at Lone Cougar.

Lone Cougar appeared embarrassed. "How the hell was I to know?" he countered defensively. "It was dark in that stairwell."

"If some people knew how to use their mind as much as they do their mouth," the Flathead in the rear section interjected, "Spotted Elk would still be with us now."

"Get off my case, Running Hare," Lone Cougar warned.

"You don't scare me," Running Hare rejoined, "as long as I don't turn my back on you."

Geronimo thought Lone Cougar was about to leap over the seats and assault Running Hare, but Rainbow intervened.

"That's enough!" she ordered. "This is no time for fighting amongst ourselves! Our people have been taken, and you spend your time engaged in petty squabbles."

Geronimo was pleased by the dissension in their ranks. Maybe he could use it to his advantage when he made his eventual bid for freedom. He studied the Flatheads, noting their buckskin clothing, long black hair, and in particular their lack of weapons. Where were their guns? In the rear section with Running Hare? Or was Lone Cougar's shotgun on the floor in the front, out of sight. Tall Oak carried a large knife in a leather sheath high on his left hip.

For that matter, Geronimo wondered, where are my guns?

"Did you know you slept all night?" Star asked Geronimo, still trying to prove her friendliness. "I was the one who bandaged your shoulder."

"I'm surprised your darling mother didn't finish the job," Geronimo remarked scornfully.

"If I'd wanted you dead," Rainbow stated, "you'd be

dead. I'm a crack shot. I just wanted you out of commission, unable to give us any problems on the way to the Citadel."

"Did you know they were your people in the hospital?" Geronimo questioned her.

"No, I didn't," Rainbow replied.

"You took a big chance," Geronimo said. "What if the ones after me weren't Flatheads? What then? They could have killed you and your daughter and taken the SEAL."

Rainbow shrugged. "Life is full of risks. You take what comes your way and do the best you can."

"Really?" Lone Cougar innocently challenged her. "Then why didn't you stay in Kalispell and take what the rest of us did?"

"You know why," Rainbow snapped, angered by the insinuation. "Golden Bull ordered us out. He wanted the Princess safe. As it was, we're fortunate to be alive today."

Lone Cougar stared at Star. "Ahhh, yes. Our sweet little Princess, destined to marry the heir apparent. We can't let anything happen to you."

"And don't you ever forget that," Rainbow said in a threatening tone.

Geronimo spotted a rusted road sign ahead, on his side of the roadway. Highway 35, it read. He caught a glimpse of a large lake through the trees over Lone Cougar's shoulder. Was it Flathead Lake, the big one on the map? He cleared his dry throat. "What do you hope to accomplish at the Citadel?"

"Like I told you," Rainbow said, driving carefully, "we need to learn what happened to my people, find out where the soldiers have taken them."

"You're just going to drive up to the front gates and ask?"

"Don't be stupid!" Rainbow replied. "We'll hide the

SEAL and reconnoiter on foot. Thousands of people don't just vanish! The army must be holding them somewhere. We'll find them," she stated confidently.

Geronimo rested his head on the top of the seat and closed his weary eyes. *This is certainly one terrific mess you've gotten yourself into, dimwit! Blade is missing. The transport has been commandeered by hostile Indians. And now you're shot. . . .*

Hostile Indians?

How could he ever have seriously considered leaving the Family to live with the Flatheads? They may be Indians, like himself, but there any resemblance ended. They viewed him as an outsider, and rightfully he was. So what if he was the only Indian in the Family? The Family loved him, cherished him as one of their own, respected his personality, and honored his ability by appointing him to Warrior status. Strange, wasn't it, how the grass did *always look greener on the other side of the fence?*

"Look!" Lone Cougar exclaimed, pointing directly ahead.

Someone was standing in the center of Highway 35, waving his brawny arms, attempting to stop the transport.

Rainbow leaned over the steering wheel. "I know him!" she stated, disbelieving her eyes. "How'd he get here?"

Geronimo, roused from his reflection, gazed at the tall figure in front of them and tensed.

It couldn't be!

"He isn't going to interfere!" Rainbow vowed angrily, and floored the accelerator.

Thirty yards separated the SEAL from their target as the vehicle picked up speed.

Forty.

Fifty.

"No!" Geronimo lunged at Rainbow, but Tall Oak was quicker. The Flathead reached over Star and grabbed Geronimo's good wrist, preventing him from obstructing Rainbow's purpose.

Sixty miles an hour and climbing.

The man in front of them still stood in the middle of Highway 35, a puzzled expression on his face.

"The fool thinks Geronimo is driving!" Rainbow said, elated.

Geronimo, weakened by his wound, unsuccessfully attempted to wrest his wrist from Tall Oak's grasp.

Sixty-five miles an hour.

Star drew her body forward, against the console, away from the struggling Geronimo and Tall Oak. She looked at the dark-haired man with his arms over his head, and dawning recognition caused panic to register on her countenance.

"Mom, no!" Star screamed. "It's Blade!"

Rainbow laughed maliciously.

19

He was in the lotus position, hidden in a stand of trees only fifteen yards from Plato's cabin. From his vantage point, he enjoyed a clear field of view to both the front and back cabin doors.

The long night, thankfully, had been uneventful.

Rikki-Tikki-Tavi listened to the morning sounds: the cool morning wind stirring the leaves, various birds greeting the new day with songs of vitality and thanksgiving, gray smoke drifting from several of the cabin chimneys as individual families prepared their initial daily sustenance, voices raised as many Family members walked to the open space between the six concrete Blocks for a period of exercise and worship, and a woman in one of the nearer cabins singing the words to "Day by Day."

Why would anyone in their right mind want to change the peaceful environment the Home afforded its residents? What was the alternative? The barbarous cruelty permeating every aspect of life in the outside world? Who would favor savagery over tranquility? If you had a system that worked, why mess with it?

Rikki thoughtfully stared at the katana in his lap. His chosen profession, as a dedicated Warrior, sometimes entailed the use of violence in the performance of his duties, but that was different. Violence utilized constructively, to preserve the standards of truth, beauty, and goodness, was not a moral evil; violence used destructively was.

Did that make Napoleon evil?

Rikki fondly recalled his philosophy classes in the Family school. What was it Confucius wrote? "Clever talk and a domineering manner have little to do with being man-at-his-best." And the Buddha was quoted as saying: "A man should hasten toward the good, and should keep his thoughts from evil." And didn't one of the Proverbs say "the way of the wicked is as darkness"?

Napoleon, so it seemed, was intentionally courting a darkness of his own devising, and exalting his ego, his vanity, over the welfare of the Family and the safety of the Home.

Why?

What made Napoleon tick?

Did it really matter?

No.

As a Warrior, as a defender of the Family, he had a duty, and his duty eclipsed any and all other considerations. His was not to reason why; his was but to kill or die.

Rikki enjoyed the many books in the Family library dealing with Oriental subjects. They suited his temperament, his inner nature, like a glove over a hand. From earliest childhood, he'd spent countless hours in the library perusing volumes on Oriental reasoning and the martial arts. Others in the Family evinced a decidedly Christian bent to their religious proclivities, and some preferred the Koran or The Circles, but he found his orientation centered on Zen.

To function as the perfected swordmaster was his only goal in life.

Ironic, wasn't it? If he'd been born before the Big Blast, before the nuclear holocaust had torn the fabric of existence asunder, he would have found himself in a sterile society, devoid of spontaneity and originality, a world designed to shape every person into the same mindless mold of cultural conformity.

He despised the very concept.

It had taken a nuclear conflagration to return—or was it advance—humanity to a free level of expression, where a man, or woman, could openly nurture the realization of his or her own unique personality without government interference or social imposition by those who claimed to "run things."

Years ago, Plato had given a seminar on "Life Before the Final Folly," an insightful examination of daily living before the Third World War. Rikki had never forgotten it. Why had the people let themselves be manipulated by those in "power"? Why had they allowed every aspect of their daily existence, from the food they consumed to the clothes they wore, to be dictated by others? And what about the ones in authority? Why had they sought to control *everything*? Whether it was by the passage of a convenient "law," or by the terrible force of "peer pressure," either you conformed or you were branded an outcast, a misfit with no redeeming social value.

A swordmaster would have been hard pressed to attain spiritual harmony in the times before the Big Blast.

Rikki placed his right hand on his katana. He wouldn't have been "allowed" to carry his sword down the street before the war. Simply amazing! His katana was as much a part of him as his arm or his leg. Maybe more so. The perfected swordmaster wasn't a swaggering bully; he used his sword only when unavoidable in the performance of his duty. His path of

rightness, the code of Bushido, perceived the katana as
the sword of justice, as an extension of his inner guide.
Before he could engage an opponent, prior to combat, he
must divest himself of all personal animosity and anger,
strip his consciousness of any feelings of revenge or
retaliation. He must become, in a sense, empty. An
emptiness with a purpose.

So Napoleon's motivation for desiring to usurp the
Family leadership from Plato was completely irrelevant.
To Rikki's mind, to the mind of the professional
Warrior, the mind of the perfecting swordmaster, the
fact of Napoleon's threat superseded any impulse toward
compassionate understanding.

The threat *must* be eliminated.

Rikki-Tikki-Tavi serenely gazed at the azure sky and
cleared his mind of all thoughts.

Today was the day.

Either Napoleon would cease to threaten the Family,
or by nightfall the Family would need a new head of
Beta Triad.

20

"... up!"

What the blazes was it? An earthquake?

"Hickok! You've got to wake up!"

Hadn't he just been through this? But hold the fort! This wasn't Sherry's voice. It was familiar, though. . . .

"What did they do to you?" the person anxiously asked.

Hickok opened his eyes and found Shane's bushy brows and full cheeks hovering inches from his face. The sixteen-year-old was wearing black pants and a black shirt, both filthy from his confinement in the dirty cell. His brown hair was matted with grime.

"Thank the Spirit!" Shane exclaimed. "You're okay!"

"That's debatable," Hickok groused, sitting up and pressing his left hand against the back of his head. "That's another one I owe."

Shane's brown eyes sparkled with excitement. "I can't begin to tell you how glad I am to see you!"

"Do tell, pard," Hickok said, frowning in annoyance. "Need I point out I wouldn't be in this fix if it wasn't for you?"

Shane, shamed, averted the gunman's gaze. "I didn't

think it would turn out like this," he mumbled.

"Let me guess. You figured you'd impress me by finding the new Troll headquarters. Right?"

"How did you know?" Shane gawked, impressed.

"It was as easy as adding two and two," Hickok informed the youth. "Your letter told me you were going to find the Trolls, and it was pretty easy to figure out why. You jerk."

"I take it you're mad at me?"

"Does a bear shit in the woods?"

There was a shuffling sound behind Hickok. "So this is the one you've been telling me about?" asked a new voice. "The one who killed fifty Trolls singlehanded?" he added doubtfully.

Hickok swiveled. The third and final occupant of the small earthern cell was a big man with short brown hair and green eyes, dressed in soiled clothes little better than tattered rags.

"Hickok," Shane said, introducing them, "this is Wally. He's from a small town south of here. . . ." Shane paused a moment. "What was the name of it again?"

"Tenstrike," Wally answered. "The Moles caught me about a year ago. Wolfe put me on one of their digging crews, but I gave 'em such a hard time they threw me in here. I don't imagine I'll be in here much longer."

"Why's that?" Hickok inquired.

Wally nodded at the iron bars comprising the cell door. A guard with a rifle stood on the other side, leaning against the far wall, his eyes closed. "These bastards put you out of your misery if you give 'em too much grief."

"Do you want to throw in with us?" Hickok questioned him.

"You have something planned?" Wally said, moving

closer so their conversation couldn't be overheard by the guard.

"I'm busting out of this calaboose," Hickok replied. "You're welcome to come along if you like."

"Calaboose?" Wally repeated, perplexed. "Oh! You mean this cell?"

Hickok nodded. "That's what I said, pard. You game?"

Wally glanced at the guard. "How do you plan to do it?"

Hickok grinned. "With my ace in the hole." He patted his right wrist, then froze, stunned.

The Mitchell's Derringer was gone!

Instantly, he leaned over and felt his left ankle under his buckskin legging.

Oh, no!

The C.O.P. was missing, too!

"If you're looking for your backups," Shane said, "you can forget it. The guards found them when they dumped you in here."

"Yeah," Wally confirmed. "The one who dropped you on the floor bumped your wrist and discovered the derringer. They both went over you from head to toe and came across the other gun. I heard them say they were taking them back to Wolfe."

"I'll have to pay him a visit on my way out of here," Hickok stated.

"You still think you can get us out?" Wally asked skeptically.

"Piece of cake."

"Mind telling us how?" Shane queried.

"When do they feed us?" Hickok asked, requesting the information essential to his budding scheme.

"Twice a day," Shane replied. "Two guards bring a bucket of slop and give us one spoon to eat it with. They wait around until we're done, then they take the bucket and the spoon and leave."

"Hmmmm." Hickok stood and slowly paced the confines of their narrow cell. Fifteen feet long by five feet wide. Not much room to maneuver. "How do they do it?"

"Do what?" Shane didn't understand.

"Exactly how do they feed us?"

"We just told you," Shane responded.

"Be specific," Hickok directed. "Give me details."

"Well, usually one of them carries in the bucket and the spoon while his buddy and the guard outside the door keep us covered," Shane detailed.

"What do they cover us with?"

"Guns."

Hickok sighed, slightly exasperated. "What kind of guns? Handguns or rifles?"

"Oh. Rifles," Shane answered.

Good. Good. Hickok nodded, satisfied with the arrangement. The five-foot width would work in their favor. It wouldn't give the Moles much space to react. He spotted a rusty bucket in the far left corner of the cell. "What's that for?" he pointed.

"What do you think?" Wally replied. "It would be too messy if we did our business in the dirt."

Hickok grinned, pleased at the prospects. "Okay." He motioned for them to step nearer. "Here's what we're going to do. . . ."

21

The warm sun on his face roused him to wakefulness. His right cheek, the one pressed against the rocks most of the night, felt sore and bruised as he opened his eyes and rolled over. The lake air was tangy and invigorating, stirring his sluggish senses.

Blade rose to his feet, taking stock. His clothes were very damp and his body cold, but overall he was all right. It was still morning, only several hours after sunrise. A pair of ducks—a colorful Wood Duck with his glossy purple-and-green head and long, downswept crest, and his mate—floated not far from shore.

There was no sign of Gremlin.

That was good.

But the M-16 was at the bottom of Flathead Lake.

And that was bad.

Blade started trekking toward Highway 35. He cut through some two hundred yards of forest before he struck the road. His mind pondered the probabilities as he walked northward toward Kalispell. What if he came across a mutate while he was unarmed? What could he use to defend himself? Find a branch he could use as a club? A lot of good it would do him against one of the larger mutates, such as the former bear they had killed a while back, before the Troll incident. And what if he ran into more Citadel soldiers? He shook his head, clearing his thoughts. It was useless to brood over potential problems. If something happened, he'd cross that bridge when he got to it. Until then, it didn't do any good to worry.

It was just that he seemed so naked without his Bowies!

He began jogging, suppressing his fatigue and ignoring his aching muscles.

Had Geronimo waited for him? Or was he stranded in enemy territory, alone and unarmed? What would happen to his darling Jenny if he failed to return to the Home? Would she . . . would she find someone new?

What was that?

There was a subdued sound, a low pitched whine, coming from up ahead.

Blade stopped, unwilling to accept his excellent fortune.

It was utterly impossible!

But there was only one thing in the world he knew of that was capable of making the noise he heard.

Was it?

Blade's emotions soared when he spied the SEAL approaching, coming around a series of curves. The transport would be visible for a moment, then disappear from view behind a cluster of conifers.

What in the world was Geronimo doing so far south of Kalispell? Looking for him?

Blade stood in the center of Highway 35, patiently waiting, smiling broadly. Everything was coming together perfectly. They could drive to the hospital and search for the equipment Plato wanted, then head for the Home as fast as the SEAL could take them.

The transport negotiated the last curve and hit the straight-away.

Blade could well imagine Geronimo's surprise at seeing him. The inexperienced Indian would probably slam on the brakes in his astonishment.

Something was wrong here.

Instead of bringing the SEAL to a stop, Geronimo was accelerating.

What was he doing, playing games?

Blade peered at the front windshield, wishing he could see inside the vehicle.

That damn tinted body!

The SEAL was speeding in his direction, and there was no indication Geronimo intended to stop.

A thought hit Blade.

What if Geronimo wasn't behind the wheel?

With the thought came action. Blade sprinted to the right side of Highway 35 as the SEAL closed in and dove for cover in the underbrush as the transport screeched to a careening halt abreast of his position. He turned, facing the road, and hugged the earth, hidden by a tangle of bushes.

For a minute, nothing transpired. The SEAL stayed still, the engine quietly purring.

Blade considered moving further into the forest and circling to the rear of the transport.

The driver's window rolled partially down.

"Blade! I know you can hear me!"

It was Rainbow's voice!

"I know you can hear me!" she repeated. "If you don't come out now, with your hands up, we'll kill Geronimo!"

Kill Geronimo? What the hell was going on here?

"You have until I count to ten," Rainbow announced.

Rainbow must be driving, which meant she was the one who had tried to run him down.

"One . . ."

Why would she try to kill him? He knew she hated

whites. Was that the reason?

"... two ..."

There had to be more to it than her loathing of the white race. How had she managed to wrest control of the SEAL from Geronimo?

"... three ..."

Where could she be heading?

"... four ..."

There were so many questions, and only one way to get the answers.

"... five ..."

Blade stood, raised his hands above his head, and strolled to the edge of Highway 35.

The driver's door was flung open and Rainbow dropped to the roadway, training the Dan Wesson .44 Magnum on its former owner. "Fancy running into you again," she said, grinning triumphantly.

Blade remained silent.

"What's the matter, Warrior?" Rainbow mocked him, accenting the last word contemptuously. "At a loss for words?"

The door on the other side of the SEAL opened and closed and two Flatheads walked around the front of the transport. The shorter of the pair, a vicious-looking specimen with a scar on his pointed chin, carried a shotgun. The other Indian, a ruggedly handsome Flathead, held a rifle.

"I say we waste him now," Scarred Chin proposed.

"We do what I decide," Rainbow countered, "when I decide it."

"What are you saying?" Scar Face objected. "You going to take this one along too? We don't need him! We don't even need the other one! If this thing breaks down, it breaks down."

Rainbow was weighing his words.

"Is Geronimo really with you?" Blade asked.

Scar Face snickered. "You bet your white ass!" He threw open the door and brutally hauled Geronimo from the transport.

"Lone Cougar! Don't!" Star yelled, trying to pull Geronimo back inside.

Lone Cougar shoved Geronimo to the cracked pavement, laughing.

Another Flathead joined them, hefting Geronimo's FNC.

Blade took a step toward his friend.

Lone Cougar swung the shotgun up, aiming at Blade's chest. "Make a move, white ass! I'll blow you away!"

Blade stared at Rainbow. "He must be related to you. Breeding shows."

Rainbow's mouth twitched. "Think you're funny, Warrior? I've got news for you. You've just sealed your fate, yours and poor Geronimo's. Help him up!"

Blade assisted Geronimo in rising. Blood was seeping from a bandage on his left shoulder. "Are you going to make it?" Blade asked.

Geronimo, clutching his wounded shoulder, grinned weakly and nodded. "Just a minor inconvenience. No worse than listening to one of Hickok's jokes."

"Move!" Rainbow barked, waving the Dan Wesson, herding them past the front of the transport.

Star's tear-streaked face appeared at the door. "Don't do it! Please!"

"Be quiet, honey," Rainbow chided her daughter. "This must be done. Watch and learn. You've got to be strong if you're going to be the wife of a chief someday."

"But they're our friends!" Star wailed.

"No white man can be our friend," Rainbow stated.

"Geronimo isn't white!"

"No, but he's one of the Family, one of them. He may be red on the outside, but inside he's as white as Blade. Trust me. One day you'll understand all of this."

Blade and Geronimo were herded fifteen yards in front of the transport and stopped in the middle of the highway.

"That's far enough!" Rainbow snapped. "Right out in the open, with no place to hide!"

The four Flatheads formed a line, Rainbow at the eastern tip, followed by Lone Cougar, Tall Oak, and Running Hare.

"A firing squad," Geronimo stated the obvious. "How original."

"You had your chance," Rainbow said. "I gave you an opportunity to join us, remember?"

"Join you!" Geronimo exploded, venting his anger in an unusual emotional display. "Why should I join a pack of murdering vultures? You constantly criticize the whites and harp on the atrocities they committed against the red race. Well, Sister, you're no better than they are. No! You're worse! Because you allowed the Family to take you in and heal you, you embraced our hospitality, and all the time you hated us, despised us with every fiber of your being. You're . . ." he paused, coughing.

"Don't bother," Blade soothed him. "It's not worth it." He gauged the distance to the nearest Flathead, Rainbow. Maybe, if he moved fast enough, he could catch her off guard and grab the Dan Wesson.

"This is a waste of our time," Lone Cougar declared. "Let's finish them and get it over with."

Rainbow, her features a grim mask, nodded. "On the count of three."

"I wish you had stayed in hiding," Geronimo mentioned, glancing affectionately at Blade.

The Flatheads aimed their weapons at the two Warriors.

"I never thought it would end like this," Blade mused aloud.

Rainbow, smiling wickedly, centered the Dan Wesson

on Geronimo's forehead. "One," she announced in a strident tone.

"I wish Hickok was here," Geronimo casually commented.

Blade glanced at Geronimo, his eyebrows knitting. "What?"

"Two," Rainbow continued her countdown.

"We do almost everything else together," Geronimo explained. "Why should he miss out on this?"

Blade, despite their predicament, threw back his head and laughed uproariously.

Rainbow, about to give the final number, hesitated, bewildered by their lighthearted attitude. "What the hell can you find so funny at a time like this?" she angrily demanded.

Geronimo winked at Blade and soberly faced Rainbow. "Your face."

Blade's mirth was seemingly uncontrollable. He actually stumbled several steps in Rainbow's direction. Doubled over, he kept laughing, but inwardly his mind was cool and calculating as he tensed his leg muscles for a leap at Rainbow.

"Let's plug these morons!" Lone Cougar urged.

Rainbow sighted again and drew back the hammer on the Dan Wesson.

At that moment, its tires squealing as it rounded the first curve to the south at high speed, a jeep roared into view.

"What the . . ." Lone Cougar blurted.

"Citadel troops!" Tall Oak shouted in alarm.

Blade, spinning, caught sight of the jeep and its occupants as he looped his steely left arm under Geronimo's armpits and bodily hoisted him from the roadway.

It was Angier and the three other soldiers!

One of the soldiers was driving, another was beside

him, and the third sat in the back behind the driver, his
hands holding an ammunition belt, about to feed the
cartridges into a swivel-mounted machine gun. Angier
was standing, gripping the .45-caliber machine gun,
steadying the lengthy barrel as the jeep closed on its
quarry, only thirty yards distant.

Blade ran, carrying Geronimo, heading for the forest
at the western border of Highway 35.

The Flatheads began to scatter, making for the
SEAL.

They weren't fast enough.

Angier opened up with the heavy machine gun, the
slugs tearing the pavement as they tore a path down the
middle of the roadway, then swerved to the left, catching
Tall Oak and Running Hare.

Tall Oak was struck first, the impact of the bullets
stitching a pattern across his chest, miniature geysers of
crimson spurting outward. He staggered and fell on his
face.

Running Hare was caught in midturn, his right side
bearing the brunt of the slugs. He screamed once, falling
in a disjointed heap onto the highway.

Angier swung the gun to the right, going after the
remaining two Flatheads.

Blade reached the woods and hastily pulled Geronimo
in after him. He glanced over his shoulder.

Lone Cougar was racing for the transport when the
machine gun zeroed in. His back erupted in a spray of
blood and he howled like a banshee as he dropped to his
knees, then toppled over.

Rainbow almost made it.

She was inches from the open driver's door when a
stray slug sped into the top of her head and exited
through her forehead. Her brains and blood smeared the
door as she sank to the road.

"Mommy!" Star shrieked in horror, too terrified to

leave the safety of the SEAL.

"Stay hidden," Blade ordered, lowering Geronimo to the ground.

"I can help," Geronimo stubbornly objected, beginning to push himself erect.

"Stay put! You're in no condition for a fight and I can do it alone. I hope."

Blade ran, weaving between the trees, bearing north. If he could come in behind the transport, interpose the vehicle as a shield, preventing the soldiers from spotting him, he could get inside the SEAL before them. If Rainbow had his Dan Wesson, then his Bowies and the A-1 must still be in the transport. None of the Flatheads had had them when they were shot.

Move! his brain clamored.

Watch out for rocks and roots. Mustn't trip now!

He was ten yards past the SEAL and he cut toward the highway. One final tree loomed in front of him. He darted behind the trunk and peered to his right.

The jeep was slowly, cautiously, rolling to a stop near the dead Indians. The soldiers weren't taking any chances. They would probably take the time to check the Flatheads and verify their victims were lifeless. The jeep braked, momentarily placing the SEAL between Blade and the soldiers.

Blade crouched and sped to the rear of the transport.

"Check them!" Angler barked. "Then look inside."

Only seconds left.

Blade eased to the corner behind the driver's door and risked a peek. The door was still wide open. Rainbow's face was visible under the door, a pool of blood forming under her.

No sign of the soldiers.

Yet.

Blade scampered to the door.

"There's another one!" one of the soldiers shouted.

Blade leaped into the SEAL as an M-16 chattered. The soldier had shot at his feet and ankles.

"Get him!" Angier commanded.

Blade slammed the door behind him and pressed the lock, quickly doing the same on the other side.

There!

The soldiers couldn't get in, and the impervious SEAL body would protect him.

And Star.

The girl was curled in the back seat, weeping, her hands over her tear filled eyes.

"Star! It's me, Blade! Don't worry! I'll get us out of here!" he promised.

The soldiers had regrouped at the jeep. Angier was preparing to fire at the SEAL's windshield.

"Blade?" Star uncovered her eyes and sat up, choking and sobbing. "They killed my mother! They killed Rainbow!"

"Your mother's hatred killed her," Blade amended, looking for the A-1. Was it in the storage section?

"Oh, Blade!" Star wailed, coming toward him for comfort, her arms held wide.

"Watch . . .!" Blade began, too late.

All hell broke loose.

Angier started blazing away at the transport's windshield, the slugs whining as they ricocheted aside, deflected by the unique iron-like plastic designed by Kurt Carpenter's scientists.

Star's right foot caught on the console between the front bucket seats. She tripped, falling forward onto the dash before Blade could reach her. Her outstretched left hand brushed against the dashboard, striking one of the four mysterious toggle switches in the center of the dash, the one marked with a large R.

Blade grabbed Star before she could fall further. He heard a peculiar whirring sound and saw the soldiers pointing at the front of the SEAL, in the direction of the grill. There was fear on their faces.

What was going on?

The transport suddenly lurched violently, as if a great force had shoved the vehicle backward.

Angier, the soldiers, and the jeep literally blew to smithereens, consumed by a mighty explosion and a spectacular fireball extending fifty feet skyward.

Star, stunned by the spectacle, gaped at Blade.

"Don't look at me," he said, watching the fireball collapse and dissipate. "I think you caused it."

"Me?" Star asked, her eyes reflecting her astonishment. "How did I do . . . that?"

Blade reached over and replaced the toggle switch in its original position. "I think you did it when you bumped this switch labeled R. It's some type of weapon. If I was to hazard a guess, I'd say the R stood for Rocket, or Rocket Launcher." He paused, pondering the implications. "Kurt Carpenter must have had armament installed in his prototype," he mused aloud. "It makes sense. Carpenter was thorough in everything he did. But it leaves us with two glaring questions."

Star was staring at the four toggle switches. "I did it? I killed the men who killed my mother?"

Blade used his right hand to wipe the tears from her cheeks. "You certainly did, sweetheart."

Star looked at the smoldering heap of debris where the jeep had stood. Her eyes gleamed and she grinned. "Good!" she stated, delighted. "Those men got what they deserved!"

"Sit here a moment," Blade directed, placing her in the other bucket seat. He clambored into the rear section, hoping they were there.

They were.

His prized Bowies and the Auto-Ordnance Model 27 A-1 were piled in one corner. He picked up the big knives and strapped them around his narrow waist. Hefting the A-1, he climbed up front.

Star's eyes were filled with tears again. "I'm sorry for what my mom was going to do to you," she said softly. "I didn't want her to do it. I didn't want her to shoot Geronimo. It wasn't right. You're our friends." She began sniffling.

"You bet we're your friends," Blade assured her. He leaned toward her. "Listen, Star. I'm very sorry about what happened to Rainbow. I wish there was time to give her a proper burial, but there isn't. We must get out of here. The shooting and the explosion might attract other soldiers, or worse. Can you stop crying? Can you be strong? We must get Geronimo and take off. Okay?"

Star struggled to compose her shattered emotions. "I'll try my best, Blade."

"Good." He reached for his door, staring thoughtfully at the toggle switches.

"Is something wrong?" Star inquired, noting his gaze.

"I was just wondering what the other three toggle switches do," he replied.

"Want to test them?" Star offered, reaching for the one marked F.

"No!" Blade grabbed her hand before she could touch the switch. "We'll discover the purpose for the F, S, and M after we return to the Home."

"You're taking me back with you?" Star asked hopefully.

"Of course."

"You won't leave me here?"

"Why would we do that?" Blade queried her.

She lowered her head in shame. "After . . . after what my mom did, I thought . . ."

"We're not going to hold what your mom did against you," Blade said, cutting her off. "You're welcome to return with us. It's up to you."

Star glanced up, smiling. "Thank you. I'd like to, very much."

"Good. Now stay put. I'm going to get Geronimo." Blade opened the door. "And don't touch anything," he stressed over his left shoulder as he exited the transport, closing the door behind him.

Dear Spirit! What was that awful stench?

He alertly moved to the front of the SEAL. His right foot bumped something, and he stared at his feet, repulsed. The grisly remnant of an arm, from the elbow to the fingertips, was on the pavement, its skin charred and blistered, strips of burnt uniform still attached. He stepped over the arm and studied the grill.

Nothing. No indication of the mechanism responsible for destroying the jeep and the soldiers.

There must be a recessed compartment, Blade reasoned, hidden from casual view until one of the toggle switches was thrown, then covered again after the armament discharged. Perfect for foiling any unwanted inspection.

One important question remained. Why wasn't the SEAL's weaponry mentioned in the Operation's Manual they had discovered inside the transport after they had excavated the vault housing the vehicle? An answer occurred to him, and although it was sheer speculation and would be impossible to confirm, it seemed logical, even probable.

Kurt Carpenter, the Home's Founder and the money behind the development and construction of the SEAL, had deliberately buried the transport in a special chamber. He had been afraid some of the Family members might give in to temptation and steal the SEAL, perhaps to search for loved ones or relatives in distant cities who might have survived the war. Carpenter had hidden the transport before his selected couples arrived at the survival site. Thereafter, knowledge of the SEAL was passed by word of mouth from one Leader to another. It was customary for a Leader to choose a successor shortly after assuming office, and to privately relay the information concerning the transport. Carpenter intended for the SEAL to be used only when absolutely necessary, and it devolved to Plato, a century after Carpenter had secreted the vehicle, to decide that the premature sensility was a bona fide emergency demanding the utilization of the SEAL.

What if, Blade conjectured, there had been a breakdown in communications? What if one of the Leaders had failed to pass on the information about the armament in the transport? He tried to recall. Had any of early Leaders died soon after taking over the reins, perhaps before relaying word on the . . .

Where was Geronimo?

Blade faced the forest, scanning for movement. Geronimo was able to walk. He should have appeared by now. Surely he had seen what happened to the Citadel soldiers? So where . . .

"Looking for something, yes?"

Blade spun to his right, his fingers on the trigger of the Auto-Ordnance.

Gremlin was calmly standing at the side of the highway, cradling Geronimo in his spindly arms. The creature's neck and face bore vivid scorch marks, and the center of the neck was bleeding.

"What have you done to him?" Blade demanded, gliding toward them.

"Nothing, no," Gremlin replied. "Found him, yes? Back in the trees. Think he's hurt bad, yes?"

Blade stopped three feet from the creature. "You expect me to believe you?"

Gremlin's expression saddened. "You do what you want, yes?" He lowered Geronimo and deposited him on the road, then wheeled and angrily stalked off, heading north.

Blade glanced at Geronimo. He was breathing regularly, evidently passed out, possibly from his loss of blood.

Gremlin was ten feet away.

"Gremlin! Wait!"

Gremlin ignored him and continued walking.

"Damn your pride, man! I said wait!"

Gremlin suddenly froze, turning slowly. "What did you call me?" he asked in a low voice.

"What?" What did it mean? "I said damn your pride, man, wait and talk to me a minute."

Gremlin covered the space between them in a rush, and before Blade could prevent him, he clasped Blade's shoulders in his skinny hands and smiled. "Thank you, Warrior."

Blade was astounded by Gremlin's reaction. If he didn't know any better, he'd swear there were tears in Gremlin's eyes. "What did I do?"

"Called me a man, yes? First to do so since . . . since operation."

"You mean to tell me . . ." Blade could scarcely believe it. ". . . you are a . . . man?"

Gremlin nodded, his face a study in abject sorrow.

"But how?"

"Doktor," Gremlin hissed between clenched teeth.

"How could he do such a thing? It isn't possible."

Gremlin motioned at his body. "Wish it weren't, yes? Doktor is wicked, is evil, evil scientist. Chemistry his specialty. Performs vile experiments, yes?"

Blade wanted more information on the nefarious Doktor, but a higher priority beckoned. "Gremlin, I want you to tell me more latter. Right now we've got to get out of here. Other soldiers might have heard the explosion and come to investigate. Will you give me a hand with Geronimo?"

Gremlin placed his right hand on Blade's left forearm in a gesture of friendship. "First, must tell, yes?" He touched his neck with his left hand. "You free me, yes?" he said in an awestruck manner. "Can hardly believe it. Freedom." He visibly sobered. "Wanted to thank you from bottom of heart, yes? You saved Gremlin, no? Gremlin always in your debt."

Blade was touched by Gremlin's evident sincerity. He felt an impulse to explain his original motive wasn't to free Gremlin, but to kill him, then thought better of it. Why rock the boat when things were finally going his way?

"Will you give me a hand?" Blade asked, bending over his fellow Warrior.

Gremlin positioned his hands under Geronimo's shoulders. "Where do we go from here?"

We? Blade, about to lift Geronimo's legs, glanced at Gremlin. "You want to come with me?"

"Nowhere else to go, yes?" Gremlin replied succinctly.

"What about the Citadel? Or anywhere else in the Civilized Zone?"

"Doktor find there, yes? Doktor kill."

"You're welcome to tag along with us," Blade offered. "I saw a lot of the things we came here for in the back of our transport, so I'm heading for our Home. Do you want to go along?"

Gremlin nodded, smiling. "Will go with, yes?" He paused, debating. "How will your people, the Family, react?"

Blade carefully raised Geronimo from the ground, assisted by Gremlin. "Let me put it this way," he said as they slowly walked toward the SEAL. "They're in for a *big* surprise."

22

"Still no sign of any tracks?"

"Nothing man-made."

"I don't like this. Something isn't right." Napoleon placed his hands on his hips and watched Seiko search for prints.

"Are you sure we're in the right area?" Spartacus inquired, his right hand on the hilt of his broadsword.

"This is the spot," Napoleon confirmed, scanning the nearby woods. "Plato told me one of the Omega Warriors on duty above the drawbridge spotted someone out here. He thought it might be another saboteur, possibly one of the Watchers spying on us. That's why Plato sent us out here."

"Then there must be someone around here," Spartacus stated.

"Why can't I find any tracks?" Seiko demanded. "I may not be as skilled a tracker as Geronimo, but I'm still one of the best in the Family."

"And one of the most modest," Spartacus rejoined.

"We must be a mile west of the Home by now," Napoleon remarked. "We'll keep going for another mile or so, but if we don't find any sign by then, we're turning back." He motioned for them to follow and led off, going

211

deeper into the forest. In addition to his revolver, he carried a Browning BPS Pump Shotgun.

They proceeded cautiously, listening for any telltale foreign sounds.

Napoleon was considering an attractive option. If there really was a Watcher out here, they might be able to capture him. Instead of taking him to the Home, a bargain might be struck. If the Watchers knew the Family leadership would be changing hands, they might be willing to agree to a truce or some form of working partnership. This little foray might be the break he needed to open negotiations with the Watchers.

"Hold," Seiko whispered.

"What is it?" Napoleon asked.

Seiko was intently scrutinizing the grass near his feet. "I thought I saw . . ." He shook his head. "No. It couldn't be. I am mistaken."

"Sounds to me like you could use some practice," Spartacus joked.

They continued through a dense stand of trees and brush. Birds chirped overhead. All seemed peaceful enough.

"If you ask me," Spartacus commented, "we're on a wild-goose chase."

The trees ended at a large clearing.

Napoleon held his right hand aloft, signaling a halt. "When we get back," he vowed, "the first thing I'm going to do is find out which of the Omega morons thought he saw someone out here and suggest he get his eyes examined by the Healers."

Spartacus, swinging his gaze to their right, suddenly tensed. "It looks like the Omega moron was right."

The others followed the direction of his stare.

"I knew it," Seiko said, an edge to his voice.

Napoleon gawked for a moment, then hastily recovered his composure.

Rikki-Tikki-Tavi was standing twenty feet away, his katana, still in its scabbard, held low in both hands, near his knees. He wore loose-fitting black clothes similar to Seiko's.

"Hi, Rikki," Napoleon greeted him. "Did Plato send you out here after the man the wall guard saw?"

Rikki walked toward them. "Plato sent me out here, all right."

"I thought so." Napoleon grinned.

"After you," Rikki stated flatly.

Napoleon moved further into the clearing. "After us?" he pretended to be surprised. "Why? Did he think we couldn't handle it by ourselves?"

Rikki stopped ten feet from Gamma Triad. "You know the reason I am here," he said quietly.

"I do?"

"I will not play word games with you, Napoleon," Rikki declared. "I will give you one chance, and one chance only, to recant and renounce your scheme to take over the Family."

Napoleon, forsaking all subterfuge, smiled sardonically. "How damn decent of you."

"I do it for Plato," Rikki clarified.

"Does the old bastard think offering clemency will change anything?" Napoleon angrily asked.

"He does," Rikki nodded, then added, "but he doesn't know how sick you are."

"And if I tell you to kiss my ass?" Napoleon snapped.

Rikki-Tikki-Tavi grinned. "Then I will kiss your ass."

"You will?"

Rikki slowly drew the katana, the blade gleaming in the afternoon sun, and dropped the scabbard. "With this."

"You're forgetting one thing, bright boy," Napoleon mocked him.

"What is that?"

Napoleon beamed confidently. "There's three of us, and only one of you."

"Uhhhhhh . . ." Spartacus interjected, glancing at Napoleon.

"What is it?" Napoleon prompted him.

"I have some news I don't think you're going to like," Spartacus informed them.

"Like what?" Napoleon queried, keeping his eyes on Rikki. What other weapons did Rikki usually incorporate in his personal arsenal? Would any of them stand a chance against a shotgun?

Spartacus took a deep breath, girding his nerves. "There's only two of you," he corrected the count, "and one of him."

Napoleon whirled on Spartacus, his face reddening. "What?" he bellowed, enraged.

"You heard me. Count me out," Spartacus stated firmly. "I want no part of this." He looked at Rikki. "I won't help them, but I won't help you either. I owe them that much. We've been together too long. You understand, don't you?"

"Perfectly," Rikki responded.

Napoleon's lips curled into a snarl. "Why, you yellow bastard!" He began to level the shotgun at Spartacus.

The broadsword was a blur as Spartacus whipped it from its scabbard. He took four quick steps and pressed the tip of the blade against Napoleon's jugular. "Don't even twitch," he threatened the Gamma leader, "or I'll take your head off!"

Napoleon's features were distorted by his unbridled fury. His mouth moved, but nothing came out.

"Lower the shotgun to the ground," Spartacus directed. "Slowly! One false move, if you so much as blink, I'll ram this through your neck!"

Napoleon complied, easing to a squatting position and

setting the Browning on the grass.

"Now back off," Spartacus ordered.

Napoleon rose and backed away about three feet.

"Far enough," Spartacus told him. "And don't touch that revolver!" He looked at Rikki-Tikki-Tavi. "That's as even as I can make it."

"I thank you," Rikki said. "This is . . . unexpected."

"You wouldn't be so surprised if you knew I was the one who informed Plato about Napoleon's plans," Spartacus revealed.

"You? Plato said one of the Family overheard a conversation concerning the rebellion," Rikki remarked.

"He made that up," Spartacus explained. "I told him I didn't want anyone to know it was me, under any circumstances." He sighed and stared at Napoleon. "I guess it doesn't matter now."

"You traitor!" Napoleon roared, taking a menacing step toward Spartacus. "You lousy, stinking traitor! I thought I could trust you! After all the years we've spent as a team!"

"You've got your nerve, jackass!" Spartacus angrily retorted. "You're the traitor here, not me! As usual, you've got everything butt backward." The broadsword made small circles in the air as Spartacus glared at Napoleon. "Did you really believe I would betray the Family, that I'd go against everything I was ever taught, against everyone who cares for me, my own family and friends, to feed your insane ambition? Did you really think I bought your stupid scheme? And Jenny! What kind of man do you think I am? I would never take a woman against her will. What good is a relationship without love? Didn't you learn anything from your parents or in school?" Spartacus paused, sadly shaking his head. "Why bother! Everything I say goes in one ear and out the other."

"You traitor!" Napoleon growled.

"See what I mean!" Spartacus said. "You made mistakes, Napoleon. You assumed I was as dissatisfied with the system at the Home as you are, and I'm not. I don't have any beef with Plato. He's a good Leader. I'm not an airhead, Napoleon, despite what you might believe."

Rikki was viewing the proceedings with intent fascination. They seemed to have momentarily forgotten his presence. Napoleon's face was an infuriated marble mask. Seiko, strangely enough, was calmly standing to one side, his arms folded across his chest. What was going through his mind? Rikki wondered.

Napoleon looked at Seiko. "Why are you just standing there? Don't tell me you're turning against me too?"

Seiko grinned. "Turning against you? Not exactly. But I will confess I wasn't very keen on your takeover idea. I was going along with you for one reason, and one reason only. I never hid that fact from you. It really doesn't interest me one way or the other as to who is in charge of the Family. There is only one thing I want out of this." He deliberately stared at the katana in Rikki's hands.

Rikki raised the sword to waist level. "Is this really that important to you?" he asked quietly.

"Let me ask you," Seiko rejoined. "How would you have felt if you lost our match and I was awarded the katana? How would you have dealt with such a tremendous loss of face?"

To carry such a burden all this time! Rikki selected his words judiciously. "Can there be a loss of face between friends, between brothers, between fellow Warriors?"

Seiko's brow furrowed thoughtfully.

"You know the Family has a huge firearms collection," Rikki went on, "but our supply of certain other weapons is limited. We only own the one katana.

You and I both wanted it. The Elders did what they thought wisest. If your loss bothered you, why didn't you come to me afterward and tell me? I thought we were close when we were younger."

Seiko gazed into the distance, frowning. "We were close," he said in a husky voice.

"Then why allow Napoleon's poison to taint you?" Rikki inquired.

Seiko raised his right hand and rubbed his palm against his forehead.

Rikki gestured with the katana toward Seiko. "If it means so much to you, my former and future friend, you may have this."

Seiko's astonishment at the offer was plainly visible. "You mean that?"

"I do," Rikki affirmed. "If it will repair the rift between us, and bring you fully back into the fold, then I will relinquish the katana to you."

"But I know how much the katana means to you," Seiko objected. "It means as much to me."

"Can a mere sword mean as much as a living, breathing brother in the Spirit?"

Seiko bowed his head. His voice was barely audible when he finally spoke. "I am shamed to my core, and I have brought dishonor to my name and my family."

"Will you lighten up?" Spartacus interjected. "We all make dumb mistakes. Don't make such a big deal out of it!"

Seiko looked at Rikki, his eyes mirroring his self-torment. "There is no apology adequate to equal the injustice I have done you. I will return to the Home and submit to whatever discipline the Elders decree." So saying, he wheeled and departed, his head hanging low.

"Go with him," Rikki said to Spartacus. "Keep an eye on him. He may try to commit seppuku."

"Seppu . . . what?"

"Ritual suicide. It was practiced by ancient samurai, especially when they suffered what they considered an irretrievable loss of honor."

"What'd they do?"

"They disemboweled themselves by slicing open their abdomen," Rikki clarified.

Spartacus began to leave. He paused and glanced at Napoleon. "I'm sorry it had to come to this, but you brought it on yourself."

Napoleon's eyes were livid pools of hatred.

Spartacus shrugged and hurried after Seiko.

Rikki moved closer to Napoleon, holding the katana in chudan-no-kumae, the middle position, with the hilt located near his navel and the blade at a slight upward angle.

"So what's it to be?" Napoleon arrogantly demanded. "A swift execution? Or do I have some say in the matter?"

"You are going to die," Rikki said coldly.

"You always were a smug son of a bitch," Napoleon said, intentionally insulting Rikki. His right hand was inches from his revolver, and he debated whether he could draw and fire before Rikki reached him with the sword. Probably not. Rikki-Tikki-Tavi was lightning fast. Psychology was called for. "So what about it? Are you going to give me a fighting chance?"

"No."

"What? Doesn't the condemned get a last meal or a final request?"

Rikki shook his head. "This is an execution, Napoleon, not a negotiation."

Napoleon's left hand slowly circled his waist, reaching for a pouch attached to his belt. His right hand hovered near his revolver, distracting Rikki-Tikki-Tavi's attention.

"What if I changed my mind?" Napoleon stalled as

his left hand stealthily opened the flap on the pouch. He had one chance to escape. His life depended on an untried, untested, antique capsule. "What if I repent and pledge never to instigate a rebellion again?"

"Do you expect me to believe you?" Rikki was carefully closing on Napoleon, keeping his eyes on Napoleon's right hand, knowing the Gamma Triad leader would not submit without a fight.

"No, I guess you wouldn't," Napoleon said, smiling broadly.

Why was Napoleon so . . . relaxed . . . about his fate? It wasn't in his nature. Something was wrong here. Rikki expected Napoleon to resist, he even welcomed the conflict, not wanting to simply murder Napoleon in cold blood, so he fixed his gaze on that right hand, expecting Napoleon to make his draw any second. With his focus on the right hand and the revolver, it took him a moment to realize the left hand was appearing from behind Napoleon's back, holding a metallic cylinder the thickness of a finger and the length of a hand. In that instant, Rikki realized he'd been guilty of a Warrior's ultimate folly: overconfidence.

Rikki was throwing his shoulders into a swing of the katana when Napoleon's thumb depressed a red button on the cylinder.

A stream of odoriferous greenish fluid shot from a small hole in the tapered end of the cylinder and struck Rikki in the face.

Rikki instinctively backed away, his left hand clutching at his face as the liquid burned his eyes, blurring his vision, and filled his nasal passages, constricting his throat and cutting off his air.

What *was* it?

A foot slammed into Rikki's stomach, doubling him over. Another blow crashed against the side of his head, dropping him to his knees.

"You won't be needing this, bastard!" Napoleon declared.

Rikki felt the katana being wrenched from his right hand. He gripped the hilt, striving to retain his grasp. His lungs seemed as if they were on fire, and he was gasping for breath and wheezing.

"Release it, damn you!"

A third time Napoleon struck, kicking Rikki-Tikki-Tavi in the abdomen.

It was no good! He couldn't concentrate, couldn't hold on to the katana.

Napoleon savagely wrenched the sword free and tossed it aside.

Tears poured from Rikki's eyes, his nose was running, and he experienced an urge to vomit.

What *was* it?

"Thought you were going to kill me, huh?" Napoleon clasped his hands together and brutally struck Rikki on the back of his head.

Rikki collapsed on the grass at Napoleon's feet.

"Guess who's going to be the one doing the killing now?" Napoleon crowed.

Rikki gagged as the foreign substance continued to sear his respiratory system.

"I'll teach you! I'll teach all of you!" Napoleon, in a frenzy, pounded on Rikki's contorted body. Finally, he straightened and raised his arms over his head. "It won't be that easy, Plato!" he shouted toward the Home.

Rikki was straining to control his bodily functions, mentally forcing the fingers of his right hand to form a fist.

"I'll be back, you son of a bitch!" Napoleon vowed, kicking the fallen Warrior in the right side. "The Family hasn't heard the last of me! I'll find some allies, maybe the Watchers, and I'll return and reduce the Home to rubble and enslave all of you. You'll see!"

His lungs were focal points of agony.

"No, you won't see," Napoleon corrected himself. "Because you won't be around when I return. You'll have been long gone!" he gloated.

My right hand! Must discipline my right hand! Rikki's mind strained, channeling his energy and strength into his right arm and hand.

Napoleon slowly drew his revolver, relishing the outcome of their confrontation. "I never did like you, Rikki. You were like all the rest. You failed to recognize my natural ability. I'll prove once and for all that I'm a master of men."

Rikki formed his right hand into a tiger claw, tensing his fingers.

Napoleon glared at Rikki's panting form. "Don't worry, Rikki. You won't die from that stuff you've inhaled. It's called tear gas. I found a carton of these cylinders in the armory. Didn't know if it'd still function after all these years. Surprise! Surprise! Although you don't look like you're too happy about it!" Napoleon laughed, cackling at his own joke.

It was not working! His fingers were too limp!

Napoleon crouched and jammed his left hand under Rikki's chin. "Do you need some air, poor boy? Let me help you." He forcefully pulled on the chin, snapping Rikki's mouth closed and rattling his teeth. Chuckling, he elevated Rikki's face until he could see the water-filled eyes.

Was it his imagination, or were the effects of the green fluid beginning to diminish?

"Can't see a thing, can you?" Napoleon facetiously inquired. "Pity. I wanted you to see what's coming, but I can't afford to dally. Plato might have sent other Warriors to cover you."

Rikki composed his racing thoughts, directing his mind to envision Napoleon's position.

"So I guess we should get this over with." Napoleon cocked his revolver.

Rikki perceived Napoleon was squatting directly in front of him. Napoleon's left hand was opening his mouth, so Napoleon's face couldn't be too far above his own. But where was Napoleon's right hand? He had to know where it was. . . .

The barrel of the revolver was rammed into his open mouth.

"Have any last requests?" Napoleon ridiculed him.

Rikki formed his right hand into the proper shape for a snake stab.

"I only wish it were Plato or Blade or Hickok," Napoleon said. "Still, you'll do. You'll serve as an example. The others will know I'm not to be trifled with!" He knew he should pull the trigger, but he hesitated, savoring the feeling of power Rikki's helplessness aroused in him.

Rikki-Tikki-Tavi was ready, but he needed the revolver barrel out of his mouth first. He tried opening his eyes, but the itching sensation was too great.

"Give my regards to the other side," Napoleon nonchalantly commented.

Rikki made his move. He deliberately gagged and choked, making motions as if he were about to puke, to regurgitate all over the revolver barrel and Napoleon.

"What the . . . !" Napoleon hastily extracted the barrel and drew his right hand away from Rikki's mouth, disgusted at the prospect of any vomit touching his person.

Rikki-Tikki-Tavi surged upward, his right hand a striking snake as it swept up and in, the calloused, compact fingers aimed at Napoleon's throat.

For an instant, Rikki thought he had missed.

Then his fingers gouged into Napoleon's neck,

shattering the windpipe and driving in up to the knuckles.

The revolver discharged, blasting near Rikki's left ear.

Now it was Napoleon's turn to gasp and wheeze, to choke and struggle. He dropped the revolver and grabbed Rikki's right wrist with both hands, frantically striving to remove Rikki's fingers from his throat.

Rikki-Tikki-Tavi, still blinded by the tear gas, grappled with the madman. His right hand, covered with a sticky liquid, was yanked from Napoleon's neck.

Napoleon made a protracted gurgling sound, and Rikki felt something splatter on his face.

Had he missed a killing blow?

Rikki, uncertain of Napoleon's position, tried to gauge the exact location of Napoleon's face.

What was he doing?

Rikki's body was lying on top of Napoleon's bulky form, covering it at an angle. He received the impression Napoleon was reaching for something, was stretching to the right.

But why? Was he in his death throes? Had he finally expired?

Napoleon, puffing and gagging, reached whatever he was after. His body suddenly coiled under Rikki's, and Rikki was staggered by a jarring blow to the left side of his head.

Napoleon had the revolver!

Wobbly, his head throbbing, the tear gas continuing to ravage his system, Rikki lunged wildly, grasping for Napoleon's gun arm. His left hand contacted Napoleon's right elbow, and he held on for dear life, forcing the arm to the grass, hoping he could prevent Napoleon from firing.

The revolver boomed again, and the slug tore a furrow

in Rikki's left side.

Rikki twisted, attempting to place his body on the other side of Napoleon, to present as small a target as possible.

The revolver fired a third time, missing.

Rikki abruptly found himself cheek to cheek with his adversary, and he instantly drove his right hand, with the first two fingers extended and stiff, into Napoleon's face, aiming for an eye. Instead, his blow struck a glancing miss off Napoleon's eyebrow.

For the fourth time, Napoleon tried to shoot Rikki.

Rikki-Tikki-Tavi was rocked by intense pain at the base of his neck, and he knew he'd been hit, knew he was losing consciousness, and realized he had better make his next strike count, because he wouldn't get another chance.

Napoleon began bucking in an effort to dislodge his foe.

Rikki, adrift in a murky sea of darkness, a whirlpool of vertigo, drew his right hand back as far as he could, then plunged it forward.

The blackness engulfed him.

23

"You call this an escape plan?" Wally demanded.

"You have any better ideas?" the gunman countered.

"Well, no," Wally admitted, "but you can bet I wouldn't come up with something as dipsy as this!"

"What's wrong with it?"

"What's wrong with it!" Wally exclaimed, shaking his head. "It's crazy! That's what's wrong with it!"

"Keep your voice down!" Hickok directed. "You'll make the guard suspicious."

"I just don't like it!"

"I thought you wanted to get out of here," Hickok said.

"I do," Wally admitted.

"Then quit being such a wimp!"

"I'm not a wimp!" Wally argued. "I've tried to bust out, several times. That's the main reason I'm in here now. But at least I didn't rely on miracles."

"Miracles?"

"What else would you call it?" Wally gestured at their cell. "If you can get two of them to come inside the cell, not just the guy with the food bucket, and if they don't notice you've moved the shit pail and Shane is now standin' in front of it, and if they don't think we're actin' a little too innocent for our own good, then maybe, just maybe, we can pull it off."

"Piece of cake," Hickok declared, checking their positions for the fiftieth time. He was standing nearest the door, leaning on the cell bars, his back to the hallway. The outside guard was about fifteen feet away, to the right. Shane stood ten feet into the cell, casually leaning against the wall. Hidden by his moccasined feet, positioned between his ankles and the wall, was the waste bucket, its handle raised directly above the pail. Wally stood in the center of the cell, nervously wringing his hands.

"It won't be long," Shane said.

"Why didn't we do it when they brought the morning meal?" Wally inquired. "Why wait until the evening feed?"

"They were prepared for trouble," Hickok answered. "It was the first time they fed me, and they probably expected me to put up a fight of some kind. Since I didn't, whoever comes now won't be anticipating any problem."

Wally anxiously stared at the waste pail. "I don't know. A shit bucket against rifles!"

"Haven't you ever heard the basic law of social relationships?" Hickok asked, grinning.

"What?" Wally absently responded, confused.

"If you can't dazzle 'em with brilliance," Hickok stated, "then baffle 'em with bullshit."

"Do you . . ." Wally began, then froze.

The guards with the food were coming, their voices carrying down the hallway as they joked and laughed.

Hickok glanced outside.

The cell guard had straightened and was watching the approaching duo.

Here goes nothing! Hickok moved to the corner behind the cell door, trying to convey an attitude of total indifference to the proceedings around him.

Shane appeared completely relaxed, his hands in his pockets, humming quietly.

The kid is good, Hickok noted. Maybe I *will* sponsor him for Warrior status after we return to the Home.

Wally was a worried wreck, glancing at the waste pail and the cell door, the waste pail and the cell door, the waste pail and . . .

"Will you cut it out, pard," Hickok whispered. "You're driving me nuts!"

"I can't help it," Wally explained. "I'm a family man, not a trained fighter like you two."

"Don't you want to see your family again?" Hickok queried.

"Of course," Wally affirmed, frowning. "If they're still alive, that is."

"There's only one way you'll find out," Hickok said.

"No problem." Wally visibly regained control of his nerves, sobered by thoughts of his loved ones.

"You're a bit early," the cell guard greeted the food bearers.

"There's a card game tonight," one of the newcomers, a hairy, burly specimen, replied.

"Yeah," said the third Mole. "We want to make our rounds as fast as we can. They won't hold the table for us."

"I wish I could get off," the cell guard complained bitterly. "Instead, I get these jerks." He waved his right hand at the cell.

"Poor baby!" the burly Mole joked, and the food bearers laughed.

Hickok recalled Silvester mentioning an auction for any captured women, and now the guards were talking about a card game. What did they use for money? he wondered.

The trio of Moles appeared at the cell door. The burly

Mole and the cell guard both carried rifles, while the Mole with the food bucket had a revolver strapped to his belt, slanted across his left hip.

"Have they been behaving themselves?" Burly Mole asked.

"Sure have," the cell guard, a thin man with a pointed chin, answered.

"Even this one?" Burly Mole questioned, swinging his rifle barrel in Hickok's direction.

"Even him."

"I'm surprised," Burly Mole said. "I heard he's a real hardcase." He glanced at the gunman. "Hey, you! How come you're being such a good little boy?"

"Because," Hickok replied, hoping he would sound convincing, "I don't want anything to happen to my woman, and I figure if I give you any grief, you just might do something to her."

Burly Mole smirked and whispered in the cell guard's ear. They both laughed at whatever he said.

"All right! Don't try any funny stuff!" Burly Mole ordered.

The cell guard unlocked the cell door, slowly swinging the iron bars open.

Hickok was now behind the open door.

The Mole holding the food bucket, a portly fellow with a perpetual grin, entered and walked toward Wally. "Here you go." He held the food bucket out. "Take it."

On cue, Shane chuckled. "You expect us to keep eating that miserable excuse for food?"

"If you don't like it," Portly Mole rejoined, "we can always let you starve to death."

"At least I wouldn't have to look at your ugly face every day," Shane snapped.

Portly Mole looked at Burly Mole. "Looks like we've got a troublemaker here, Frank."

"Do tell," Frank stated ominously as he came into the cell.

The cell guard, Pointy Chin, stood in the doorway, covering the prisoners.

What a bunch of amateurs! Hickok, faking disinterest, toyed with the frayed hem on his buckskin shirt.

Frank passed Portly Mole and Wally and stopped, his rifle aimed at Shane's midsection. "Now what were you saying?" he arrogantly demanded.

"I said," Shane angrily responded, "you can take this shit and eat it yourselves! I'm not taking another bite!"

"Is that so?" Frank, grinning, turned slightly, winking at Portly Mole. He reached for the food bucket with his left hand. "Pass that food to me. We're going to help our young friend change his mind."

Portly Mole started to extend his arm, the food bucket dangling from his hand, its putrid contents steaming.

"*Now!*" Hickok shouted.

The cell exploded into action.

Wally lunged, grabbing Portly Mole's arm and sweeping it backward, causing the food to fly from the bucket, the reeking mess catching the Mole in the face, covering his eyes and his nose and momentarily leaving him open and vulnerable. Before the startled Mole could react, Wally had the revolver in his hand. He brought the long barrel crashing down on Portly Mole's head as the Mole tried to wipe the food from his eyes.

Frank, spinning to assist Portly Mole, detected a motion out of the corner of his right eye. He swiveled again, expecting Shane to be coming at him.

Instead, Shane had looped his right foot through the handle on the waste pail. As Frank began his swivel, Shane swept his foot back and up, instinctively judging the angle and the trajectory and praying he was right.

Frank was on the verge of completing his turn when
the contents of the waste pail, a week's worth of
accumulated excrement, struck him in his enraged
visage. He tried to duck under the filthy barrage, but the
urine and the feces peppered his upper torso.

Shane, seizing the initiative, kicked with his left foot,
striking Frank's right knee.

There was a popping noise, and Frank cried out and
stumbled, wildly striving to recover his lost balance.

Shane stepped in and grabbed the rifle, a Marlin 1894
lever action. He savagely slammed the stock again and
again against the Mole's head.

Simultaneously with the activity in the cell, Pointy
Chin took a step inside, raising his rifle to his shoulder.

Hickok threw his entire weight against the cell door,
propelling the heavy iron bars into the hapless guard and
smashing him between the cell door and the fixed bars
on one side.

Pointy Chin's rifle dropped to the dirt floor as Hickok
rammed him three more times for good measure.

Satisfied, the gunman stood back and allowed Pointy
Chin to tumble to the floor. He gazed around the cell.
The other two Moles were likewise down and out. Shane
held the Marlin and Wally was armed with the revolver,
a High Standard Double Action.

Hickok retrieved Pointy Chin's rifle, a Winchester.
"See?" he said to Wally. "Like I told you, it was a piece
of cake."

Wally was gaping at the fallen Moles, amazed at their
good fortune. "And you say you do this kind of thing a
lot?"

"All the time," Hickok confirmed, removing Pointy
Chin's shirt.

"I don't see how you do it," Wally stated. "I don't
think my nerves could take it."

"You get used to it, pard," Hickok said, shredding the shirt.

"So what's our next move?" Shane asked. He walked to the cell door and looked both ways. The hallway, illuminated by candles at ten-yard intervals, was empty. "No sign of anyone," he informed the others.

Hickok was staring thoughtfully at Wally. "You say the Moles have had you here about a year?" He began binding the Moles.

"Near as I can tell," Wally replied. He knelt and searched Portly Mole for additional ammunition.

"Then you must be pretty familiar with the tunnels," Hickok deduced, gagging the first of the Moles, Pointy Chin.

"I can get around okay," Wally said, "but I don't have the tunnels memorized, if that's what you mean."

"It'll do," Hickok stated. He started securing Portly Mole.

Wally glanced up. "What are you getting at?"

"Can you get us from here to Wolfe's personal chambers?" Hickok inquired, moving to Frank, working quickly.

"To Wolfe's per . . ." Wally quickly stood, shaking his head. "No way, Hickok! It's suicide. We'd never make it. His private chambers are guarded all the time. Why the hell do you want to go there?"

"Two reasons," Hickok explained, joining Shane at the door. "First, the varmint has my guns, and I aim to get them back. . . ."

"Who cares about some measly guns?" Wally interrupted. "Are they worth dying for?"

"They're my guns," Hickok said coldly, "and the only way anybody is going to get them from me is by prying them from my lifeless fingers!"

"What's the second reason?" Wally asked, hastily

changing the subject.

"I came across a female type I've developed a real hankerin' for," Hickok admitted, "and I don't reckon to leave her behind." He led the way into the hallway.

Wally tapped Shane on the shoulder.

Shane glanced back.

"Has anyone ever told you," Wally curiously inquired, "that your friend talks kind of weird?"

"Just about everybody," Shane acknowledged, grinning. "It's one of the things that makes Hickok . . . Hickok." He followed on the heels of his mentor.

"I'm trying to escape from the Mole Mound," Wally mumbled as he brought up the rear, "with a kid and a mental defective. How do I get myself into these things?"

They reached the first intersection and stopped.

"Still no Moles," Hickok said, pleased. "Probably wouldn't expect to find too many hanging around the cells anyway." He looked at Wally. "The rest is up to you. Lead us to Wolfe's chambers."

"The tunnels will be full of Moles," Wally objected. "We'll never make it."

"You'll never get anywhere in this life with a negative attitude," Hickok commented. "Besides, we'll stick to the less-frequented tunnels. Stay in the shadows. There are hundreds of Moles in the Mound. Odds are, they don't all know each other on sight. If we're careful, we won't even be noticed."

"You hope," Wally muttered.

"We're wasting time. Move it out," Hickok ordered, gesturing with the Winchester.

Wally, grumbling under his breath, reluctantly led them to the left. They traversed tunnel after tunnel, always avoiding those tunnels filled with traffic where possible. Where they couldn't avoid them, they bluffed their way through, walking in the darker areas and smiling at everyone they passed. Several times Wally became lost and they were forced to retrace their steps. Hours passed.

"Can't we take a break?" Wally asked at one point. "My feet are killing me?"

"And what do you think the Moles will do if they find us?" Hickok reminded him.

Wally kept walking.

More time elapsed.

Shane, now behind the other two, was reflecting on his recent actions and dreading his homecoming. His father might tan his hide from one end of the Home to the other; if not physically, then at least verbally. Plato might censure him in front of the assembled Family for his blatant stupidity. Hickok would likely never consent to sponsor him to become a Warrior. His girlfriend, Jane, would undoubtedly drop him for someone else. And all because he wanted to make an impression.

He'd made an impression, all right.

As a first-class jackass!

Dumb! Dumb! Dumb!

Shane frowned, recalling his motives. He wanted to become a Warrior because he was bored with the dull routine of Family life. Excitement! That's what he craved. Excitement and adventure, lured by the illusion of a Warrior's glamorous life. Maybe, he realized, his motives were all wrong. Maybe the reason Hickok, Blade, Geronimo, and the rest made such outstanding Warriors was because they were devoted to protecting the Family and safeguarding the Home. They cared about each and every Family member. Look at Hickok! The gunman had traveled all those miles, through hostile territory, just to rescue him from his own foolishness. Why didn't Hickok just let him reap the results of his own stupidity? Because the gunfighter cared. Hickok would have done the same for any Family member because the family came first, his own life second. He put the welfare of the Family above his own safety.

That, Shane decided, was what made the difference. Caring.

To qualify as a Warrior, you had to sincerely care.

Which only left one question.

Did he?

"Guard," Wally whispered, terminating Shane's reverie.

They were in a narrow tunnel with sparse lighting. A single Mole, armed with a rifle, was casually strolling toward them.

Shane hugged the shadows, trying to be inconspicuous.

"Good evening," the Mole greeted them as he passed.

"Howdy, pard," Hickok, from habit, replied.

The Mole stopped and turned, puzzled. "What did you just say?"

"Blast!" Hickok exclaimed. He whirled and bashed the unprepared Mole on the forehead with the Winchester stock twice in rapid succession.

The Mole staggered against the wall, then slid soundlessly to the floor.

Wally was watching the incident, grinning.

"You have something to say?" Hickok demanded, annoyed at his own carelessness.

"Nothing at all," Wally said.

"I did it so you'd have a rifle too," Hickok fibbed.

"Uh-huh." Wally nodded, picking the Mole's weapon up from the floor. He resumed their trek, glancing over his right shoulder at Hickok. "Nothing at all," he repeated.

The tunnels seemed endless.

"How much farther?" Shane inquired after a while.

"It shouldn't be too much longer," Wally answered. "We should reach a major intersection, and that's when the hard . . ."

Without warning, the tunnel curved sharply and branched at the junction of five other tunnels. The volume of traffic was considerably heavier as the Moles hurried about their business.

Wally motioned for them to back away from the intersection until they were out of sight. "Wolfe's private chambers are down the hall to the right. He's the only one who lives along that tunnel and there will be guards."

"How many?" Hickok asked.

"Beats me." Wally shrugged.

"Okay. Here's what we'll do." Hickok detailed his plan, took their rifles, and marched them to the intersection, their arms in the air. They turned to the right and discovered a well-lit tunnel leading to a huge wooden door.

A pair of guards were on duty.

Evidently, Hickok mused, Wolfe isn't expecting a revolution.

The taller of the two guards noticed them first. "Hey. What do we have here?"

"Hold it right there!" Hickok barked at Shane and Wally.

"What is this?" the tall Mole demanded.

"Is Wolfe here?" Hickok asked.

"He's in," the guard replied. "Why . . . ?"

"I was ordered to bring these two here. Wolfe wants to see them right away," Hickok said, fabricating a reason for their presence.

"I wasn't told anything about this," the tall guard stated suspiciously. "You wait right here while I check with Wolfe." He reached for the door handle, then paused, staring at Hickok's buckskins. "Wait a minute!

Those clothes! I heard about you! You're the . . ."

Hickok was on him before the Mole could move, the barrel of the Winchester pressed against the man's right ear. "One word," Hickok warned, "and I'll splatter your brains all over the door. The same goes for your friend!"

The second guard, like the tall one, was armed with a pistol. His left hand hovered above his holster.

"Don't do it!" the tall Mole urged. "He'll kill me!"

Hickok waited until the smaller guard relaxed his hand, then tossed the other rifles to Wally and Shane. "Cover them," he directed.

"Where the hell are you going?" Wally queried nervously.

"Hold the door until I get back," Hickok said over his shoulder as he slowly opened the door and eased inside.

Wally, covering the guards, glanced at Shane. The youth was facing the intersection, twenty yards distant. "You say you have others like him at this Home of yours?"

"We have other Warriors, yes," Shane answered.

Wally shook his head. "I'm surprised your Family has lasted as long as it has."

Hickok, closing the door behind him, overheard Wally's comments and smiled. As he released the handle, a glimmer of reflected candlelight caught his attention. He glanced down, to his left.

The Navy Arms Henry Carbine was leaning against the wall.

Eureka! He exchanged the Winchester he was carrying for his Henry, happily cradling the Carbine in his arms. Now all he needed was his Pythons and Sherry and he'd be a happy man.

The antechamber he was in, about five square yards in size, was littered with Wolfe's clothing and personal effects.

The man is a lousy housekeeper, Hickok noted as he crossed to another door on the far side of the antechamber.

Voices.

Hickok levered a round into the chamber and cautiously cracked the door.

". . . want you willingly, but I'll take you by force if need be." It was Wolfe speaking.

"You just try it and I'll bite your nose off!"

Hickok grinned. Sherry was as feisty as ever!

The spacious room beyond was decorated with plunder from the Moles' many raids. Plush furniture and fixtures were positioned in random fashion. The center of the room was dominated by a pair of king-size beds placed side by side, both covered with immaculate purple blankets.

What's with all this purple, Hickok wondered? He vaguely remembered reading in the Family school about the practice of ancient royalty adorning themselves with the color purple. Why, he couldn't recall. Personally, he didn't think the color was so hot. Give him a blue or a green any day.

Wolfe was reclining on the bed, propped up on four large pillows. "Come, my dear. It's useless to resist."

Sherry was standing at the foot of the bed, her back to Hickok. Her entire bearing was one of sheer defiance. "You don't hear very well, do you? There's no way you're going to get me in this bed with you!"

Wolfe, smiling like a giant cat preparing to pounce on its helpless prey, reached overhead and pulled on a rope hanging from the ceiling.

From his vantage point, Hickok was unable to see what the rope was attached to, but he did spot his cherished Colts, still strapped to Wolfe's lean waist.

A door at the other end of the room suddenly opened and Goldman entered. He crossed to the bed and bowed.

"Your orders, sir?"

Goldman was unarmed.

Hickok inched his door open, thankful a dresser partially obscured him from the others.

"This wench refuses the honor of sleeping with me," Wolfe declared indignantly. "You will strip her and bind her arms for me."

"As you wish," Goldman obediently responded, bowing.

"Just try it!" Sherry warned.

Goldman, relishing his task, walked toward the blonde, his lips curled in a vicious sneer. "You'll do as you're told, bitch!" He lunged for the woman.

Sherry, retreating, lost her footing and fell.

Goldman covered the three feet between them and stood at her feet, gloating. "I'm looking forward to this," he growled.

"Then I sure hope you can handle disappointment," said a new voice, and Hickok stepped into view, the Henry leveled and ready.

"You!" Goldman hissed, enraged. "Here!"

"Did you think I would leave without saying so long?" Hickok asked sarcastically. "After all we've meant to each other?"

Wolfe, incredibly, was smiling, at ease. "It appears I have greatly underestimated you, Hickok. I won't make that mistake ever again."

"You won't get the chance," Hickok assured him. "Undo your belt and slide my Pythons over here. Slowly! One hasty move, and the Moles will need a new leader."

Wolfe carefully complied, depositing the Colts at the foot of his bed.

"Now, Sherry," Hickok said, keeping his eyes on the two Moles. "Stand up. Don't get between Goldman and me! That's it! Come over here and take the Henry."

Sherry's affection was radiating from her relieved face as she raised the Henry to her shoulder.

"Keep it on Wolfe," Hickok advised. "If he reaches for that rope, put a bullet between his eyes."

"With pleasure," Sherry assured him.

Hickok, warily watching the red-faced Goldman, sauntered to the bed and lifted his Colts. "I'll never let these babies out of my sight again," he vowed.

"What's next?" Wolfe inquired as the gunfighter slid the Pythons into his own empty holsters.

"If you're a good little boy, and keep your big mouth shut, you may come out of this alive," Hickok stated.

"How do I rate?" Wolfe, surprised, questioned him.

"Let's just say I'm in a generous mood," Hickok replied. "Plus you're going to give me your word that you'll stop your raids until we send a delegation from the Family and hold a conference with you."

"Why should I give my word?"

"Do you care about your people?"

"Of course I do!"

"Then why shouldn't you give your word? What have you got to lose? My Family can assist your people in learning to live off the land, in improving their lives. You keep on the way you're going, and sooner or later the Moles will run into someone bigger and stronger. Your Mound will be reduced to a pile of rubble." Hickok paused, studying the Mole leader. Had he read the man right? Was there a chance of striking a deal with this pompous ass?

"Stop . . . raiding?" Wolfe said, his brow creased. "I don't know if my people are ready to change."

"Oh, come off it!" Hickok retorted. "Are you going to spend all eternity in this mud heap? Wouldn't you like to live above ground again, breathing fresh air and enjoying the sunlight?"

Wolfe stared at Hickok. "You are a constant source of

amazement to me."

"What about it?" Hickok pressed him. "Do I have your word? Prove you're a real leader, and not just a walking hard-on with a cock for brains."

Wolfe, offended, almost returned the insult. Instead, he composed himself and smiled. "I give you my word I will not order any more raids until I hear from you. But I must warn you. I think you expect too much from my people."

"I thought you said you'd never underestimate anyone again," Hickok remarked.

"I take back what I said before," Wolfe commented. "You do have an intellect. You simply hide it well."

"What about me?" Goldman snarled.

"Ahhhhh. You." Hickok faced Goldman and deliberately drew his Pythons.

Goldman, expecting to be gunned down, flinched.

Hickok moved forward, stopping a foot from his implacable foe.

"Go ahead! Shoot!" Goldman defiantly blustered. "I didn't think you had the guts to take me on one-on-one."

Hickok, grinning, shoved his lefthand Colt under Goldman's leather belt, underneath the waistband near the navel, leaving the butt free. He took two steps backward and aligned his other Python in a similar position under his belt. "Any time," he said in a menacing tone, "you think you're ready."

Goldman, slack-jawed, gaped at the revolver at his waist.

"Something wrong?" Hickok asked.

Goldman glanced at Wolfe.

"He challenged you," the Mole leader stated matter-of-factly. "Don't look at me for help."

Goldman, pale and sweating, stared at Hickok. "I don't want to do this," he protested.

"Pretty feeble excuse," Hickok remarked. "You have

no other choice."

"What if I don't draw?" Goldman inquired hopefully.

"I'll shoot you anyway."

"You would, wouldn't you?" Goldman took a deep breath and relaxed his hands.

"Any time you're ready," Hickok repeated, patiently standing with his arms at his side.

"I might beat you," Goldman commented. "I'm not bad with a handgun."

Hickok waited.

"You're not as tough as you think you are," Goldman said, hoping his chatter would distract the gunfighter.

Hickok's blue eyes were centered on Goldman's navel.

"Silvester seemed to think you're a dangerous man," Goldman mentioned. "Personally, I think you're an asshole. A dumb asshole, at that."

Sherry's heavy breathing filled the chamber.

"Go on!" Goldman suddenly shouted. "Make your play!"

Instead, he made his.

Goldman fancied himself fast, he'd often practiced a quick draw with a pistol he possessed, so as his hand flashed toward the Python, his astonishment was all the more compounded when Hickok's Colt was already out and up before he even touched the butt on his revolver.

Hickok rammed the barrel of his Python into Goldman's stomach and pulled the trigger.

The blast of the Colt was effectively muffled by Goldman's abdomen. He literally flew backward as the slug exited his back, splintering his spinal column. Blood sprayed over the furniture as he stumbled and fell onto his back, his bearded features frozen in a contorted death mask, his green eyes wide in disbelief.

Hickok slowly walked over to the body and picked up his other Colt. He wiped the Python against his pant leg, removing crimson splotches from the pearl handles.

Finally, he twirled the Colts into their respective holsters, shook his blond head, and smiled. "Piece of cake," he said to himself.

Wolfe was gazing at the gunfighter in awe. "I've never seen anyone as fast as you."

Hickok patted his Pythons. "Lots of practice."

"You can't wring water from a stone," Wolfe observed. "I could practice all my life and never be as fast as you. It takes talent, and you have it."

"Flattery from you?"

"No. The truth."

Hickok glanced around the room. "Would there happen to be a knife in the house?"

Wolfe, chuckling, reached into his right front pocket and withdrew a small folding knife. "Will this suffice?"

Hickok moved to the bed and took the proffered pen-knife. "You do understand I have to do this? Just as a precaution."

Wolfe nodded. "I understand. Do what you must."

"Lie face down on the bed," Hickok directed. After the Mole leader obeyed, Hickok climbed onto the bed and used the knife to cut a two-foot length from the rope Wolfe used to signal Goldman. He was careful not to pull too hard on the rope as he sliced it. No sense in inviting any more Moles to their farewell party.

"Now put your hands behind your back," Hickok ordered. As he securely tied Wolfe's wrists, he winked at Sherry. "Hang in there, babe. Before you know it, we'll be safe and sound back at the Home." Satisfied with his knots, he jumped from the bed and began pulling the purple blankets from under the mattresses on the two king-size beds.

Wolfe, watching the proceedings, nodded appreciatively. "You don't take chances. I'll give you that."

Hickok paused, holding the corners of one of the blankets. "Before I wrap this up," he said, amused by his pun, "I have a few words to say to you. I don't know how seriously you took what I said before, but you better. You've been lucky so far. The Trolls never found your Mound, or you'd be dog meat by now. Oh, sure, you were able to defeat those who survived their fight with us. But if the Trolls had been at full strength, the outcome might have been completely different. There's another bunch we've tangled with, called the Watchers. They're one mean passel of hombres. I'm not exaggerating when I tell you they have more firepower than you can ever hope to muster. The point I'm trying to make is this. You could use some friends in this world, an ally you could rely on to help you out if things got tough. My Family has been lucky too. We've been pretty insulated in our Home, out of touch with the rest of the world. We've survived as a close-knit clan all these years. But I've got this feeling all that is about to change. A lot of people know about us now, and for better or for worse, that spells change. My Family could use some friends. You think about it, Wolfe. The future of the Moles is in your hands."

"I will consider everything you have said," Wolfe promised.

Hickok nodded and started wrapping the purple blankets around the lean giant.

Sherry joined him. "And here I thought all you did was kill, kill, kill."

"What do you mean?"

"All those things you just said to him," Sherry said. "I never thought of you as a man of peace."

"I have this friend," Hickok began.

"The one named Joshua?" Sherry interrupted.

"Yeah. Josh. He taught me an important lesson when we were in the Twin Cities. Killing isn't everything. There are other ways of dealing with enemies, if you can take the time to talk about your differences."

"I'm looking forward to meeting this Joshua," Sherry remarked.

"I hope your ears are in good shape," Hickok wryly commented.

"What?"

"Nothing." Hickok surveyed his handiwork.

Wolfe was enclosed in a cocoon of purple blankets, covered from head to toe.

"You okay in there?" Hickok asked him.

"Just fine," came the muted response. "A little hot."

"I just thought of something," Hickok said, snapping his fingers. "Is there another way out of here?" he inquired, tapping on the bundled blankets. "I don't want to kill any more of your people if I can help it."

"Look behind the big cabinet in the corner," Wolfe replied. "There's a hidden air shaft and a ladder. It'll take you straight up to the surface. You'll be in the forest north of the Mound proper."

"Thanks," Hickok said, walking toward the door he'd used to enter.

"Where are you going?" Sherry questioned him.

"To get some friends," Hickok answered, stopping at the door. "I'll be right back." He crossed the antechamber and stepped outside.

Shane and Wally were now training their guns on three Moles.

"This one showed up with a tray of food while you were inside," Wally informed him, motioning toward the newcomer.

The terrified Mole, still holding the tray of food, was visibly quaking, his knobby knees shaking violently.

Hickok laughed. "Howdy, Silvester. You in the food business now?"

"Hickok!" Silvester cried, his delight lighting up his face. "Am I glad to see you."

"I'll bet." Hickok glanced at Shane. "Take the two

guards inside and find something to tie them up with. Make sure they can't free themselves."

Shane nodded and led the guards into the antechamber, Wally bringing up the rear.

"You escaped from the cells!" Silvester marveled. "No one has ever done that before."

Hickok draped his left arm across Silvester's narrow shoulders. "I'd like to take the time to shoot the breeze with you, but I've got to run. You'll be seeing me again." He stared along the tunnel, insuring it was empty.

Silvester noticed his gaze. "No one comes here unless Wolfe tells them to," he explained.

"Speaking of your fearless leader," Hickok said, "didn't you tell me you were on the outs with him?"

"I'm not one of his favorite people," Silvester admitted. "I saw my sister. Gloria still hasn't gone to bed with him."

"I'm surprised he hasn't forced her," Hickok commented.

"No. He only does that with outside women."

"Well, anyway, how would you like to be one of his favorite people?" Hickok asked.

"I don't see how. . . ."

"Trust me. After I go through that door, count to one hundred. Can you do that?"

"I know how to count," Silvester stated indignantly. "I can even read a little bit."

"Good. Then count to one hundred and go inside. You'll find Wolfe on his bed. You'll know what to do."

"What do you . . ."

Hickok waved and walked to the door. "You'll know what to do. Believe me, Wolfe will thank you for it. Take care, pard." He stepped into the antechamber.

Shane and Wally were tying the guards with strips of torn clothing.

"Tie them tight," Hickok advised, then re-entered the bedroom.

Sherry ran into his arms. "I can't believe you've done it! I'll never doubt you again."

"You're a woman. Want to bet?"

"Since when are men any better?" Sherry rejoined.

Hickok chuckled.

Shane and Wally joined them.

"They won't be getting loose this year," Wally boasted. He spotted Goldman and his mouth dropped. "Do you always leave bodies wherever you go?"

"He does have that habit," Sherry answered for him.

"Follow me," Hickok directed.

It was a simple matter for them to lift the cabinet from the wall, locate the hidden air shaft, and scale the ladder to the surface. They pushed aside a camouflaged trap door and clambered out of the shaft.

"The air smells so sweet," Sherry mentioned, taking deep breaths and brimming with happiness.

The night sky was filled with stars and a half-moon.

"Are you coming with us?" Hickok asked Wally.

The big man shook his head. "I've got to go to Tenstrike and see if I can find my family."

"Good luck," Sherry offered.

"May the Spirit guide you," Hickok stated. "You're welcome at our Home any time."

"I'll keep that in mind."

"So long," Shane said.

Wally, carrying a rifle, with a pistol around his waist, waved and walked into the woods.

"Which way?" Shane asked, likewise armed with one of the door guard's pistols and a rifle.

"Which way do you think?" Hickok retorted. "I'm not about to sponsor someone for Warrior status if they can't read the stars."

"Spon . . ." Shane sputtered, staring at the gunman

in disbelief. "You can't mean it! Not after the way I've handled myself."

"I intend to do it because of the way you've handled yourself," Hickok explained. "You did real well down there. Although," he paused, "you're a mite too quiet for my tastes."

"I've had a lot on my mind," Shane explained. "I've felt like I've failed everybody. You. My father. Plato. I've been dreading going back, thinking everyone would laugh at me."

"When you make stupid mistakes," Hickok said, "you've got to expect folks to laugh at you. If you have a sense of humor, you'll get through it okay."

"Then you're really going to sponsor me?" Shane inquired hopefully.

"I'm a man of my word."

Shane clenched his fists and spun in his tracks, laughing.

"Try to control your enthusiasm," Hickok stated. "We'd best put as much distance between the Moles and us as we can, and do it fast."

"Don't you trust Wolfe?" Sherry asked.

"Not until he proves he's trustworthy," Hickok replied. He reached out and grabbed her, pulling her into his arms and embracing her.

"Please! Shane's right here!"

"So he'll learn something. What's with the sudden modesty?"

Sherry squirmed playfully in his arms. "You said we had to get out of here," she reminded him.

"There's always time for this," Hickok declared, kissing her passionately on the lips.

Shane, embarrassed, politely turned away, keeping his eyes on the trap door and the surrounding forest.

The kiss lingered and lingered.

Sherry, at last, pulled back, her eyes closed, her warm

form straining against his hard body. "MMMMMMmmmmmmm. Nice."

"Did you just hear something?" Shane inquired.

"Like what?" Hickok asked, nibbling on Sherry's left ear.

"I don't know. . . ." the youth stated uncertainly.

"Don't move!"

The harsh command, barked from the concealing cover of the encircling forest, riveted the trio where they stood.

Blast! How could he have been so dumb? Hickok abruptly realized they were standing in the center of a clearing approximately twenty feet in diameter, completely enclosed by the dense forest.

"Don't move!" the deep voice bellowed again.

"It was a trap!" Sherry whispered to Hickok. "They were waiting for us!"

"They sure were," Hickok replied through clenched teeth.

"But how . . . ?"

"Wolfe," Hickok deduced. "They found the guards we overpowered before we reached his chambers. He must have figured we'd come after you and set this whole thing up. Pretty clever of the bastard! And I fell for it, like the prize sucker of the year!"

Moles were cautiously emerging from the woods. One of them, the apparent leader, held a rifle barrel to Wally's head.

Six. Seven. Nine. Ten counting the guy shoving Wally. Hickok took a step to his left, away from Sherry.

One of the Moles fired his rifle, the slug narrowly missing the gunfighter's moccasins.

"I warned you not to move," the tall leader reiterated. "Do it again and we'll finish you off right here and now, no matter what Wolfe wants."

"My compliments to Wolfe," Hickok said, grinning.

"This shows real finesse. I didn't think he had it in him."

"Shut your face!" the tall Mole ordered. "We could care less what you think. Drop your weapons. Now!"

"Sorry, Hickok," Wally apologized. "They caught me by surprise." His hands were raised over his head and he was unarmed.

"Quiet!" the leader snapped, ramming his rifle barrel into Wally's lower back.

Wally grimaced and doubled over, clutching his back.

Perfect! Now he had a better shot. Hickok slowly inched his body sideways.

The tall Mole was glaring at Wally. "You speak when you're spoken to, and not before!"

Six of the Moles sported rifles, the rest handguns. They encircled their prisoners, but only five of the ten actually had their guns aimed at the three in the middle of the clearing.

Doubly perfect! Hickok almost laughed. The Moles were confident in their superior numbers, and some of them manifested an air of nonchalance, evidently convinced there wouldn't be any resistance.

Were they in for a surprise!"

"Drop your guns!" the leader angrily demanded. "I won't say it again!" he threatened.

Sherry released the Henry and it fell to the ground.

Shane dropped his rifle and reached for his pistol.

"When I move," Hickok whispered, "you two hit the dirt."

Shane held the pistol in his right hand.

"Toss it," Hickok said out of the corner of his mouth.

Shane, puzzled, looked at Hickok.

"I'm waiting!" the tall Mole barked.

"Toss it!" Hickok hissed. "Up!"

Shane glanced at Sherry, shrugged, and obeyed. He flipped the pistol into the air.

It was the moment Hickok needed.

The Moles, taken unawares by this unforeseen maneuver, automatically fixed their attention on the pistol, watching the weapon fly end over end upward. For an instant, their collective gaze was distracted from their intended captives.

In a blur of motion, Hickok drew his Colt Pythons, thankful the night was dark, limiting their reaction time. In the three seconds it took the Moles to wake up to the ruse played on them, the Family's pre-eminent gunman fired four times.

Hickok's first shot took out the tall Mole, the leader of the ambush, catching him in the forehead and flipping him backward.

The second shot downed the Mole on the leader's right.

Hickok continued his turn, going for the head as he invariably did, felling two more Moles.

Sherry dived for the Henry as the Moles opened fire. Something buzzed near her head as she grabbed the 44-40, quickly sighted, and pulled the trigger. The big gun boomed, jarring her shoulder. One of the Moles was flung four feet to the ground.

Shane experienced a stinging sensation in his left arm and knew he'd been creased. He used his right hand to snatch the pistol as it descended, whirling and firing three times at the nearest foe.

The blasting of the gunfire attained a staggering intensity, becoming a thunderous din, deafening to the ear, shattering the serenity of the night and startling all the wildlife for a mile in every direction.

Then abrupt silence.

The perimeter of the clearing was littered with bodies contorted in the throes of violent death. An acrid, burning odor filled the air.

Hickok, his Pythons held at waist level, searched the

Moles for any indication of life.

There was none.

"Anyone hit?" Hickok asked, reluctant to glance at Sherry for fear she was a casualty of the conflict.

"I'm in one piece." Her voice floated up to him, and relief washed over him like a cold bath on a hot day. She rose, staring in amazement at the Moles. "We did it! I don't believe it!"

"I was hit," Shane announced. "Looks like a nick, is all."

Wally was still doubled over, his hands on his back, his mouth slack.

"You can stand now, pard," Hickok said. "I want to thank you for your assistance."

Wally slowly straightened. "Any time," he mumbled, dazed.

"Better get your guns and skedaddle," Hickok advised. "More Moles are bound to show up."

Wally absently retrieved his firearms and walked to the edge of the woods. "I'll never forget you!" he said, and was gone.

"Still think you can make a pact with Wolfe?" Sherry queried.

"Won't hurt to try," Hickok replied, scanning the trees. "We'd better vamoose. Can you wait a spell for the rest of those kisses?"

Sherry pouted at him. "When do I get them?"

"As soon as we return to the Home," Hickok assured her.

"Can we run?"

24

The Family held it wildest celebration in anyone's memory.

Blade, Geronimo, Gremlin, and Star arrived at the Home a day after Hickok, Sherry, and Shane. Their collective homecoming prompted Plato to announce a special holiday. He was particularly elated because, with the generator taken from the Watchers in Thief River Falls and the equipment Geronimo had found in Kalispell, he as confident the Elders would discover the cause of the premature senility and a cure. Gremlin, claiming he knew something about the source of the senility, offered his assistance. The Family, while initially shocked by Gremlin's appearance, soon accepted him into the fold, especially the younger children. They followed him everywhere, besieging him with constant questions and marveling at his features. Gremlin was thrilled at all the attention.

Geronimo was treated by the Healers. They pronounced him well enough to participate in the festivities, but advised him to take it easy.

Jenny smothered Blade with kisses and clung to him throughout the party.

Shane received a verbal tongue-lashing from his father

and the Elders, but after Hickok stood up in his defense, extolling his courage and endurance, they desisted.

Jane, Shane's girlfriend, professed her undying devotion for her "hero." The object of her admiration was confounded by his reception. He decided Hickok was right in his assessment of the opposite gender. Women *were* strange.

Nadine, Plato's wife, took Star under her wing.

Toward midnight, three figures detached themselves from the laughter and the fun, the food and the drink, and walked to C Block, the infirmary, to visit the one Family member not able to attend the jubilee.

Rikki-Tikki-Tavi, reclining on a cot in a spacious room lit by a dozen candles, looked up as Alpha Triad entered the room.

"Sorry it took us so long to come see you," Blade remarked. "You wouldn't believe how busy we've been."

"I understand," Rikki informed him, smiling. "I am pleased you came, but shouldn't you be with the others?"

"They won't miss us for a spell," Hickok said. "They're singing and dancing and generally making fools of themselves."

"How are you?" Geronimo solicitously inquired, staring at the bandage covering Rikki's neck.

"Napoleon came close," Rikki replied. "They tell me another inch and I would be in the worlds on high."

"The Family doesn't seem upset about Napoleon," Blade mentioned. "They've taken the news of his defection in stride."

"Once they learned of his plans," Rikki said, "all sympathy for the rebel died with him." He pointed at Geronimo's bandaged shoulder. "How are you doing?"

"As well as can be expected," Geronimo answered. "It's not too serious."

"Speaking of Chrome Dome," Hickok interjected, "they tell me you drove your fingers through his eye socket into his brain. Nice touch."

"I can't remember," Rikki admitted. "It's all a blur."

"Yama and Teucer told us they thought you were dead when they found you," Geronimo commented, referring to the other Warriors from Rikki's Beta Triad.

Blade strolled to the doorway and stared outside. "Listen to them. They're having the time of their lives."

"They deserve it, pard," Hickok stated. "I bet those Citadel creeps you told us about won't leave us alone for long."

"We'll be ready for them when they come," Geronimo vowed.

"Yeah." Blade glanced at Hickok. "Plato likes the idea of an alliance with the Moles, if it can be arranged. We still must travel to the Twin Cities again and bring back those people who want to join us." He paused, reflecting. "At the rate we're going, we could end up with a genuine confederation on our hands."

"Wouldn't the Watchers be surprised!" Geronimo deduced.

"All these folks backing our play is well and good," Hickok declared, "but when it gets right down to it, the only ones I really trust to protect the Family, the only ones we can completely rely on, are the Warriors."

"That's why we're here." Geronimo grinned. "The safest, most boring occupation anyone could ask for."

Blade, his arms folded across his massive chest, nodded. "Reminds me of something we read in one of the books in the library when we were kids. How did it go? Oh, yes. All for one and one for all."

"You got it, pard," Hickok said, walking to the doorway and standing next to Blade. He nodded at Rikki. "I'll come visit you again tomorrow," he pledged.

"I heard about your new . . . companion," Rikki

stated. "Why don't you bring her along? I'd like to meet her."

"Will do." Hickok stepped outside onto the front steps.

"Going somewhere?" Blade casually inquired.

"You better believe it," Hickok replied. "I have some serious kissin' to attend to, and my lips are rarin' to go."

"Need any help?" Geronimo offered, and the others laughed.

Hickok faced them, perched on the threshold, affectionately gazing at his three closest friends, and patted his Colts. "Thanks for wanting to help, but I can handle this mission by my lonesome. It'll be a piece of cake. If I run into a mutate, though, I'll be sure and give a yell."

"If you bump into a mutate in the dark," Geronimo quipped, "the poor thing would probably die of fright."

Hickok, grinning, turned, inhaling the cool night air. He strolled toward the joyous gathering, reflecting. All for one, and one for all. It would make a dandy motto for the Warriors. He recalled another saying, a phrase imprinted on a wooden plaque hanging on one of the walls in his parents' cabin when he was a child, and for the first time he experienced a real appreciation for the words and their meaning.

There's no place like Home.

THE END . . . FOR NOW

ABOUT THE AUTHOR

Dave Robbins was raised in southeastern Pennsylvania, amidst dense forest and rolling farm fields. At seventeen, he enlisted in the Armed Forces and, after serving overseas, returned to travel through America. He currently resides near the majestic splendor of the Rocky Mountains. A happily married family man, an outdoorsman, writer, and broadcaster—among other pursuits— Robbins is acquiring a devoted core of readers who enjoy his finely crafted tales of adventure, romance, mystery, and excitement.

Among his other books you will enjoy reading are:

BLOOD CULT
THE WERELING
THE ENDWORLD SERIES #1:
  THE FOX RUN
THE ENDWORLD SERIES #2:
  THE THIEF RIVER FALLS RUN
THE ENDWORLD SERIES #3:
  THE TWIN CITIES RUN

Ask for them at your favorite bookstore.